THE OTHER PRINCE

ALICE DOLMAN

ISBN 978-0-6451497-0-8

The Other Prince is a work of fiction. The characters and events portrayed in this book are fictitious. Any similarity to real people, alive or dead, is coincidental and not intended but the author.

Cover by www.yummybookcovers.com

Editing by www.loptandcropt.com

Copyright © 2021 by Alice Dolman

❀ Created with Vellum

For Gerard

House of Huntington

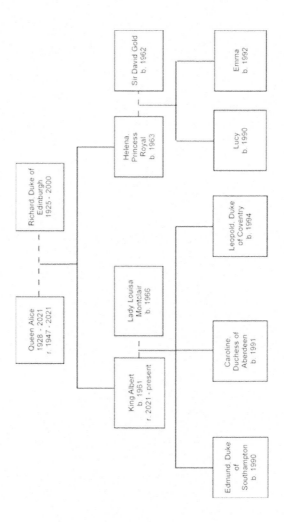

Queen Alice
1928 - 2021
r. 1947 - 2021

Richard Duke of
Edinburgh
1925 - 2000

King Albert
b. 1961
r. 2021 - present

Lady Louisa
Montclair
b. 1966

Helena
Princess
Royal
b. 1963

Sir David Gold
b. 1962

Edmund, Duke
of
Southampton
b. 1990

Caroline,
Duchess of
Aberdeen
b. 1991

Leopold, Duke
of Coventry
b. 1994

Lucy
b. 1990

Emma
b. 1992

CHAPTER 1

Thursday 8 July 2021

"ARE YOU CRYING?"

"I am not crying!" I say, trying—and failing—to hold back the tears. "Okay, I'm crying a bit. But can you blame me? She's been part of our lives from birth, and she *is* kind of my boss."

Was. She *was* kind of my boss.

Although I am—or was—technically employed by Her Majesty Queen Alice of England and Wales, I haven't actually met her in the three years I've worked at the Queen's Charitable Foundation. The closest I've come is spotting her in one of her signature jewel-toned skirt suits across the ballroom at our annual major donors gala. One year, I walked past and tried to sniff her so I'd know how she smelt. Is that weird? It's weird, right? Still, it was worth it, because now I know she smelt like gardenias. That's the kind of insider information you don't get from a biography.

A cushion flies across the room and hits me in the head.

"Cheer up, Amelia. To be fair, she was ninety-three."

"I know, I know. I just don't enjoy change. She was queen for seventy-four years. Seventy-four years, Penny! I can't even commit to a twelve-month phone plan. Meanwhile, she survived a world war, seventeen prime ministers, entering the EU *and* leaving the EU. She's been such a constant in our lives. If she can die, you can't count on anything to be around forever."

"Okay, Ms. McSerious. Snap out of it. I'm sad too, but we need to maintain some perspective here: it's the queen, not Ryan Reynolds or a Hemsworth."

"Penny, I'm genuinely upset about this and would like to watch the funeral in peace. Joke all you want, but she really did feel like a big part of my life, and I need some closure."

"Are you watching this for closure, or because a televised funeral is a prime opportunity to watch your future husband march around in full naval uniform? I've never understood what you see in Leo, but I'll admit, the uniform does it for me."

"Pen! For the last time, I am not in love with Prince Leo. I just respect his charity work. Do you even know how many schools he's built in Africa?"

Penny purses her lips and gives me a pointed look. "Lady, do you forget that I've been to your office? Does anyone else at work keep royal family memorabilia on their desks?"

"As a matter of fact, they do. I'm positively normal by Foundation standards."

"Whatever. I maintain it's not normal. Do I need to go and check if you still sleep with a picture of him under your pillow like a sixteen-year-old?"

I don't dignify Penny's teasing with a response, but she's not entirely wrong. I'm not sixteen anymore, but I do still have a little crush on Leo. Just a little one though, I swear. Okay, fine, a moderate-sized crush.

Leo is the new king's third child. His older brother Prince Edmund and older sister Princess Caroline are both reserved and hard-working. Leo, on the other hand, has more than lived up to the stereotype of the playboy prince in the past. But after some rebellious years involving quite a few questionable life choices and unflattering tabloid headlines, he has matured into a community-minded philanthropist and naval captain. He famously spends at least a month each year living and working in one of the African orphanages or schools he supports. The tabloid photos of him playing around and giving grinning children piggyback rides always make my heart and ovaries do a flip. Let's be honest, who wouldn't be a little in love with him?

"I'm taking your silence to mean you have no interest in seeing Leo all kitted out, and I should switch to *The Bachelor* now," Penny says, her finger hovering over the channel button.

"Oh, no you don't!" I say as I lunge for the remote. Penny shrieks as I wrestle it out of her hands.

"You can't take away my chance to check out Leo covered in medals without a fight," I say. "Besides, you loved the Queen too. You won't want to miss this."

"Fine. I did admire her. And as a New Zealander, she was my queen, too, so I feel a certain sense of national obligation to farewell her."

"I knew you'd come around. Come sit with me. I'm going to need some moral support to get through this."

Penny sits down and sighs. "She's really gone, isn't she?"

I wipe my eyes with my sleeve. "I don't want to believe it, but she really is."

We fall into silence and watch the funeral procession down the Mall from Buckingham Palace to Westminster Abbey. I cry the whole time.

Friday 9 July

PENNY IS STILL ASLEEP when I get ready for work the next morning. We share what I would generously describe as a 'cosy'—read:

tiny—flat in Camden. On the plus side, I lucked out in the flat-mate lottery. Penny, who went to high school with a friend of mine, was moving to London from New Zealand at the same time I was moving from Australia, so we joined forces to pay the hideously expensive rent and have been inseparable ever since.

In the last four years, we've laughed, cried and watched a lot of *Keeping Up with the Kardashians*. It's lucky we get along, because our exorbitantly expensive flat would fit three times over in Kim K-W's glam room. If we weren't such good friends, sharing this tiny space might have ended in a murder-suicide by now.

I flip on the TV—making sure the volume is low so I don't wake up Penny before she's had her required eight hours—while I'm making my coffee. It's been a week since Queen Alice passed away, and every station is still showing the same obituary reel they've been broadcasting on repeat since the palace announced her death. At least today, they've updated the reel with footage from the funeral. I know I shouldn't ogle mourners, but Penny was right—the naval uniform *really* works for Leo.

At eight fifteen, I run out the door and down the street to the Tube station. My trip is about twenty-five minutes, but it feels like at least two hours of desperately trying not to touch, smell or make eye contact with anyone. If you like personal space and are generally awkward around people like I am, travelling on the Tube in rush hour is the stuff of nightmares. Depending on who's standing around you, the smells can also be nightmarish.

When we pull up at Southwark Station, I push my way off the train and am swept up the stairs by a wave of commuters. I emerge onto the street, take a big breath of the relatively fresh air and thank god that I survived another morning of being wedged against someone's armpit. By London standards, the weather is lovely, so I take the long way and walk along the banks of the Thames towards the Queen's Charitable Foundation offices in South Bank.

When I stroll into the office just after nine, I'm surprised to see my boss Soph sitting at her desk scribbling notes on a contract. Lady Sophia Sumner-Jones has worked for the foundation since she graduated from law school thirty-five years ago. While she's brilliant, she's also social to a fault and spends much more time out for long lunches and boozy dinners than working. If she isn't catching up for coffee with Amal Clooney or having lunch with Victoria Beckham, she's playing bowls on a Kensington Palace lawn with Queen Alice's daughter, Princess Helena. That's why she has me and the two other women on our team to do the grunt work.

I met Soph not long after I moved to London from Melbourne four years ago to take a job in the project finance team at a magic circle firm. The recruiter who approached me about the role sold me on the London dream. At twenty-five, I had visions of glamorous international work and exciting weekend jaunts around Europe. I didn't realise until later that London firms recruit Australians because of their high-quality education, strong work ethic and ability to focus purely on work because moving halfway around the world from everyone you've ever known means you don't have much else to do on a Saturday night. Six months later, I had left the office before ten p.m. a total of three times—including on weekends—and had seen nothing in London that wasn't the Tube, my office or my flat. Needless to say, the European sojourns had not materialised.

One night I was sitting under the fluorescent lights in my office at eleven p.m., rewriting an indemnity clause for the seventh time, when I started crying and couldn't stop. I was under so much pressure to be perfect—from my boss, from my clients, and most of all, from myself. I was exhausted and depressed and hadn't even had time to notice. I knew if I was going to stay in London, things needed to change. I needed to be doing work I cared about and only during something that I could reasonably describe as "business hours."

When I stopped crying, I jumped in a taxi back to my flat—

after finishing my indemnity clause, of course, because even a minor breakdown can't take the A-type out of a lawyer—and sent Soph a message on LinkedIn. I had met her a couple of months earlier at one of the networking dinners that the firm expects its lawyers to find time to attend (and look like they're enjoying) while working eighty-hour weeks. Soph and I had sat next to each other at dinner. I immediately recognised her as Princess Helena's best friend, but obviously played it cool and pretended I had no idea who she was. She told me about the amazing projects she was working on and complained about funding agreements giving her migraines. Meanwhile, I tried not to ask a million embarrassing questions about Leo.

We met for coffee the day after my breakdown and made a deal: I'd get a job doing rewarding work, and she'd never have to read a funding agreement again.

Two weeks later, I set up my stack of Moleskine notebooks and—much to Soph's amusement—my Leo mug on my new desk at the foundation's office, and the rest is history. Three years later, I almost always leave the office before the sun goes down, and I've been able to make liberal use of the short flights between London and other European cities. Most importantly though, I feel like the work I do has a real purpose and contributes to improving people's lives, instead of just moving money around from one big company to another. It's what I've always wanted to do, with the bonus thrill of being associated with royalty.

~

"SOPH! YOU'RE IN EARLY. COFFEE?" I ask as I walk past her desk on my way to the kitchen.

"Yes, please. I'm dying for caffeine. I don't know how you get into work so early," she says, sighing.

"Turns out nine isn't that early if you go to bed before

midnight," I tease. I dodge out of the way of the balled up Post-it Note Soph throws across her desk at me in response.

"If you must know, I was working last night. Well, talking about work, anyway. I had dinner with Helena and was trying to dig up some dirt on the direction that Bertie is planning to take the foundation in now that he's in charge."

"Bertie—as in King Albert, ruler of this fair nation and owner of more country estates than you can poke a stick at?" I ask, raising an eyebrow.

Queen Alice had two children, the now-King Albert, and Helena, Princess Royal. One reason Soph got her job here, and why she's so good at it, is that she's firmly cemented in the royal family's inner circle. She grew up at her family's "country seat" neighbouring the royal family's Scottish castle at Balmoral and then shared a room with Princess Helena at boarding school. She's so upper-crust, she's basically a loaf of bread. There are even rumours that at one stage the family were set on her marrying King Albert, but we don't quite have the kind of relationship where I can ask her to confirm or deny that particular rumour. It's a bit of a moot point now anyway, given that both Soph and King Albert have been married for decades.

"So, what's the inside word?" I ask, worrying that as well as being devastating to me on a personal level, the queen's death might end up impacting me professionally.

"Oh, who knows," she says, shrugging. "It doesn't sound like Bertie's given it much thought yet. I expect that like most things, we'll be re-named the King's Charitable Foundation and keep on as we've always been. Regardless, nothing will happen until after the coronation and wedding. They're absolutely frantic at the palace right now."

In an inconvenient twist of fate, Queen Alice passed away only four weeks before King Albert's eldest child, Prince Edmund, was scheduled to marry his long-term girlfriend, Lady Sibella Cavendish. The timing means that both the palace and royal souvenir sellers everywhere are now in a state of complete panic trying to deal with a royal funeral, coronation and wedding all within a month of each other.

"Trying to undertake any kind of major restructure at the same time he and his team adjust to new roles wouldn't make any sense," I say.

"No, it wouldn't," Soph says. "I expect we'll hear officially after the wedding."

Surely he won't change things straight away—it's just not the way that the royal family works. When you're dealing with a centuries-old institution, change happens at a glacial pace. Even so, doubt niggles at me. I don't know King Albert, but from what I've read—yes, mainly in the tabloids—he wasn't always on the same page as Queen Alice. What if he decides he wants to strike out on his own and scrap Alice's foundation and projects? What would that mean for me?

"Amelia, are you alright? You're looking a tad pale."

I shudder. "I'm fine, just a bit worried about what's going to happen with us."

Soph pats my hand. "Oh, Amelia. I know you're a worrier, but I promise that if there's something to be concerned about, I'll tell you. Nothing happens in a rush around here."

She's right—having seen how the business side of royalty works, I'd be shocked if Albert made any major changes. But it would be worth having a backup plan just in case. I could always quit lawyering and bake cakes for a living. I would have to learn how to bake first, though.

Okay, new plan. I'm going to *buy* a cake and hope that the sugar hit takes my mind off things.

CHAPTER 2

Saturday 10 July

"CUCUMBER? Pen, unless you're an eighty-year-old woman in an extremely impressive disguise, you can't possibly think that cucumber is the best finger sandwich." I say, outraged.

"I absolutely can and do. I'm a traditionalist. What do you prefer, smoked salmon? Chicken? *Egg*? Please tell me it's not egg. Please."

I mumble indistinctly and take a big swig of my champagne.

"Oh my god!" she says, before shrieking with laughter. "It is egg! What kind of monster am I living with? I would never have agreed to move in with you if I'd known about this."

We both laugh as we soak up the sunshine. It's coronation day, and the combination of champagne and an unseasonably warm twenty-six-degree-Celsius day is making us significantly more passionate about finger sandwiches than we might be otherwise.

Penny, her man of the week, Steph and Jane from the flat upstairs and I are squeezed around the table in our postage stamp of a courtyard to watch the BBC coverage on an iPad.

Albert, his rather cold and aloof wife Queen Louisa and their three children are riding down the Mall in an open carriage.

"He's so stiff! He looks like he's going to another funeral," Steph from upstairs says.

"Stiff? He's a bloody toff, that's what he is," says man-of-the-week (Joe? John? Who knows, they never last long enough for me to remember their names), slapping his palm down on the table. "Look at him up there. Years of media training, and he can't even wave like a normal person!"

"You'd probably look uncomfortable too if you had tens of thousands of people screaming at you on the street. He's never liked the huge public events. One of the biographies I read about him claimed that he's been known to have panic attacks before events that are going to draw a big crowd."

King Albert isn't the universally beloved monarch that his mother was. Queen Alice took the throne as a nineteen-year-old following the sudden death of her father. She grew up, got married, and built a family, all as queen. Through it all, the public grew to know and love her. She had a down-to-earth, relatable attitude that endeared her to everyone. During the Second World War, she often spent time at factories packing care packages for soldiers and is said to have had her private secretary read the daily dispatches to her aloud so she could knit socks for the troops while she listened. There was just something so soothing about her quiet mumsiness and never-quite-perfect hair.

King Albert however is not a homespun, "bake a cake for the soup kitchen you're cutting the ribbon at" sort of leader. Having recently turned sixty, Albert has faced a long wait to become king. In the meantime, he pursued a range of elitist hobbies. He's big on dressage and international art auctions, and his watch collection is supposedly worth millions. The fact that he travels almost exclusively by helicopter and refuses to stay in hotels that don't have a private landing pad doesn't help his reputation for being out of touch. When it comes down to it, he's just not the kind of person who inspires five-year-old girls to stand in the street waving flags for hours on end.

Luckily for Albert and the palace PR team, while King Albert isn't particularly likeable, the world loves his children and nieces. Who doesn't love a flock of young, attractive princes and princesses?

"OK," says Steph, clapping her hands together. "Edmund or Leo?"

"Leo," I reply without missing a beat. "The answer is always Leo."

"*Your* answer is always Leo," says Penny. "You've been in love with him since you were twelve."

"I have not! I mean, yes, I once spent four hours queuing to see him walk past when he was on an Australian tour, and I've had a mug with his face on it on my desk since I started work, and I occasionally walk past Kensington Palace even if it's not on my way. But I maintain the mug started out as a joke. Going to see him in the street is showing a normal level of interest, and the streets around KP are more scenic than other streets."

Man-of-the-week scoffs. "A normal level of interest, hey?" he says. "Sounds like you're a full-blown stalker to me!"

"He's right, Mils," says Penny. "I go along with it because I love you, but you're a bit obsessed."

"I'm not obsessed! And even if I was, is that so wrong? He's an objectively attractive person who is also heavily invested in improving the lives of impoverished orphans. Is that not at least a bit swoon-worthy?"

"Please, he saves orphans one month a year and then waltzes off on holiday to shag his way through Europe for the other eleven months of the year," replies Jane.

"Maybe he used to, but I think he's matured a lot over the last few years," I say. "I've heard that he's getting much more involved in the strategic direction of the charities he's involved in, and these days he spends more time on naval ships than luxury yachts."

Joe (I'm pretty sure it's Joe) slams his beer down. "Whatever you say. All I'm saying is that a lotta girls think they want a Leo, but they'd be better off with an Edmund." He adds, winking at Penny, "I'm an Edmund, just FYI."

Although they were born four years apart, Edmund and Leo have always looked remarkably similar. They're both tall and broad with sandy hair and chiselled jaws, having inherited more of their mother's looks than their father's. In another life, Louisa might have been a famous actress, but as every *Daily Mail* article about her will tell you, growing up in the same circles as Albert, she set her sights on becoming a princess early, and her dogged pursuit was rewarded with an heirloom diamond just shy of her twenty-second birthday.

Despite their similar appearance, the princes are easy to tell apart thanks to their very distinct personalities. While it's almost impossible to find a photo of Edmund smiling, Leo is the life of the party—but in a much more likeable and responsible way than a few years ago. I swear.

"To be fair, there's a lot more pressure on Edmund as heir to the throne than there is on Leo. I'm sure he's a perfectly nice guy, but he's just so *serious* all the time," I say. "He spends half his life on holiday, has hundreds of millions of pounds and lives in an actual palace. You'd think he could smile once in a while."

"He's hard-working and reliable. He doesn't have to be exciting," says Joe.

"Plus, he doesn't have a lot to smile about at the moment," says Jane. "His grandmother just died, he's being thrown into a new job with way more responsibility and he's about to marry a boring aristocrat who is probably way more interested in horses and jewels than she'll ever be in him."

"She *is* a total bore, isn't she?" Steph says.

Lady Sibella Cavendish is the eldest daughter of the twelfth

Duke of Chester. Her family home, Ellingsworth House, was built in the early seventeen-hundreds and has been used as a set in dozens of movies. Calling it a house is perhaps the biggest understatement of the eighteenth century. They even used it in *The Crown* for some of the Buckingham Palace sets. Now I don't profess to be an expert on Buckingham Palace, but I've been on the summer tour more than once, and let me tell you, I can see why Netflix used it—Ellingsworth looks much more like a palace than the actual palace.

"She may be a bore, but she's also scandal-free, which in the royal family counts for a lot. Strategically, I think she's a solid choice," I say.

"Call me a romantic, but I think they love each other," Jane says.

"Mm, maybe. In his position, love is nice, but what he needs is someone who won't cause any public image problems, and he knows that. Can you even really love someone when being married to them is a job description in itself?"

Steph snorts. "Of course you can!" she says. "Just look at Barack and Michelle. They definitely love each other!"

"Sure, I can't argue with that. But when they got married, he was 'future lawyer' Barack, not 'future president' Barack. There's a big difference between marrying someone before they even think about taking on that kind of position and marrying someone who's known nothing else."

"Lucky your boy Leo will never be king then, eh?" says Joe, laughing. "You can marry him purely for his body."

"His body of philanthropy? Of course."

Joe slaps me on the back jovially. "Keep telling yourself that, Amelia, keep telling yourself."

Tuesday 13 July

THREE DAYS AFTER THE CORONATION, I'm sitting at my desk proofing a contract when Soph walks up to me.

"Morning, Amelia. Can you please come by to see me later this afternoon? Pop some time in my diary when you get a chance."

"Sure . . . but I'm happy to just chat now if that suits you?" I reply.

"No, no. I don't want to interrupt what you're working on. Check my calendar to find a time that works, and we'll talk then," Soph says before proceeding into her office and closing the door.

Our junior lawyer Daisy shoots me a confused look across the room. "What's that all about?" she asks.

"No idea. Maybe it's just a new project she wants me to help with," I say, trying to sound casual. But on the inside, I'm anything but casual. Alarm bells are ringing left, right and centre. Soph never books times to talk to people in the team, and she never has her office door shut. Ever.

My mind is racing, wondering what is going on. The timing of this mysterious chat so soon after the coronation doesn't bode well. Has Albert decided to shut down the foundation? Am I being restructured out of a job? I check Soph's calendar and send her a calendar invite for her first available slot after lunch.

After a long morning where I achieved exactly nothing (unless you count thinking of at least six hundred and thirty different disasters that Soph could be planning to tell me about), I go over and knock on her door, which has remained firmly shut since she got into the office. A few seconds later, I'm ushered into the office and take a seat. As I sit down, my pulse is racing and my skin is hot and prickly. I haven't felt this panicked about a meeting since I was at my last firm and had to go through the belittling ritual of taking a contract in to my senior partner's office and then sitting in silence while he read through the document and covered it in red pen, occasionally shaking his head or looking up at me and giving very useful feedback like "what were you thinking?" or "this is terrible."

I force myself to look Soph in the eyes. She looks serious, but not angry. I'm still trying to calm myself down by focusing on my breath when I realise that she's speaking.

"Thanks for coming by, Amelia," she says. "I wanted to talk to you before we make anything public."

I scrunch up my face. "Public?"

"Now that the coronation is done and dusted, Bertie's team is moving ahead with the broader transition work," she continues.

I nod and make some indistinct "mm" sounds.

"There are going to be some changes around here. I know I said I was expecting us to be re-named and continue as is, but the position has changed a bit. Turns out that Bertie has decided to keep managing all his charity work through *his* existing trust. He's handing the foundation over to the boys," she says.

"The boys?" I ask, confused.

"Yes, to Edmund and Leo. Bertie thinks it's about time that their charity work becomes more organised, and given that we're a ready-made foundation with a fabulous team and oodles of experience, he thought it made sense to leverage us to help them," she says.

"What about Princess Caroline?"

"She already has her own team up with her in Scotland, so she doesn't need the help. The boys have never been as organised as she is."

"Right. So, are they keeping on the team?" I ask, wondering how this is all going to impact me.

"Yes, yes," Soph replies, waving her hand around. "They'll need a full team on board."

"So what happens to our charities and projects?" I continue.

"The family will sit down and divvy up the Queen's causes, I suppose. Anything the boys take on will stay here, and everything else will be dropped or moved out to someone else's portfolio," Soph says.

"Right," I say. "Well, I guess there'll be some big changes around here then."

"Yes, there will be," Soph says before pausing and looking at me. "Amelia, there's something else. Bertie's offered me a job heading up his trust. Not just legal, the whole shebang. It's quite an honour, and I've decided to take it."

"You're leaving? Oh, Soph! We're going to miss you so much! How are we going to manage this without you?"

"You'll all be okay. You do the proper work anyway, you know," she says with a smile.

"Not true. We only do the technical legal work. That's the easy part! You're the one who knows how this world works and who to talk to to make things happen. I don't know how anyone will fill your shoes."

"Well, you're going to have to figure it out, because I've recommended to the board that you replace me."

I shake my head and try to play back what I've just heard. Did she just say that she's making me head of legal for the foundation? I'm filled with a mix of pride and sheer panic. Mainly panic.

"You want me to take your job?"

"Yes, I do. You're capable and always calm under pressure. You can do this. You were number four in the *Financial Times'* top not-for-profit lawyers list last year, for heavens' sake."

Despite having achieved a two line mention in a news article, I wouldn't refer to myself as either capable or calm. Most of the time I'm just bluffing my way through things and hoping that no one figures it out.

"Soph, I'm so honoured. But I can't, I can't. I just... I've only been here for three years. I've only been a lawyer for eight. I'm way too junior to run a legal department like this. I wouldn't even know where to start!"

"You can, and you will. You're smart, you're good at your job and you're passionate about what we do here. I believe you can do this, but I won't force it on you. You have to want to take the leap and do it for yourself," Soph says.

She's wrong. I can't do this. Sure, people often tell me that I do good work, and things usually seem to go pretty smoothly when I'm involved, but I always feel like I'm one wrong step away from total disaster or someone realising I have no idea what I'm doing. I'm just not good enough.

Soph looks me straight in the eyes, willing me to step up.

As she stares at me, a little voice creeps into my mind. A man (even a hideously under qualified one) wouldn't question this, it says. He'd take the opportunity and run with it. No questions asked.

Trying to block out the panic, I clench my fists and look back at Soph. "Okay, I'll do it."

"Excellent!" she says, clapping her hands together. "You start tomorrow."

I think I might pass out.

CHAPTER 3

Thursday 15 July

LUCKILY FOR EVERYONE INVOLVED, when Soph said I started tomorrow, she didn't mean that she was going to walk out the door that afternoon and never come back. I was officially starting my new job as head of legal the following day, but Soph was staying on for two weeks to help me with the transition. The first (and, if I'm honest, most exciting) part of the transition was packing up my desk and moving everything into my new office—complete with its very own window, walls and door. That's right, a proper door I can close when I'm busy and people will have to knock on before they come in. Even though it's not enormous, and there's duct tape holding the carpet together in a couple of places, I've done it—I've escaped the hellhole of the open-plan office. No more trying to talk in code on phone calls to the doctor or spending all day smelling someone's leftover lunch.

A couple of days into the handover, I'm horrified that I ever considered turning the job down. Taking on a management role seemed like a big stretch, but in the last few days I've realised how ready I was to challenge myself with something bigger. It's not a simple job by any means, but I might be able to do it after all. There's something exhilarating about knowing that I've got a voice with management, that I can have a say in the strategic direction of the foundation at a time when so much is changing. I've stayed up way too late the last couple of nights researching new projects to pitch to the princes' team.

Today, though, I am not confident at all. Today, I'm both terrified and incredibly excited, because in less than two hours, I'm meeting Prince Leo. In person. In real life. I tossed and turned all night and then spent three hours getting dressed and changing my outfit again and again before sweating and hyperventilating through my Tube trip. I was not popular on the Jubilee Line this morning.

Leo is coming into the office to discuss his annual Africa trip, which the foundation will now manage. As part of this year's trip, Leo will work at a school in Kenya that the King's Trust has recently helped to construct. He's scheduled to leave in a month, and I need to sort out all the funding and sponsorship arrangements before he goes. There will be a film crew following Leo on the trip, so there are broadcasting and publicity deals to deal with, too.

"What time is Leo coming in this morning, Amelia?" Soph asks, flipping through some notes.

I open my laptop to check my Outlook calendar, even though obviously I've memorised the details, but I don't want Soph to think I'm too excited. "He's due at eleven. Should we have a quick pre-meet to prep?"

"Yes, good idea. Can we meet at ten? I'm due in another meeting at ten thirty."

My head snaps up. "Wait. You're not coming to see the prince with me?"

"No, I've got a clash, sorry. You'll be fine. You can take a junior along with you if you like."

Everything screeches to a halt in my mind. This is not what I prepared for. I'd expected that Soph, who has known Leo since he was born, would be in the room with me and could run things. I did not expect to have to speak coherently while seated less than two metres away from someone I had a poster of in my bedroom as a teenager.

"Are you sure you can't reschedule?" I ask, my eyes darting around the room. "Please. I'm begging you."

"Sorry, it's a meet-and-greet with the board of the King's Trust. Nothing I can do," says Soph, giving me a half-hearted smile.

Slight hysteria is rising within me. "Can we reschedule Leo?"

Soph's eyes crinkle as she laughs. "Amelia," she says. "I've known you for a while now, and I know you're quite keen on Leo, but working in this job you're going to have to be able to handle being star-struck sometimes. Think of this as practice."

An hour later, I've had my prep session with Soph and am standing in a locked bathroom stall in a superhero style power-pose. I once saw a TED talk about how standing like this makes you feel more confident. If it's in a TED talk, it must be true; everyone knows that. Right now, though, it's mainly making me feel like a bit of an idiot.

I persevere though, and ten minutes of intense posing later, I think it's worked. I'm calmer than I was before, and more confident. A quick hair and make-up check, and I'll be ready to do this.

Wait, why do I look like death? I'm not that nervous. There might just be weird light in here? I lean in and peer at my skin in the mirror. It's not the light, it's that in my stress this morning I forgot to put on any blush, bronzer or highlighter. All I've got on is a lightweight foundation. *So what, who even needs make-up?* I hear you say. Me, I need make-up. My pale, blotchy skin won't allow me to go without in public. I'm the person who forgets to wear make-up to work, and suddenly has everyone in the office asking if I'm sick.

Why would I do this to myself on the one day I'm going to be in the same room as a prince? I dig around the bottom of my bag to see if, by some miracle, I have any make-up in there. All I find is a tube of lipstick. I wonder if I could improvise, surely a tiny bit of lipstick rubbed on my fingers is basically the same as a cream blush? I wouldn't normally try, but these are desperate times.

Oh my god! I look like a clown. And not a glamorous French mime artist clown, a toddler nightmare clown. I grab some toilet paper and rub at my face madly. At least I can scrub it off—no harm done, right? Wrong. I now have two big, pale spots on my cheeks where there's no make-up at all. Pulling at my hair, I check the time. I'm already four minutes late. There's nothing else for it. Time to use my hands to blend the foundation from the rest of my face back onto my cheeks. With any luck, there'll be a power outage and no one will be able to see me properly. What a disaster.

I'm utterly flustered and looking worse than when I started when I walk into our biggest conference room and see him there, sitting in the corner gazing out at the view along South Bank, just like anyone else might be.

On either side of Leo sit a middle-aged man who I recognise as his private secretary, and a blonde woman in her mid-twenties who I understand is part of his press team. He turns around as he hears me approach but stays seated as he gives me a leisurely look up and down. I curtsy as gracefully as I can manage with what feels like an army of butterflies practising tactical manoeuvres in my stomach.

"You should probably acknowledge him first, he's the important one," Leo says, jerking his thumb across the table. I spin around and realise that there's a fourth person in the room.

Prince Edmund, heir to the throne, in the flesh.

"I'm so sorry, Your Highness," I stammer, dropping into a curtsy. "I wasn't expecting you."

Edmund gives me a tight-lipped smile. "No need to apologise. I was a last-minute addition."

I turn back to Leo. "Your Royal Highness, it's a pleasure to meet you. I'm a long-time admirer of your work in..." I stop speaking abruptly when I see he has his hand held up to signal me to stop and is staring at his phone.

"Water. Sparkling. Three ice cubes."

I blink, momentarily confused. Wait, does he think that I'm a waitress?

"Your Highness," I say, trying desperately to summon some confidence I had in that brief window of time between trying to look like a superhero and ending up looking like a clown. "I'm Amelia Glendale, head of legal for the foundation. I'm here to discuss preparations for the Kenya trip."

"There won't be much of a discussion if you let me die of thirst now, will there?" he says without so much as glancing up from his phone.

I stand, staring at him for a moment, unsure what to do.

"Chop chop," he says, scrolling through his Instagram feed and gesturing with his spare hand to shoo me out of the room.

Too shocked to do anything else, I rush out of the room and flag down someone to organise drinks.

When I have glasses in hand, I force myself to walk back into the conference room. Edmund thanks me politely for the water I place in front of him, while Leo makes no attempt to acknowledge me.

The next hour passes in a bit of a blur and goes about as well as you'd expect. I hand Leo a stack of draft terms sheets that he doesn't even pretend to read. Then I try to hold it together while I run him through a detailed list of questions about how he wants the arrangement with the school and broader aspects of the trip to run. Either his private secretary Francis or the press woman Charli answer each of the questions. Edmund sits and listens quietly, but Leo is absorbed playing on his phone. Now and then, he looks up, but adds nothing to the discussion and seems entirely disengaged from planning what he claims is his passion project.

At the end of the meeting, I stand to leave. "Thank you for coming in today, Your Highnesses. The team here at the foundation and I are looking forward to working with you on this project."

"Yes, I expect so," is all Leo says as he walks out of the room without looking me in the eye.

"Thank you for the water," Edmund adds before following Leo out of the room.

I show Francis and Charli to reception and amble back to my desk. When I sit down, I see my pathetic Leo mug sitting there on my desk and burn with embarrassment. I turn it around so I don't have Leo's smug, smiling face staring at me. I close my eyes and put my head in my hands. As I sit there and breathe out for what feels like the first time in an hour, my heart breaks into a thousand little pieces. I know that it's silly—I'd never met him before and I wasn't actually in love with him or anything—but I somehow feel like I've lost something real by discovering that the man who I've had a crush on for almost twenty years, and who is my new kind-of-boss, is indisputably a total prick.

I walk in the door after work, and Penny is waiting in our tiny lounge room, looking at me with anticipation. I nod to her and start walking to my room to get changed. As I try to walk past the sofa, she grabs my arm to stop me.

"Amelia Marie Glendale! You met a prince today, and you walk in here without even saying hi?"

Penny likes to play it cool and pretend not to be bothered by the royal family most of the time, but I know the truth. Deep down, she loves the monarchy. Coming from a Commonwealth country like I did, she grew up with a deeply entrenched sense of Anglophilia. It also didn't hurt that Princes Edmund and Leo are total heartthrobs. Show me a woman who was a teenager in the mid-2000s who didn't have a crush on one of them, and I'll show you a liar.

"I don't want to talk about it," I say, sniffling and trying to pull away. But Penny isn't having it and keeps a firm grip on my arm.

"Excuse me? Five hours ago, you were in a room with a prince who you've been in love with for more than half your life. A room he had go to with the express intent of having a conversation with you," she says. *And you don't want to talk about it?*

"There's not much to tell."

Penny rolls her eyes at me.

"Look, I'm super tired and just want to change into PJs. Okay?" I snap.

Penny throws her arms up in frustration. "Mils, spill! Something happened. What was it? Did he not show up? Did he say something dumb? Did he say something sleazy? Oh my god!" she says, her eyes growing wide. "He sexually harassed you, didn't he? Did you tell the CEO? Are you going to go to the papers? How much do you think *The Sun* would pay for that story? Did you record anything? Someone would pay a fortune for the story if you had recordings."

"Calm down there, Piers Morgan. He didn't sexually harass me. He just wasn't what I expecting," I say with a sigh.

"In what way?"

"From everything I've watched and read, I had this image of him being so charismatic and passionate. He wasn't rude. Actually, that's a lie. He was pretty rude. But the key thing was that he was so disengaged. This Kenya trip is his baby, and he just... didn't care. He wasn't interested in any of the details. He was way too busy playing on his phone while his secretary and PR rep made all the decisions." I say. "I thought he cared about trying to improve people's lives, but I guess it's more about his image."

Penny jumps up and gives me a big hug. "I'm so sorry. I know how disappointing that must have been for you. At least being at the foundation means that you still get to use his money to do good, regardless of whether he cares. That's something, right?"

I give a feeble laugh. "I suppose so. Oh, and Edmund was there too and I didn't even see him when I came in, so it looked like I was ignoring him. I can't do anything right."

"You met Edmund too! I'm so jealous. Was he even worse than Leo?"

"No, surprisingly he was fine. He didn't contribute much either, but at least he was paying attention and wasn't rude." I wrap my arms around myself and hang my head. "Oh Pen, how am I meant to work for them after this? Less than a week into my new job, and it's already a disaster. I should never have taken the promotion."

"It's not a disaster, hon. You can recover from this. You just need a pick-me-up. Go get changed, and I'll bring out the big guns. Ice cream, chocolate mug cake and new Kardashians ep coming up. We can try to figure out if Khloe has another new nose or has just gone overboard with the contouring again."

I slump back into the sofa. "Sounds perfect."

An hour of trash reality TV and two mug cakes later, I'm starting to feel better about everything. Still disillusioned, but better. I need to make sure that from here on out I never look up to or admire anyone; that way no one can ever disappoint me again. Easy.

We've moved on to *Love Island*, where the contestants are competing in some kind of challenge that involves being blind-folded and making out with every other contestant. I don't understand how the scoring system works at all, but it's both disgusting and fascinating at the same time. I hope they have an industrial amount of mouthwash in that house. And maybe hazmat suits for the crew. I must still seem upset because Penny tosses me another chocolate.

"Cheer up," she says. "At least we've got the wedding to look forward to next weekend."

Prince Edmund's wedding to Lady Sibella is on Saturday afternoon, and we'd planned another little viewing party complete with high tea and lots of bubbles.

I sigh. "Ugh, the wedding. I don't know if I can even be bothered with it anymore. I think it will trigger me after today. We should cancel."

"I'm not letting you miss a once-in-a-generation royal watching event just because you've realised that your imaginary boyfriend isn't all he's cracked up to be."

"I'm not saying you can't watch! I just think I've had enough royalty for one week."

"Rubbish," she says. "How many times in our lives will we get to see a royal wedding? I insist you at least watch the arrivals. Think—fashion, celebrities and ridiculous hats. You'll regret it if you don't watch and have to find out who had the most outrageous outfit from some terrible *Buzzfeed* listicle."

I hesitate. Today wasn't a great day for my inner sixteen-year-old, but maybe she's right.

"Besides, just because you've found out that Leo is kind of a dick doesn't mean that you can't enjoy watching him walk around in a dress coat carrying a sword," she says with a sly grin.

I sigh. "Okay, you convinced me with the sword."

CHAPTER 4

Saturday 24 July

BRIGHT AND EARLY ON the morning of the wedding, Penny and I go for a walk through Camden Market. It's a sunny day with clear skies, and as we walk between the stalls, the festive atmosphere is infectious. The streets and stalls are bursting with decorations, professional bunting and balloons hanging alongside kitschy homemade flags and posters. From the souvenir sellers to goth clothing vendors, everyone is involved. There was a buzz around the coronation, but it was nothing like this. It turns out people enjoy weddings a lot more than they enjoy events which remind them that their collective honorary grandmother is dead. Who knew?

"Teapot or bag?" Penny asks as we pass a souvenir stall—she's holding up a Union Jack bag with a picture of Edmund's head in the middle of it and a teapot featuring a bad paparazzi photo of Edmund and Sibella.

"I'm not sure that I'm in the market for any more royal family merchandise after my recent experiences."

"Come on!" says Penny. "You can't let one run in with an arrogant prince ruin your love of the monarchy! We're experiencing history here. I know you—you'll regret it if you don't buy any memorabilia to bring out and bore your grandchildren with in fifty years."

"Fine. One commemorative plate, but that's it."

I pick out a plate from the display in front of us. It has a copy of Edmund and Sibella's official engagement portrait printed on it. In the portrait Edmund is wearing a charcoal suit and sitting on an antique gilded sofa next to Sibella who is wearing a high-necked, floral Erdem dress. They're both smiling small, tight-lipped smiles and not touching each other. To be honest, it looks more like a political headshot than an engagement photo.

Walking by the river, there are dozens of boats coming and going, all decked out in flags and playing a cacophony of music. The occupants wave and cheer as they float by. The atmosphere buoys my mood. Penny's right, I shouldn't let my disappointment with Leo turn me against the royal family altogether. The romance of living in a city of kings and queens is half the reason I moved to London. I'm also partial to them because they pay my salary.

EVERY CHANNEL IS SHOWING the wedding. Coverage on most of them started at eight a.m., six hours before the actual ceremony. After lunch, we set up our tea platters in the courtyard with Steph, Jane and Penny's fresh man of the week and settle in to watch the coverage. We've landed on switching between the classy BBC coverage and the much less restrained E! News version to get the best of both worlds.

With three hours to go until the ceremony, everyone is still showing canned backstory footage. But once we hit the T-minus two-hour mark, the arrivals start.

"Here we go! This is what we've all been waiting for!" I say as the first guests trickle through the gates to Westminster Abbey.

"It'll be ages until anyone important shows up," says Steph.

"For sure. No way the king shows his face until right on four," agrees Penny.

"Don't go trying to bring down my mood, ladies! All I want to do is laugh at some ridiculous hats, and I don't care whose hats they are."

"Fair call. Look at her! I have no idea who she is, but that outfit is next-level." Penny says.

A group of aristocrats are walking through the gates towards the abbey—two men in charcoal morning suits complete with waistcoats, tie clips and colourful pocket squares, and a tall blonde woman in... I'm not sure what that is.

"Is it a dress or pants?"

"I think they're asymmetrical wide-legged culottes?" says Jane hesitantly.

I tilt my head to study the woman from a different angle. "Or maybe she ripped half a leg off on a sharp fence on the way in and it was too late to go home and change?"

"Either way, the puff ball sleeves are not helping," Steph adds.

"Neither is the colour," says Penny, wrinkling her nose. "What would you even call that? Neon tangerine?"

"At least the hat is simple. It looks like an upside-down ice cream tub, but it's simple."

"Well, you wouldn't want to take away from everything else that's going on here," Steph says, gesturing wildly at the screen.

"Is this what we're going to be doing all afternoon?" interrupts Penny's man of the week.

"Yes," Penny and I say in unison.

"Why am I even here?" he asks, shaking his head.

I'd like to know the answer to that, too. Penny always has questionable taste in men, but this one doesn't seem to have any redeeming features.

"Oh," Jane says. "There's Victoria Beckham in another navy dress and pillbox hat."

Penny nods. "It's her royal event uniform."

"Well, I guess if you find something that works, you may as well stick to it. It's not exciting, but no one is putting her on a worst-dressed list for it."

"How do they even get invited to all these royal events?" Steph asks.

"I think it's all part of David's quest to make friends with enough royals that he ends up getting knighted. It's not enough for him to have squillions of pounds." Penny says.

"I think it's also a bit of a quid pro quo. I've heard they give serious money to the King's Trust. Enough to make sure that he can't ignore them."

"Is that Kayla Monroe walking next to them?" Penny asks.

"From *Ex on the Beach*?" Jane says. "I think it is."

"How on earth did *she* get an invitation?"

"She must be dating some aristocrat, I guess," replies Steph.

Half an hour, and a considerable amount of champagne later, I call out. "Everyone, it's Soph!" I do my best to shush everyone while Soph is on screen. She's walking towards the abbey, deep in conversation with Amal and George. Of course.

"I wonder where Barry is?" I say to no one in particular. Soph is married to Lord Henry Barrington, one of those tweedy country aristocrat types, who's been the royal family's head horse trainer for twenty five years and is affectionately known to everyone as Barry.

"Elizabeth, we can now see George and Amal Clooney arriving with Lady Sophia Sumner-Jones and her daughter Lady Isla Barrington," BBC special royal correspondent Cyril Bingham narrates.

Soph and Amal both look stunning in their own unique ways. Soph is elegant and understated in an ice-blue coat dress and reserved Philip Treacy hat, while Amal is more attention-grabbing in a skin-tight knee-length red Givenchy gown with a low-cut square neck and a large satin hat. George of course looks smooth as always, as though he might offer you a Nespresso at any minute.

"Yes, Cyril, for viewers who aren't aware, Lady Sumner-Jones is a well-known socialite, lawyer and philanthropist. She's a close personal friend of Princess Helena's and now the CEO of the King's Trust," Elizabeth adds.

"That's right, Elizabeth. I hear that she's recently separated from her husband Lord Barrington," says Cyril before moving on to the next arrival.

"You never told me that Soph and Barry broke up!" Penny exclaims.

"I didn't know. She never mentioned it."

"Weird."

It is strange that she didn't tell me. It could have happened after she moved to the King's Trust, I suppose. She never let on that anything was wrong.

A bit after three thirty, we get to the good stuff—the royal family arrivals. A stream of minor royal cousins make their way into the abbey before a car carrying Princess Helena, her ex-husband Sir David Gold and their daughters Princesses Lucy and Emma arrives.

Next up is Edmund accompanied by Caroline and Leo. Caroline is elegant in a slate-grey knit dress with a built-in cape which, according to Elizabeth, is custom Valentino. Edmund and Leo are both in their military uniforms. I shouldn't admit it after my recent encounter with Prince Ego (as I've taken to calling him), but both of them look pretty damn hot. Edmund in his red army dress coat with a chest full of medals, and Leo in black complete with gold buttons, ridiculous gold rope embellishments, and, yes, a sword on his belt. It's a shame that Edmund is going to be married in an hour and Leo is dead to me.

Finally, the king and queen arrive. Even on his son's wedding day, Albert couldn't let Edmund upstage him.

The only person missing now is Sibella.

~

THE CAMERA CUTS to a hotel in central London, with Cyril and Elizabeth's heads superimposed in at the top of the screen.

"Here we are at the Dorchester Hotel, where Lady Sibella spent her last night as a single woman."

"Yes, Cyril. As we speak, Lady Sibella and her parents the Duke and Duchess of Chester will be entering their car in the private courtyard at the rear of the hotel. We should be able to catch a glimpse of them any moment now. Ah! Yes, there we are!" Elizabeth says as a dark Rolls Royce appears in view.

"Can we see anything?" Penny asks as we all strain to see through the windows of the car as it drives down the street.

"I think I see full-length sleeves," Steph says. "And a boat neck?"

"The sleeves are lace," Penny says, peering at the screen.

From the BBC commentary box, Elizabeth jumps in. "Cyril, I can confirm that we've just had word from Lady Sibella's team that Jenny Packham, a favourite of the royal family, designed her gown. I can't wait to get an unobstructed view when she arrives at the Abbey in just a few moments now."

True to Elizabeth's word, a few minutes later, the Rolls arrives at Westminster and pulls to a stop at the front steps. An aide appears and opens the door to the car, standing by waiting for Sibella to step out.

"What's going on? Get on with it, love!" the man of the week calls out two minutes later when the palace aide is still dutifully standing and holding the car door open with all occupants still inside.

"I don't know, she might have to fix her make-up," I say. But as I do, a hand appears from within the car and pulls the door shut. The Rolls Royce moves, and we all glance at each other in confusion.

"Is she... is she leaving?"

"Oh my god! I think she's leaving!" shrieks Steph.

The car speeds up, and just like that, it's out of view. The TV footage then cuts back to the camera in the abbey where Edmund and Leo are standing in the nave, Edmund looking jittery as he keeps glancing down the aisle. Leo nudges Edmund and makes a comment that's not caught by the microphones before giving him a goofy grin. Edmund smiles tightly back at Leo and seems to relax a fraction.

"They don't know," I blurt out. "They don't know that she's left. Is Prince Edmund being left at the altar on live TV? Is that what we're watching here?"

Before anyone can answer, an aide appears on screen, running from the side of the church towards Edmund.

"What's he doing? Is he going to tell Edmund that she's gone in front of everyone?" Penny squeals.

But when he reaches Edmund, red-faced and shaking, he says nothing. Instead, he just holds out a phone. Looking confused, Edmund takes the phone. We all watch in silence as Edmund stands at the end of the aisle, in front of two thousand guests and millions of people at home. In an instant, his face crumples. He shakes his head twice, as if in disbelief, and then turns, throws the phone on the ground and storms down the aisle.

The footage cuts back to the BBC commentary team. "Elizabeth, it's not entirely clear what's happening right now. There's no official word from the palace as yet, but it appears that Lady Sibella Cavendish has turned runaway bride."

"This is unprecedented, Cyril. Absolutely unprecedented," Elizabeth says, shaking her head, the feathers on her hat bobbing around madly. "Let's not jump to conclusions. It's possible that Lady Sibella has taken ill or there has been some kind of accident. Prince Edmund looked rather concerned during that phone call."

"That is possible, Elizabeth, although I have to say... wait, we're going to cross live back to inside Westminster now. We've just been informed that there will be a statement made momentarily," Cyril announces before the feed cuts back to show the scene inside the abbey.

Guests are looking around and whispering to each other, but everyone falls silent as a palace aide speaks briefly to the king and then ascends the steps to the nave. The archbishop steps aside as the aide strides up to the pulpit and clears his throat. "Ladies and gentlemen, thank you for your patience. Unfortunately, because of unforeseen circumstances, the wedding will not be going ahead today. We will not be making any further statement at this time. "

The camera cuts back to Elizabeth and Cyril, who continue chattering away, trying in vain to make the situation less awkward.

"This is insane," Penny says.

"Did she just run away from her own wedding?" Steph asks.

"I can't blame her," cuts in Penny's man of the week. "Who wants to get married and trapped with one person for the rest of your life?"

Note to self: remember to talk to Penny later and make sure this one doesn't somehow survive for a second week.

"Edmund looked devastated."

"What do you think she said? How do you tell someone that you're leaving them when they're live on camera with millions of people watching?" Jane asks.

"Well, she might not have left him," I say. "Maybe she's just freaked out and couldn't go through with the wedding."

"When you're marrying a prince, you don't get to 'freak out' on the day," says Penny. "Today was planned and choreographed within an inch of its life. No way she's staying in the picture after that stunt."

"I just can't believe she did that. I already bought a plate with her face on it! Do you think I can get a refund?"

"Don't you dare get rid of that plate, Amelia! It's a piece of porcelain history."

CHAPTER 5

Monday 26 July

"I STILL CAN'T BELIEVE she ran away from the church," I say as I pour my coffee on Monday morning.

"Have you seen the *Daily Mail* today? She didn't just run away from the church," Penny replies.

"No! I haven't seen it yet!" I say, pulling out my phone.

The page loads and a trashy headline screams at me '*EDMUND DUMPED! Sibella spotted fleeing country!*' Above the headline are two pictures—one taken from the TV footage of Edmund on the phone, looking devastated, the other a grainy photo of what appears to be Sibella at a Heathrow check-in desk wearing jeans and a baseball cap low over her face.

The other tabloids are full of similar headlines: '*Sibella splits after wedding disaster,*' '*EDMUND ALL ALONE,*' and '*ROYAL RUNAWAY! Sibella says I DON'T*'. The list goes on.

"She left the country? They're properly done, then."

"Looks like it. No word on where she went, but I'm sure there'll be photos soon," Penny says.

"I assume so. Where would you go if you were running away from a royal wedding?"

"Nowhere in the Commonwealth, that's for sure. You wouldn't want Albert's henchmen tracking you down."

"True. You'd want somewhere warm, though. Somewhere warm where people wouldn't recognise you too often."

"South East Asia? A Pacific island?" Penny muses.

"I wouldn't go South East Asia, but mainly because my hair is a total nightmare when it's humid. Sibella's hair always seems perfect though, so she could definitely be relaxing at a resort in Laos by now."

"Ooh, that sounds nice. A nice resort with over-water bunga-lows and in-room massage services. That's what I'd do," Penny declares. "I'd go to Bora Bora or the Maldives, though. Laos isn't bougie enough for my tastes. Or it wouldn't be if I had Cavendish-level money, anyway."

WHEN I WALK INTO WORK, there's an unusual buzz around the floor. Everywhere I look, groups of staff are talking frantically. As I walk towards my office, I catch snippets of conversations.

"Can you believe she didn't tell him before the church?"

"I feel so sorry for him. You could see the moment his heart broke."

"She'll be better off without him. Who wants all that respon-sibility?"

"Imagine letting it go that far!"

"Well, she doesn't need him for the money."

"She must have been cheating on him, surely!"

"He could have been cheating on her?"

When I make it through the gossip circles to my office, I check a range of news sites to see if anything new has happened. *The Sun* has now published an article claiming they spotted

Sibella boarding a yacht in Croatia with a cousin of the Earl of Derby.

Sibella sails into the horizon!

Fresh from her disaster of a royal wedding, Lady Sibella Cavendish has been spotted boarding a Croatian yacht with Sir James Parker, younger cousin of the Earl of Derby. Is romance on the cards between the world's most famous runaway bride and the Cambridge drop-out?

Sibella attempted to go incognito, dressed down in jeans and the same baseball cap she sported at Heathrow last night. Parker, on the other hand, did nothing to disguise his identity as he walked down the dock with his hand conspicuously placed on Sibella's back.

Sources close to the pair say they've been growing closer for months after an encounter at a charity ball earlier this year. There are whispers that the relationship is the reason Sibella sensationally ditched Edmund at the altar. Palace insiders say Sibella hadn't been seen at Edmund's Kensington Palace pad in months and speculate that she may have been shacked up elsewhere.

The Earl of Derby bought the yacht the pair were seen boarding— the Lady Salvation—in 2017 for a reported twenty-seven million pounds. The yacht features five state rooms, an indoor salon, two outdoor dining areas and a hot tub. It has a crew of eight and has played host to celeb-filled parties across Europe.

More to come.

There's a photo included in the article that looks like someone took it on a phone at max zoom. It could be Sibella, but it's blurry enough that it could be anyone.

I send Penny a quick text:

Me: *Looks like she's gone to Croatia. Wouldn't be my first choice, but I might not say no to the guy she's with...*

Her reply comes through straight away.

Penny: *A new guy already?! She must have been cheating on him, right? Even people as attractive as her can't find a new guy that fast.*

I tap out my response, but am interrupted by a calendar reminder popping up on my screen. Ugh. I totally forgot that I'm meeting with Leo's team again today. Lucky for me, Leo isn't on the invite list because he was meant to be busy with a post-wedding engagement, so I'll be able to have a civil, productive meeting with his team instead.

"Daisy, can you please pop in when you get a minute?" I call out from the doorway into my office.

"Sure, let me just grab a pen, and I'll come now," Daisy says. A moment later, she appears in my office, notepad in hand.

"I'd like you to come to a meeting with me this afternoon about the Kenya trip," I say, seated back at my desk.

"Of course. Who are we meeting with?" Daisy asks.

"Prince Leo's team. We're meeting to discuss the financing arrangements for the new school and the fundraising plans for before the trip."

"Is the prince coming here? Today?" Daisy asks, eyebrows raised.

"He's not meant to be coming, no. He's probably got a few other things going on after the wedding drama. I assume they've locked the entire family up in crisis talks. Besides, last time I met with him and his team, he didn't seem particularly interested in the project, so I doubt he'll be coming to any more of our meetings."

"I thought this project was his thing," she says.

"I thought so too, but trust me, based on our last meeting, I can tell you he's far more interested in his Insta feed than in educating poverty-stricken children."

"What a shame," she replies. "Doesn't surprise me, though. I've always expected he was a bit of a tosser. What do you need me to do to prep for the meeting?"

"If you could read through the background pack and pull together the details of how the funding arrangements were structured for the last couple of schools established by the King's Trust, that would be great."

"No worries, I'm on it," she says, beaming.

～

DAISY and I chat about one of our other projects as we walk down the corridor to the nice conference room. Charli from Leo's PR team is standing outside the door speaking quickly on her phone. She gives us a harried smile as we approach. She looks far less put together than last time we met—her clothes are creased, her face is pale and her hair is frizzy.

"Looks like she's had an all-nighter," whispers Daisy.

"Half the palace probably haven't slept in days between the wedding lead-up and then trying to deal with the fallout."

"I assume so. Don't feel too bad for her, though. I'm sure everyone on the princes' PR team knows what they're getting into when they choose to work at the palace," Daisy says.

It doesn't appear Charli is going to wrap up her call anytime soon, so Daisy and I walk through into the conference room. Inside, we're greeted by the sight of both Francis and Prince Leo sitting at the table drinking coffee. Ugh. I didn't want to deal with Leo today, but apparently I'm going to have to. Oh well, on with the show.

As Leo looks up, I give a small curtsy. "Good afternoon, Your Highness. I'd like to introduce Daisy Mellington, one of the lawyers in my team."

Leo gives Daisy the same appraising stare that he gave me the first time we met, but this time he seems to be impressed by what he sees. He stands and extends his hand.

"It's a pleasure to meet you, Daisy."

Daisy hesitates for a beat before shaking his hand.

An hour later, Leo is staring off into space as we continue running through the draft funding agreements and clarifying details with Francis and Charli. As Henry and I discuss claw-back arrangements for unused funds, Leo looks across the table.

"So, how long have you worked here, Daisy?"

Daisy looks up from her papers. "About three years now," she replies before going back to making notes on her draft.

"Three years," says Leo. "So you must be at least twenty-six then?"

"Yes, I'm twenty-six."

"You don't look it," says Leo. "I would have guessed about twenty. You must get that a lot though, given how beautiful you are."

Charli visibly stiffens across the table, wondering if she's going to have another long night dealing with a new PR problem.

"If you don't mind, I think we should focus on these contracts, Your Highness," Daisy says, looking Leo in the eye.

Leo laughs. "All business, eh? You're no fun."

Daisy makes an irritated tsk sound without looking back up from her notes.

"I didn't mean to offend you," Leo says, smirking. "Don't worry, though. I'll find a way to make it up to you, love." He winks at Daisy across the table.

"OK," Charli says, clapping and shooting Leo a sharp glance. "We're out of time for today. Thank you for your time, ladies. If you have any follow-up questions, do you want to email them through to Francis and me?"

"We'll be in touch," I say, before nodding to Leo and walking Daisy out of the room.

The silence is deafening as we walk down the hallway. As soon as we're out of earshot, I stop walking.

"Daisy, I am so, so sorry. That was totally inappropriate, and I never would have brought you to the meeting if I had any idea that would happen."

"Don't worry about it," Daisy says, shaking her head. "I'd never met Leo before today, but I went to school with his cousin Emma. I've heard all the stories."

I'm fuming. "It's not okay. You shouldn't have to deal with that kind of thing at work. It's not 1980. I'm going to talk to his office about it. I don't want him coming back for any more meetings."

"Don't cause any problems on my account. I can handle myself."

"I know you can, but I'm still going to say something to his office. It's completely unprofessional."

Daisy shrugs, and I give a long sigh as we walk back to our desks.

IT'S INCREDIBLY STIFLING on the Tube. Too many bodies and not enough space creates that awful kind of humidity where you can almost taste the surrounding people. I love London, but some days the commute is almost enough to send me packing back to Australia.

I'm scrolling through my social feeds and trying to block out the woman next to me who is having a conversation at megaphone volumes, when I get a text from Steph in our group chat.

Steph: *Looks like Sibella isn't the only one running away.*

Under her message is a link to a *TMZ* post showing a series of paparazzi photos of Edmund driving a Range Rover with tinted windows out of the gates at Kensington Palace and away from London. Based on the photos, it looks like the paparazzi followed him all the way to Heathrow before picking him up in Scotland where they followed him from the airport up to Balmoral.

"I feel so sorry for him. I can't even imagine how humiliating it would all be," Penny says later over dinner.

"Don't feel too sorry for him, he's still a prince."

Penny laughs. "Exactly, he's going to be king one day, and he *still* wasn't likeable enough for Sibella to stay with him!"

"Well, based on my recent experiences with the royal family, I'm not that surprised."

"Experiences plural?" Penny says, perking up. "Have you seen Leo again?"

"Yeah, I met with him again today."

"And you didn't think to lead with that piece of news? What's the point of having a roommate who works for the royal family if you don't even remember to tell me your gossip?" Penny throws her hands up in the air dramatically.

"There's not much to tell. I was scheduled to meet with Leo's team about the Kenya trip. I didn't expect him to turn up with everything going on, but he did. He spent half the time hitting on my junior lawyer. Totally inappropriate and slimy." I shake my head. "He still wasn't at all interested in the project either. He's way too wrapped up in his own life to pay much attention to anyone else. Other than attractive girls, of course."

Penny's eyes gleam. "Maybe he and Edmund aren't as different as the press makes them out to be, and that's why Sibella left."

"Who knows? Unfortunately for you, I'll never be friendly enough with them to find out anything we can't read in the *Daily Mail*."

CHAPTER 6

Tuesday 27 July

ON TUESDAY MORNING, I'm sitting in my office preparing some slides for a seminar I'm giving on fundraising for not-for-profits, when I hear a sharp rap on my open door.

"Morning, Amelia. Do you have a minute?" William Longchamp-Boel, the CEO of the foundation, strides into my office before I can respond.

"Sure. How can I help you?"

"How have you been finding the new role?" he asks, ignoring my question.

"It's been great. I've been enjoying the challenge and love being able to have more strategic involvement."

"Very good, very good," William says, pacing around the room. "And how's your team? All good sorts?"

"Uh, yes. It's a wonderful team." That seems like a strange question to ask given that we've all been here for at least two years.

"You trust them all?"

Now that is a very strange question. What's going on here?

"Of course. I wouldn't be working with them if I didn't trust them. Has there been an issue?"

"No, no," he says. He looks at me for a moment before speaking again. "You're aware of the recent unpleasantness with His Highness?"

Is he talking about the Leo and Daisy situation? Not long after our meeting the other day, I called and spoke to Charli and said that I didn't want Leo attending any more meetings at the offices unless he was going to behave professionally. Perhaps news of my call has gotten back to William, and he thinks I overstepped. Is this going to be a boys' club situation where I complain about a man being sleazy and somehow I'm the one who gets in trouble?

"With which prince?" I ask, deciding to hedge my bets.

"Edmund, of course!" William replies, looking at me as if I have three heads. "The wedding! What on earth did you think I was talking about?"

"Of course, the wedding. Sorry, I'm a bit distracted today."

"Right. Well anyway, as you know, Edmund's wedding didn't quite go to plan on Saturday and this week he's been taking some time out of the public eye to recover in Scotland."

"Didn't quite go to plan" is an understatement.

"Yes, I'd heard that."

"Well, His Royal Highness is planning to return to the city on the weekend and wants to get back to work on some planning for his patronages."

"Sounds very sensible." I'm still not sure where this is going.

"After some recent press, it appears there may be a leak in the princes' offices at Kensington Palace. So, Edmund wants to stay away from the offices there for a while," William continues.

"Okay."

"Edmund is going to base himself here for the next couple of months while he tries to fly under the radar."

"Oh!" I say, surprised. "That's a good idea. Let me know if

45

there's anything I can do to help. You can trust that no one in my team will leak anything to the press."

"Thank you, Amelia. As a matter of fact, there is something you can do."

"Sure, whatever you need."

"Edmund is going to use your office while he's here. Being out on the open floor would be far too exposed for him."

I crinkle my nose. "He's going to share my office?"

William chuckles, his waistcoat shaking. "No, no. The prince will be using your office. You'll need to make other arrangements."

Oh, so I'm being evicted to accommodate the potentially even more arrogant version of Leo? Lovely.

I guess I'll have to find a spare desk somewhere out on the floor. On the plus side, if he's anything like Leo, he won't be doing much work and will probably stop coming in after a few days, so I'll able to reclaim my territory.

William narrows his eyes and speaks. "I trust this won't be an issue for you, Amelia?"

Clearly I'm not doing that good a job of concealing my annoyance.

"Of course not, William," I say, plastering a bright smile on my face. "Happy to help. I'll clean up my things this afternoon."

"Oh, and Amelia, please remind everyone in your team of the confidentiality clause in their employment contracts. I won't stand for anyone in this office providing information about the prince to the press."

"Absolutely, William."

"See that you keep it in mind yourself too, Amelia."

Hm, maybe I'd better cancel my plan to call Penny as soon as William leaves the room and tell her what's going on.

Wednesday 28 July

I DID NOT END up cleaning up my things. Someone did, though. The next morning the files that had been strewn around the office are neatly piled on my bookcase. Someone has also rearranged my furniture.

My desk that normally sits in the corner to avoid any glare from the sun on my monitors has been moved to sit in a sunny spot by the window and kitted out with a teapot and collection of fancy pens. The room even smells better. Has someone been in here overnight with a scent diffuser? And the carpet! They've replaced it overnight. I guess that's the treatment you get when you have country-ruling DNA. What a waste for someone who'll turn up once, drink a cup of tea and play on his phone for an hour before disappearing, never to be seen again. Maybe I'll get to keep the pens.

I rummage through the piles of papers on the bookcase and pull out everything I'll need for the day. Clutching my stack of documents I pull the door closed behind me and make my way back out onto the floor to search around for an empty desk. I spot one in the middle of the room and plop myself down with a sigh. Immediately Mervin from finance, who's sitting at the desk next to me, knocks his cup over, sending coffee spilling over his desk and dripping down onto my handbag. Oh, open plan, we meet again.

Half an hour later, I get an email asking a question about a software licence we signed last week. Flipping through my papers, I realise I must have left it in the office. I know it's 2021 and people are all pro-paperless office... but I can't do it. I need to see things on paper to process them properly.

I walk over to my office to find it, open the door and run right into William, who splutters.

"Agh, William! Sorry, I didn't realise you were here."

He brushes himself off and tuts. "Amelia, good of you to join us."

Us? I swing around and my eyes go wide. Oh my god, he's here.

"Your Royal Highness," William says, turning to Prince Edmund. "May I introduce Amelia Glendale? Amelia is our head of legal here at the foundation."

The prince is dressed casually in jeans and a cream linen button-up shirt. His face is pale, and the dark circles under his eyes tell me he has slept little in the last week. Understandable.

"Thank you, William, but we actually met the other week."

Great, he remembers. I was hoping he would have forgotten our previous meeting given how terribly it went.

I curtsy. "It's a pleasure to see you again, Your Highness."

Edmund waves off the curtsy. "No need for the formality. And please, call me Edmund."

Huh. Not the attitude I expected from Leo's more important brother.

"Alright, then," says William. "I'm running late for a meeting so will leave you to it."

With that, William disappears, and I'm left standing in my office with Prince Edmund Louis Albert George Huntington, Duke of Southampton and future King of England.

"I hope everything here is to your liking, sir. Let me know if you need a hand finding anything."

"Please. It's Edmund," he says, extending his hand for me to shake.

"Okay, Edmund," I say, accepting his hand. "Do you mind if I just take a few of my things quickly?"

He smiles as he sits and leans back in my swivel chair. "Not at all." He swings around in the chair, surveying the room before abruptly coming to a stop. "Hold on a tick. Why are your things in here?"

"Oh, this is normally my office. I took some papers with me earlier but wasn't able to carry everything."

The prince raises his eyebrows. "This is your office?"

"It is. My name's right there on the door," I say, smiling and gesturing to the name plaque on the front of the open door.

"So where are you working now?"

"Out on the floor." I flinch involuntarily.

Prince Edmund cranes his neck to look out the door. "You're sitting at one of the little desks out there?"

"I am."

"Because I'm here?"

I slowly nod my head.

He slams his hand down on the desk. "Well. We can't have that."

"Sorry?"

"I'm hardly going to displace you from your office. It wouldn't be particularly gentlemanly of me, would it? You should move back in immediately."

I assume that this is some sort of test where he offers me my desk back to be polite but doesn't expect me to say yes.

"Oh no, Your Highness. It's absolutely fine, I'm more than happy to sit outside while you're here."

Prince Edmund purses his lips and raises an eyebrow. "Really, you're 'happy' to work there for the next two months?"

I laugh nervously. "Alright, 'happy' is a bit of an overstatement. I do really enjoy having a door."

"I knew it!" He grins. "I must insist that you retake your rightful place."

"Where would you go?"

He glances around the room. "I'll stay too. There's room to put another desk over in the corner there."

He wants me to share an office with him for two months? I'm not loving that idea. If Leo is anything to go by, I don't think I particularly want to spend weeks of my life in a confined space with a member of the House of Huntington.

"Uh…"

"Don't bother arguing, Amelia, I'm not planning to take no for an answer."

What am I meant to do here, fight with the heir to the throne? That's a career-limiting move if I've ever seen one.

"This isn't necessary, but thank you."

"It's the least I can do. I've heard about all the great work that you've done here over the last few years. I don't want to interfere with that or cause you any inconvenience by being here."

I smile. "I appreciate it. You have no idea how awful it is out there."

LATER THAT MORNING, someone has brought in a second desk and I'm safely nestled back where I belong. I'm replying to an email when I hear Prince Edmund speak.

"So, how long have you worked here?" he asks.

"I've been here for about three years now," I respond.

"Nice. What are you working on at the moment?"

"A few things. Mainly bits and pieces for establishing the new school in Kenya and Prince Leo's trip there next month," I say. "But Edmund, please don't feel you need to make small talk. This is your office for the next couple of months, too. Just make yourself at home, and I'll stay out of your way."

Edmund gives me a look that I can't quite make out. Amused? Offended? I can't tell. It's not the aloof expression I'm used to seeing on him in tabloid photos.

"I didn't intend it to be small talk. I thought we were just having a conversation so we could get to know each other. Believe it or not, I was asking you the questions because I'm interested in knowing more about the people I work with." He smirks at me. "But I understand if you don't want to talk. Looks like you're more of a Leo fan anyway."

I scoff. "A Leo fan? I don't think so."

"Are you sure?" Edmund says, nodding towards my desk. "Your choice of decor suggests otherwise."

I follow his gaze towards my desk. Shit. The mug.

My cheeks burn, and I mumble something incoherent as I swipe the mug off my desk and throw it in a drawer. Edmund leans back and lets out a deep laugh.

I bury my head in my hands and groan. This is so humiliating.

"I didn't even buy that mug, I swear. My grandma gave it to me."

"Don't worry, Amelia," Edmund says, chuckling. "I'm aware that Leo is the heartthrob of the family. I won't take it personally."

I peek out at him through my fingers. He looks into my eyes and speaks in a hushed, mock-serious tone. "Amelia, I know it must be incredibly disappointing for you to be stuck here with me when you're desperately in love with my brother. So, I'm going to let you in on a little secret that might cure you of your Leo-itis." Edmund shoots me a conspiratorial look and whispers, "He wears pyjamas with pictures of puppy dogs on them that our mother bought him. Do you honestly want to spend the rest of your life sleeping next to a man in puppy jammies?"

I drop my hands, and we both burst out laughing.

"My grandma really did buy that mug for me, you know. She's always loved your family. When I was little, she even took me out to see your parents walk by when they were on a tour of Australia."

"Ah yes, I remember that tour. My parents left Caroline, Leo and I at home with the nannies. We didn't see them for four months."

Parents of the year, right there.

"I can't imagine that. I don't think I ever spent more than two nights in a row away from my parents until I moved out."

"Are you close to your parents and grandmother?" Edmund asks.

I sigh. "I'm still pretty close to my parents. My grandmother and I were very close."

His eyes soften. "When did she pass away?"

"A few years ago now, not long after I moved to London."

"That must have been difficult losing her when you were so far from home. Do you miss her?"

I nod.

Edmund grimaces. "Does it get any better? My grandmother and I, we didn't have quite what you'd call a traditional grandparent-grandchild relationship, but she meant a lot to me." He looks away, eyes focused on something in the distance out the window.

No, I imagine they didn't have a particularly traditional relationship. Not many people have to dress up in military uniform and parade around the city to celebrate their grandmother's birthday. Most people's jobs don't depend on their grandparents dying either.

"It hurts less with time."

"Mm, we shall see." He swivels to look back at his computer screen. "Anyway, I've distracted you for long enough. I'm sure we both have work to do."

The rest of the morning passes without event. Edmund sits at his desk and reads through stacks of papers, making notes and sometimes furrowing his brow and tapping his pen on the desk as he thinks about something.

When my stomach starts audibly rumbling, he shoots me an amused look across the desk. "Sounds like you could do with a sandwich."

I shrug. "Ran out of time for breakfast again this morning."

I finish typing out the thought I was in the middle of and then pack up to head out for lunch.

"Will you be staying for the afternoon?" I ask Edmund.

"Of course," he responds.

"No ribbon cuttings today?"

"No," he says, looking down and clearing his throat. "My schedule is clear for the next couple of weeks."

"Oh," I say, pausing. "You were meant to be on your honeymoon, weren't you?"

"Yes," he says, looking down at his phone.

"I'm so sorry. I didn't mean to bring it up like that. This whole thing must be awful for you."

He looks up at me with a forced cheerfulness. "Don't worry about it at all. It's a good chance to catch up on the back office work and take some time to plan new projects."

"Right, of course. Well, I'll see you after lunch then," I say, giving him a small smile.

Edmund nods, and I walk as quickly as I can away from the office without running. Did I just bring up the fact that he was dumped a week ago in front of hundreds of millions of live TV viewers? Hiding out in our office was meant to let him get away from the drama, not be an opportunity for random people to bring it up in conversation. I'm such an idiot. I assume he'll disappear back to Kensington Palace while I'm out at lunch and never speak to me again.

When I skulk back into my office after lunch, I'm surprised to see that, true to his word, Edmund is still sitting there.

"Did you get out over lunch?" I ask as I settle back down at my desk.

"No, Walters brought me a salad to eat here."

"Walters?" I ask, confused.

"One of my personal protection officers."

"Oh. I haven't seen any security guards around, but I guess that makes sense. Do they go everywhere with you?"

"Pretty much," he says, shrugging. "Now and then, they give me a free pass to slip out somewhere pre-screened by myself, but

I have to go incognito and I always assume they're watching from a distance."

"Wow," I say. "That must make popping to the shops or out for lunch pretty tough."

Edmund laughs warmly. "It certainly does. Hence, Walters delivering lunch to my desk."

"Sounds pretty annoying."

"Oh, it comes with the territory," he says. "I'm used to it. Besides, if I didn't have PPOs following me around, how would anyone know how terribly important I am?"

"So?" Penny practically yells at me as soon as I walk through the door. "What's he like? Is he as tall in real life as he looks in photos?"

"Penny! I shouldn't have even told you that he was going to be at the office. I can't tell you anything else."

"Are you seriously not going to tell me anything about him? I know you—you're so excited by this you can't possibly keep it to yourself. You practically bounced in the door tonight."

"If I tell you something and it gets out, I will for sure get fired."

"Excuse me! Are you suggesting that I would sell you out to the press?"

"Well, you are always talking about wanting to be quoted as a 'source close to the star' in a celebrity news story."

Penny rolls her eyes. "Mils, you know I'm joking about that. I'm your best friend! I would never tell anyone something you told me in confidence."

"Do you absolutely promise you won't tell anyone anything? I mean no one. I could lose my job if you do."

"Cross my heart," Penny replies, hand on her chest.

I sigh. "Fine."

Penny squeals and claps like a toddler. Or a performing seal, either way.

"I can confirm he is quite tall," I say.

"Did you get to talk to him?"

"I did. Quite a bit, actually— he insisted I share the office with him."

"No, he didn't!"

"He did."

"So you're going to be within spitting distance of him for weeks?" Penny says, sipping her tea. "Tell me everything."

"I'm not planning to spit on him, but yes, we'll be pretty close. I don't know what else to tell you about him. He seemed pretty down to earth and much friendlier than last time I met him. Not nearly as arrogant as Leo. We just chatted like he was a normal person."

"Did he seem devastated about the wedding? It's only been a week."

"Not particularly. If I hadn't watched him be publicly dumped a week ago and read nine thousand articles about it since, I wouldn't have known anything was wrong," I reply. "Other than when I accidentally brought it up, of course."

"You *what?*"

"I asked him why he didn't have any other engagements on, and he had to explain that his schedule is clear because he should have been on honeymoon at the moment."

"You didn't!" says Penny, laughing. "I bet that made for an awkward day!"

"It wasn't as awkward as you'd expect, thank god. He seemed kind of unfazed by it, to be honest."

"Weird. He could have been cheating on her? Or maybe he's taking lots of Valium? Or on something else..." Penny muses.

"Pen, I don't think he's on drugs!"

"You don't know that. Don't you read all those articles about normal, high-functioning people being addicted to meth?" Penny asks. "Watch him tomorrow and see if you think he's high. Check his arms for track marks if you can."

I laugh. "I doubt I'll have an opportunity to inspect his arms. I'm sure one day of office time will be plenty for this week. He probably called his private secretary on the way home to book a holiday to replace the aborted honeymoon."

CHAPTER 7

Thursday 29 July

"Are we still on for dinner tonight, lady?" I ask Penny as we're getting ready for work on Thursday morning.

"Oh, love, I forgot!"

"You've made other plans, haven't you?"

She murmurs something I can't make out.

"Scratch that. You've organised a date with another internet guy, haven't you?"

"Mils, I know you're on an app cleanse, but at some stage you're going to have to accept that this is how dating works these days."

"Ugh, I know," I say, exasperated. "But I don't know how you do it. I just hate the whole drama of it. How many bad Tinder dates am I expected to go on? I just want to do things the old-fashioned way and meet a drunk guy in a pub."

"Poor, sweet Amelia. Bless your heart," Penny says, shaking her head. "Things don't happen that way anymore. Dating these days is a numbers game. You've gotta be on the apps and chatting to as many guys as possible to give yourself any chance of finding a good one."

"That's so depressing! Most of the good guys are already gone, and I don't want to spend hours of my life combing through the dregs."

"With that attitude, you're going to be single forever, Little Miss Sunshine."

"Most likely," I say. "I can't do it, though. I don't need the cheesy pick-up lines and dick pics in my life."

Penny shudders. "I'm on your side there. The dick pics are almost enough to make me delete all my accounts. How many more of them can I subject my poor phone to?"

"I'll never understand why guys even send them. Are there actual women out there who find blurry and poorly lit pictures of penises attractive? Has a woman ever asked a man for a picture of his genitals? If you're going to send me a picture, send me one of your face or abs. Or arms. God, anything else."

"Trust me, I'm with you. I'm convinced the whole thing is weirdly homoerotic. One day they'll figure it out."

"I hope so. Until then though, I'm off the apps."

"Fair enough. Well, tonight's prospect hasn't sent me any not-safe-for-work pics yet, so he could be a winner."

"I hope it goes well. But I also hope that's not your only criteria. You deserve better than that." I say. "I'd better get going. No hard feelings about you standing me up for dinner. I'll make sure there's ice cream in the freezer so we can debrief after."

BY THE TIME I arrive at the office, I've decided yesterday was some kind of blip and by today Edmund will have found something more interesting to do at the palace or flown to Algeria to buy polo ponies. So I'm surprised when I walk through my office door at eight forty-five and find Edmund sitting at his desk flipping through a stack of reports.

I have to say, I'm genuinely impressed by his work ethic, especially with everything he has going on at the moment.

"Good morning, Edmund," I say, trying not to sound too surprised.

"Good morning, Amelia. By the way, my friends call me Eddie."

I raise an eyebrow. "Are we friends?"

"Yet to be determined, but I'll allow you to use the name on a probationary basis."

"Why, thank you, Eddie. I'm honoured."

"The honour is all mine," he says with a wink.

As I'm waiting for my computer to turn on, Daisy careers into the office looking pale and breathing quickly.

"Amelia! Thank god you're here."

"Hey Daisy, are you okay?"

She makes a high-pitched squeak as she slaps a piece of paper down on my desk.

"What is this?"

"It's a letter."

I laugh. "I can see that. What's it a letter about?"

When Daisy doesn't respond, I look down and start reading.

Dear Mr Longchamps-Boel:

As we have not received notice of renewal of your lease, we require The Princes' Charitable Foundation to vacate the premises by 20 September at the latest.

Please confirm your proposed vacation date by return letter at your earliest convenience.

Yours sincerely,

London General Property Trust

I carefully place the letter down on my desk and look up at Daisy who is quietly hyperventilating in front of me.

"Daisy, did you forget to renew our lease?"

She yelps. "I'm so sorry, I didn't mean to! I wrote the letter, but then I got distracted and I forgot to send it and I guess I must have missed the deadline and now we're being thrown out but I only missed it by a week! How am I going to tell William? How are we going to find a new office in less than two months? I can't believe I let this happen."

"Hey, it's okay. We can deal with this."

"How?" Daisy asks me, her eyes bulging.

"Well, I haven't seen any for lease signs around, so I assume the landlord hasn't got a new tenant lined up yet. I'll just call and see if we can extend."

"Do you really think we'll be able to? What if we can't?"

"We should be able to extend, but if we can't, we'll find a solution. I believe someone in this room happens to have access to quite a few offices at the palace that we could probably use if we needed a temporary space."

I glance across at Eddie who winks back at me.

"See? Nothing to worry about. Why don't you go and get yourself a cup of tea and I'll call the landlord?"

"Thank you so much, Amelia. I can't tell you how sorry I am about this."

"Honestly, it's fine. I'll let you know when I've sorted it out."

Daisy wipes the sweat from her forehead and gives me a shaky smile before leaving the room. A quick phone call confirms that our offices are in fact still available. We agree to extend the lease for the next three years. All I have to do is send a follow-up email, and we're done.

I hang up and exhale. "Crisis averted."

"Do things like that happen often?" Eddie asks.

"Ha! Not if I'm doing my job properly."

"Looks like you're doing a pretty good job to me."

I wave my hand. "Please. I'm passably competent at best."

"Is that how you found your way onto the top not-for-profit lawyers list?"

I blush furiously. "You know about that?"

"I make it my business to know about my star employees. Actually, that's a lie. Soph told me. She's very close to the family and has been bragging about how great you are for years now."

I can't believe that a freaking prince knew who I was. I might faint.

I look up and my stomach does a little flip as Eddie meets my gaze. I've never noticed before how striking his eyes are. In photos and on TV they always look cold and distant, but up close there's a warmth there. And now I've been staring at him in silence for an awkwardly long time. Quick, say something.

"Uh, so what are you working on today?"

"Nothing nearly so dramatic as what you've just been doing. I'm just reviewing some reports about my brother's African projects. As you know from the meeting the other week, he's asked me to get involved. He's hoping that both of us promoting it will create more publicity and attract more donations."

More like he's hoping he'll be off the hook because he'll have someone else to do the work.

"Sounds like a good idea," I say in an even tone, trying not to betray my scepticism.

"These schools are doing wonderful work," Edmund muses. "But I feel like we could do more. Education provides tremendous benefits in the long term, but is it enough?"

"I don't think we can ever do 'enough.' There are so many problems out in the world, but I believe that everything we do here makes a difference. We're so lucky to be in a position where we can have a genuine impact on people's lives."

I realise that I'm starting to sound quite sentimental. Edmund is studying me silently, with a look I can't read in his eyes. Nice work, Amelia, you've gone and made this into a much more awkward conversation than it had to be.

"I'm sorry," I say, tugging at my earlobe. "That was so cheesy. I get carried away sometimes."

Edmund looks at me for a moment. "Did you mean it, though?"

"Did I... did I mean it? Of course. The reason I'm here is that I believe we can help people."

"Well, you're right. It was very cheesy," Edmund says. "But I believe it too."

We both sit in silence for a minute before Edmund clears his throat nervously and speaks again.

"I've got a meeting in a minute with Henry, my private secretary." He looks back at me as he gets up to walk out the door. "We should talk more later about what more we can do with the schools."

I watch the door swing shut behind Edmund and sit for a minute twirling my hair and gazing out the window. He seems so genuine and not at all like Leo.

After an endless phone call with a hospital's team of lawyers about naming rights for a hospital wing, Edmund is back at his desk reading over meeting notes. I check the time and see that it's almost twelve thirty. As if on cue, my stomach rumbles.

"Skipped breakfast again, did you?" Edmund asks, eyebrow raised.

"Does coffee count as breakfast?"

Edmund tuts and shakes his head at me.

"Ugh, I know you're right. I should eat something. Can I pick anything up for you while I'm out?"

"A chicken salad from the place down the street would be great, if it's not too much trouble? No issues at all if it's out of your way, though. I can send a PPO down later."

"No, no trouble at all. Just the salad?"

"Yes, thanks. Need to watch my figure being in the public eye, natch." Edmund says, grinning at me.

"Salad it is."

CHAPTER 8

Friday 30 July

WHEN I WALK into my office on Friday morning, there's no sign of Eddie, but there is a mysterious brown paper bag on my desk. I open it and see a little plastic tub of Bircher muesli and a ham and cheese croissant wrapped in red and white chequered wax paper. At the bottom of the bag there's a Post-it Note: *'Can't do your best work on an empty stomach—E.'*

I look at the note and smile to myself. I'm sure he sent a PPO or some other minion out to buy this for me, but it's still a surprisingly thoughtful gesture. As I bite into the croissant, I inadvertently let out a moan that sounds entirely inappropriate for an office environment. This might be the greatest pastry I've ever eaten. There are perks to being a prince.

I'm halfway through a phone call when Eddie walks into the office and nods towards me in greeting as he shrugs off his coat. I wave my arms around towards the now-empty paper bag sitting on my desk, trying to convey my how delicious the breakfast was. He watches with a raised brow and amused smile. I'll admit, my mime skills are not world-class. There may have been stomach rubbing and mock-swooning involved.

"So," Eddie says with a laugh when I hang up the phone. "I take it you enjoyed eating breakfast for a change?"

"I did. It was amazing!"

"You should try doing it more often. Did you know many people eat breakfast every day? Most important meal of the day, set you up for success and all that," he says officiously.

"I always *try* to eat breakfast, but it doesn't seem to happen most of the time. Do these magical people who eat breakfast every morning have extra time in their days?"

"Not that I'm aware of, but they may get more done later in the day given that they're not weak with hunger by ten a.m."

I laugh, "That could be it. Why didn't anyone teach me this in school?"

"Maybe they did, and you just weren't paying attention. Which, to be honest, is a bit concerning because I generally prefer my head of legal to pay attention to detail."

Funny, attractive and genuinely passionate about helping people—I'm starting to wonder why more people don't swoon over Eddie instead of Leo. I'm starting to wonder why I never did.

I wave off his comment. "Details, details."

I look out into the empty corridor outside my office, straining to spot the PPOs who like to melt into the walls and pretend they're not there. "Seriously, though, is Walters around? I'd like to ask him where he bought that croissant. It was something else."

Edmund rests his chin in his hand and looks across the room at me, "Something else good, you mean?"

"The best. Mind-blowing. Life-changing," I say before closing my eyes and exhaling, daydreaming about the initial crunch of the pastry and its delicious buttery-ness melting in my mouth.

"Quite good, then," he says, grinning. As he does, a little dimple appears to the left of his mouth. I've never seen it before, in pictures or in real life. I like it, though—quite a lot, in fact. I might not like it as much as I liked that croissant, but it's pretty close. Edmund sits looking back at me, and I realise that I've been staring at his face—and his mouth—for way too long. My cheeks burn, and I force myself to turn back to my computer screen and pretend to check my email while I try to steer myself back to a more work-appropriate tone.

"So," I say briskly, "do you know where Walters got them? I'd like to buy some for a friend."

"He didn't. I brought them from home." Edmund responds.

From home. As in Kensington Palace, where he lives. And has private pastry chefs on call. The thought makes the warm, fuzzy feeling that had started to bubble up inside of me disappear. I don't know exactly what's going on here with Edmund and me and this easy banter we have, but whatever it is, he isn't just another guy from work. He's next in line to the throne, and when the PR storm dies down and he moves back to his office at the palace, I won't see him again other than in occasional meetings full of palace advisors and handlers.

Wednesday 4 August

A few days later we're sitting in the office, Eddie absorbed in writing an email. "Hey Eddie?" I say across the desk. "Do you have a minute?"

"Of course. Do you mind if I just finish this thought? I get so much done here without all the distractions of home."

"Sure."

I sit and watch him finish his email, brow creased in concentration and a pen clenched between his teeth. He finishes typing and reads back over his email. As he gets to the end, his brow relaxes and I see a flash of satisfaction in his hazel eyes. He's so cute when he's proud of what he's done.

Wait, did I just call Prince Edmund cute? Danger, Amelia, danger. Finding him attractive in photos online is one thing, but sitting here with him a metre away and obsessing about how cute he is is a different thing altogether. A thing that can only end in awkwardness and disappointment.

As I'm thinking, Eddie turns around to face me and catches me looking at him.

"There was something you wanted to talk about?" he asks with a small, amused smile.

"Something I wanted to talk about?" I say, feeling flustered, worried that he could somehow see what I'd been thinking about. "Oh, right, yes. Kenya! I wanted to talk about Kenya."

"Okay," he replies. "What about Kenya?"

I try to collect myself and push all thoughts of cute Eddie out of my mind. "It's the schools. You were talking the other day about how you wanted to do more, and I wonder if the schools are the answer."

"Go on…"

"Well, the African programs have focussed pretty heavily so far on building schools and trying to educate children who otherwise wouldn't be able to go to school, right?"

"You are correct."

"What's being overlooked is that building schools has given us a strong physical presence and connection to communities that we could leverage to do more. Why aren't we using the schools to provide other services? Immunisation programs, visiting nurses for health screenings, training in agricultural methods or trades for adults. There are so many possibilities."

I take a breath and continue. "When I was studying, I did some volunteer work in Peru one summer, and the logistics of providing health services to remote communities were so complicated. We could make access much easier."

He looks at me, a spark in his eyes. "How do we make it happen?"

"How do we what?"

"I love the idea. We should do it. So where do we start?"

"Just like that?" I ask, flabbergasted.

"It's a good idea, and it could help a lot of people. So why wouldn't we do it?"

"Uh, well, for starters, we'd need a lot of money."

"Did you know," Eddie stage-whispers, "that I happen to have quite a bit of money?"

I stare at him. "You want to fund this? Yourself?"

"I do. Part of what I've been trying to do here is find something new to work on in my personal capacity. That, and just stay out of the public eye for a while. I want to be involved in creating something from the start. Selfishly, I also want to show people what I care about and who I am. I need that fresh start right now."

Silence falls over the room. A new start after being dumped at the altar and slammed in the tabloids for weeks as someone too boring to marry, even if it meant being an instant millionaire and future queen. What on earth do I say to that? More importantly, why do I keep accidentally bringing this up?

"Great, well, best to talk to Simone, our head of project development. She'll know how to get something started." I say, deciding to take the coward's way out and just ignore the awkwardness.

"Only if you come with me."

I shake my head. "Me? I don't do the operational side of things. I just take care of the legals once the rest of the team sort out the details. And let's be honest, I'm barely across the legal side half the time."

"That may be how you usually work, but this was your idea, and I want you to get involved. And you're far more talented than you give yourself credit for, you know. We're going to need to work on your self-confidence. I'm not taking no for an answer."

I hesitate. This would mean working more closely with Edmund to get the project set up, and I'm already worried that I'm getting too close. It's not a good idea. But then Edmund smiles expectantly, and my stomach does its little flip again.

Screw it.

"Well..." I say. "I guess my answer has to be yes then."

～

ONCE EDMUND DECIDES to make something happen, things move *fast*. It turns out that when the first in line to the throne calls people directly and asks them to do something, they pull out all the stops. Imagine what I could achieve with that kind of influence! I could probably even convince the cafe downstairs to start delivering coffee directly to my desk.

By Monday, Simone has blocked out my morning for a Project Phoenix (as it's apparently being called) strategy meeting.

Edmund strolls into the office a bit before nine and places a coffee and paper bag on my desk.

"Is this... is this another croissant? What have I done to deserve this?"

"Don't get too excited, Amelia, it's raspberry banana bread today. Croissants are not an everyday food, you know. Do you know how long they take to make?"

"Well, I'm sure palace banana bread is also amazing. You have no idea how lucky you are to have in-house chefs."

"Hmm..." Eddie looks down and fidgets with his watch. "There are definitely some perks, but it's not all rowing regattas and tasting menus. When was the last time you had to ask your security team to sweep a shop three days in advance if you want to pop in for a loaf of bread? Or wonder if every person you meet is going to be the next one to sell a story about you to the papers?"

I stare at Eddie, taken aback. He is still staring at the series of little dials on his watch with a dark cloud over his normally relaxed face. I didn't expect my throw away comment to trigger anything serious.

"Eddie, I'm sorry. I didn't mean it that way. I can't even imagine what your life outside this office is like, but I know enough to understand that it's not all good."

"It's fine. I don't expect you to understand. I just get a tad frustrated when people assume my life is perfect."

He lifts his gaze, and I gaze into his warm hazel eyes. I hate seeing the weariness in him. Working with the royal family, I like to think that I have a better understanding of what their day-to-day lives are like than most people do, but I've never stopped to understand how exhausting it all must be for them as people. Even working here and getting glimpses behind the curtain, at heart I'm still just an everyday royal watcher. When I look at Albert, Louisa, Edmund and the rest of them, I still see jewels and privilege. To outsiders, it's a fairy tale, but to Eddie, it's just life, and not always an easy one. I sit, looking into his eyes, unsure of what to say until our phones beep in unison.

"Time for us to get to the meeting," says Eddie, not breaking eye contact.

He looks so tired and defeated, I just want to give him a hug. I'd probably be tackled to the ground by a PPO if I tried, though.

We both collect our things and walk in silence to the conference room. Edmund pushes the door open and steps aside to allow me to walk in ahead of him. I make my way into the room and am overwhelmed to see Edmund's private secretary Henry, Leo's private secretary Francis, Charli and her assistant from the princes' PR team, Simone from project development and five other people I recognise as foundation employees sitting around the table waiting to kick off.

I inhale sharply and bite my lip. Are these people really here because of my idea? I can't quite wrap my mind around the fact that I made a comment to Eddie less than a week ago, and now I've walked into a room of ten people who are working furiously to make it a reality. I've never had this kind of power before. It's both exhilarating and slightly terrifying. What if it's a terrible idea, or it doesn't work? Eddie is putting his own money into this, and I don't want to let him down. I'm not meant to be able to decide serious things.

"Your Royal Highness! So, so glad you could make it! Please take a seat," Simone gushes as she attempts to curtsy and gesture to the seat at the head of the table at the same time.

I scribble notes for the next few hours while the team runs through the status of various tasks. We're going to partner with Doctors Without Borders to run immunisation clinics and UNICEF to run adult trade and farming courses. I jump in every now and then with comments about the legal arrangements, but mostly I'm a bit out of my depth. I've never worked on the operational side of a project before, so I don't have a clue about how to organise visas for visiting nurses or where to find refrigerated trucks to transport vaccines.

Towards lunchtime, Charli speaks. "So, last order of business." she says grinning. "My fabulous team has pulled off a minor miracle. There was a last-minute scheduling change at the king's office, so we were able to snag Buckingham for a launch gala on Saturday night!"

"Amazing!" enthuses Simone.

"My team has taken care of everything, and the guest list is looking great. All you need to do, Your Highness, is to be there in a tux by seven p.m."

"Very good," responds Eddie. I look over at him. He doesn't seem particularly excited about this announcement. The spark he had in his eyes earlier in the meeting has disappeared and been replaced by a dull, empty expression. I assume this is all part of

Charli's plan to divert attention from the wedding disaster and put Eddie back in the news for a positive reason, but somehow I don't think he is on board.

My train of thought is broken when I hear Eddie speak again. "Will the entire team be attending?"

"No, not the *entire* team." Charli responds, glancing around the room at the junior staff who she has clearly not invited. "William Longchamp-Boel and Simone will attend on behalf of the foundation."

"And Amelia, obviously," adds Eddie.

"Pardon?" Charli says, her forehead wrinkling.

"I assume Amelia will also attend, given she initiated the project."

"Of course, Your Highness. Apologies, I"—Charli clears her throat—"forgot to mention her."

She most definitely did not just "forget" to mention me.

"Right." says Eddie, clapping his hands together and standing abruptly. "We all know what we're doing, so let's break for today. Excellent work, everyone. I commend you on the tremendous efforts you've made so far. It's been fantastic working with you."

The group around the table disperses as I gather up my notes and stand to leave. Edmund is waiting for me by the door.

As we stroll back towards our office I turn to Eddie, who is still looking distant. "You didn't need to invite me like that, you know. I don't normally go to that kind of event."

He keeps walking and responds without looking at me directly. "I know I didn't have to, but I wanted to. I'd like you to be there."

"Do *you* want to be there, though? When I broke up with my ex before I left Melbourne, I hid in bed for a month. I definitely wouldn't have wanted to go to a huge party where everyone would be staring at me."

Eddie exhales slowly. "It's not at the top of my 'things I'd like to do' list, but what the palace wants, the palace gets. I don't have much choice in the matter. But I'd be happier about it if you came too."

~

Tuesday 10 August

I'M EATING a salad for lunch at my desk on Tuesday when Penny calls.

"Hey, Pen. What's up?"

"Just calling to say hi. I just got out of a four-hour 'brand story development' meeting and need something fun in my life. Entertain me!"

Penny has always worked in fashion, which it turns out is way less glamorous than you might think. At the moment, she works as a marketing manager at Zara and spends an inordinate amount of time in meetings with more jargon than coffee.

"Hmm, did you see the *Daily Mail* article today about Holly from *Geordie Shore*'s latest surgery?"

"Someone should tell the girls on that show that the idea of plastic surgery isn't to end up looking like a blow-up doll."

"It might be the fashion in some crowds?"

"Surely not! Oh speaking of next-level plastic surgery, have you seen that photo of Khloe that's going around? She's unrecognisable!"

"It's all filters!" calls out a sing-song voice. My head snaps up, and I see Edmund walking into the office.

"I'm sorry, what?"

"That photo of Khloe Kardashian," Eddie replies as he rummages through his briefcase and pulls out a muffin and bottle of water. "I'd put money on her not actually looking like that. It's all filters."

"Oh my god!" Penny whispers on the other end of the phone. "Is that him?"

"How would you know anything about Khloe Kardashian?" I ask, bewildered.

"Oh, I follow the whole Kardashian-Jenner clan on Instagram. I enjoy the drama too much not to."

"Just one second," I say, holding a hand up to Eddie. "Pen, I'm going to have to call you back." I hang up over her protests and swing around to face Eddie.

"My friend Penny is going to kill me for hanging up on her, but you can't drop a bomb like that in conversation without any follow-up. I have so many questions. You care about the Kardashians?"

"I absolutely do. Don't forget the Jenners too, because let's be honest, Kylie and Kendall are the true stars these days."

I open and close my mouth a few times, totally unsure of what to say.

"I've been watching *Keeping Up with the Kardashians* with my sister and cousins for years," he says. "Watching TV shows about people with utterly ridiculous lives makes our lives seem almost normal in comparison."

"That makes sense. Besides, I'll never hold being a Kardashian fan against anyone."

"Lucky, I was worried for a second that you were going to banish me back to KP."

"I'd never do that!" I exclaim, a little too forcefully. "So, wait, you follow the KarJenners on Instagram, on your palace-certified account?"

Eddie pulls a horrified face. "On my public account? Dear god, no. Can you imagine the tabloid headlines? They'd have it out for me even more than they do already! Dad would also murder me. Sometimes it seems his sole focus in life is controlling the family's public image. No, I follow them on my private account."

He pulls out his phone and taps away for a minute.

"There you go, I've just followed you—Frank Jones."

I open the app on my phone and click into his feed. Up pop dozens of photos of Eddie looking way more casual than he does in the office. Eddie in jeans and a T-shirt playing croquet with Princesses Lucy and Emma. Eddie at Lucy's thirtieth birthday. Eddie on a boat with Leo. Eddie and Caroline in front of a fireplace with mugs of hot chocolate. And then... "Hold on a second! Who is this?!" I thrust my phone into his face.

"Ah, Poppy. She's my cavoodle. Six years old, loves sitting on the sofa and hiding my shoes."

"You have a fluffy dog you never mentioned? You, sir, have been holding out on me!"

Eddie laughs, still looking at the picture on my phone. It's a shot of him relaxing on a picnic blanket on a lush lawn with a golden pile of fluff in his lap.

"Why is she not all over your public social media? People would love this."

"Trust me, Charli has tried to convince me to post artfully posed photos of Poppy and me on the palace accounts hundreds of times now. She thinks it would 'humanise' me. But I'd rather keep her to myself. She's part of my private life, and the world doesn't get to share her."

"I suppose I can understand wanting to keep some things to yourself. Especially something so cute."

"She's so great. You'd love her. Maybe you can come over and meet her sometime."

Is Eddie inviting me to visit him at home? Calm down, Amelia, he's just saying it to be polite. He doesn't expect you to ever actually visit and meet his dog. Don't let yourself get carried away and say anything that might make him think you expect an actual invitation.

"I'd love that." I hear myself say. Oops.

I glance down at my phone and see a stream of messages from Penny.

DID YOU JUST HANG UP ON ME?

YOU ARE SO DEAD!

Was I hearing things or did he say he follows the Kardashians on Instagram? Is that even allowed?

Why aren't you answering me?

What is he saying now?

WHY DID YOU HANG UP! THIS IS KILLING ME!

Is he still there?

CALL ME

CALL ME

CALL ME

I'd better call her before she explodes.

CHAPTER 9

"So let me get this straight." Penny says, fixing me with a glare over her gin and tonic. She insisted on meeting me at a bar near my office as soon as I finished work so that she didn't have to wait until I got home to get all the goss. "Ed—"

"Frank," I interrupt, glancing furtively around the busy third-floor bar at the Royal Festival Hall. I'm sure no one is listening to our conversation, but given how anxious about press coverage Eddie is, I don't want there to be any risk of me inadvertently feeding a reporter a new story.

"Okay" Penny says, rolling her eyes. "So 'Frank' invited you to a 'dinner party' at his 'house,' and you neglected to mention it to me for over twenty-four hours?"

"Technically he asked someone in marketing to invite me to a work function for a project I am heavily involved in."

"Uh-huh."

"And I didn't tell you last night because I went to bed before you came home."

"Don't think I'm buying that excuse for a second, lady. For starters, you saw me this morning and could have told me then.

Also... phones. You may have heard of them? They help us communicate when we're in different places."

I sigh and look out at the view over the Thames through the floor-to-ceiling windows. It's coming up to sunset and everything outside seems to glow in the soft dusk light. I find myself thinking that spontaneously stopping in for a drink on the way home from work is only one of the countless small joys I take for granted, but Eddie can never experience.

"Hello? Earth to Amelia!"

"Sorry, I got distracted for a sec."

"Mm..." says Amelia, looking at me intently. Her glare from earlier has been replaced with a smug, knowing look. "I assume you were distracted thinking about a certain someone who, based on what I overheard on the phone, you're spending a lot of time flirting with. Spill!"

"I... I just didn't think to message you about it. It's a boring work event, it's not a big deal, so I didn't think I needed to tell you about it."

"Mils, we've lived together for four years now. I know when you're lying, and I don't believe this story at all."

I lift my head and stare up at the ceiling for a minute. She's not going to let this go.

"Fine," I say nervously, looking back at Penny. "I didn't tell you because I don't know what's going on here—with me and 'Frank', I mean—and I didn't want to tell you about the party because I knew that you'd ask me all these questions."

Penny squeals and slams her hands down on the table. "I knew it! There is something going on with you two!"

"No, I swear there's nothing going on."

Penny smiles knowingly. "But you want there to be."

"No. Maybe. I don't know. All I know is that he's surprisingly easy to talk to and I enjoy spending time with him."

"Mm-hmm. Whatever you say. I think you want him. Bad."

"Pen! Stop it! Even if I did like him, he's him, he's completely out of my league. Nothing could ever happen."

Could it?

~

Friday 13 August

AFTER PULLING out everything in both our wardrobes trying to find a suitable outfit for me to wear to the gala, Penny and I decide that an emergency shopping trip is needed. It turns out that nothing in our collective wardrobe cost more than a hundred quid. Somehow I don't think that quite cuts it in the throne room at BP. So here I am on Friday morning, keeping my head down and trying to rush through my work so that I can leave the office early to buy a dress.

I'm concentrating so much that I don't even realise that Eddie has arrived in the office until I hear him speaking to me.

"You're very focused today, aren't you, Amelia? Busy saving the world?"

"Oh! Hi. Sorry, I didn't see you come in," I stammer.

Eddie chuckles. "I know, I noticed. I don't want to sound arrogant, but people generally pay attention when I walk into a room. You'll find that it's a grave insult to the monarchy not to greet me. If you were a foreign royal, I might have to insist that we invade your country."

"I'm so sorry, Your Highness!" I exclaim, dripping with sarcasm.

"So you should be. I bet you wouldn't have ignored my brother walking in here."

"Oh that's not fair. Just because I have photos of him on my crockery doesn't mean I like him more than you."

"Just checking." Eddie winks before flashing me one of those dimple-creating grins and going back to his work.

Did it just get hotter in here?

After hours of trying desperately to get my work done and equally desperately not to get caught up in daydreaming about Eddie's smile, I'm ready to go shopping.

"Heading off?" he asks as he watches me sweep my phone and make-up off my desk and into my bag.

"I am."

"It's a bit early, isn't it? We don't pay you a premium salary to waltz out of work at three p.m. Actually, do we pay you well? I have no idea."

"You pay me just fine, thank you. And I wouldn't normally leave so early, but I had a last-minute invitation to a fancy-pants party tomorrow night and have nothing to wear."

"Very well then, you're dismissed. Although, given your etiquette faux pas earlier, I feel that it's my duty to point out that by convention, you should curtsy when leaving the room."

"Of course, Your Highness." I demur, sweeping into an awkward curtsy-bow hybrid while still sitting at my desk. As I go to raise my head again, I feel a tug and realise that as I tried to bow I must have rolled a wheel of my chair onto the hem of my maxi skirt. I try to roll myself free, but somehow manage to roll the wrong way and become even more tangled. As I stand up, everything slips into slow motion as I fall face first towards the floor.

Now I'm lying face down on the ground, frozen in a combination of shock and embarrassment. Did I just fall off a chair in front of the first in line to the throne of the most important monarchy in the world? Classy as always, Amelia, classy as always.

I'm still lying there when I sense someone nearby. I look up and see Eddie standing over me looking concerned.

"Are you okay?"

"Yes," I say, trying to sound nonchalant instead of completely humiliated. "I'm fine. Clumsy, but fine."

"Here, let me help you up." I feel Eddie's hand taking mine and pulling me up off the floor. He's surprisingly strong for someone who spends all day in offices or at tea parties. We're standing next to my desk now, with Eddie still holding firmly onto my arm. I open my mouth and then close it again, not sure what to say. Then I look down at his hand. As soon as I do, he drops it from my arm and takes a step back.

"Right, I'd better be going then I guess. Thanks for the, er, help."

I walk as calmly as I can out of the office and towards the lift without looking back. My cheeks are burning, and my whole body is buzzing. Once I'm out of the lift and into the foyer, I basically run out the door and all the way to the Tube. How am I ever going to live that down?

I TAKE the Tube over to Bond Street Station and emerge onto bustling Oxford Street. A quick walk down the street, and I spot Penny waiting outside Selfridges.

"Penny!"

"Mils, thank god you're here. We've got some serious shopping to do."

"Aren't I lucky I've got you to help me spend my money?"

"You sure are, kiddo," Penny replies, hooking her arm through mine and steering me through the revolving door.

We weave our way through the perfume floor towards the lifts.

"Where are we going?" I ask as we emerge from the lift and Penny walks away from the dress department.

"Okay, don't get mad…"

"Penny, why would I get mad?" I narrow my eyes. "What have you done?"

The warm glow in my chest is replaced with sheer panic.

"Nothing bad, I promise." Penny bats her eyelashes at me and gives me her most angelic smile.

I'm still trying to figure out what she's up to when I notice where we are, standing right in front of the personal shopping suites.

"Pen, you know I don't like attention." I sigh, resigned to what's about to happen. "Why did you think I'd be okay with trying on dresses in front of a stylist who is being paid to judge me?"

"Because, missy, this is an important occasion, and while I obviously have exceptional taste, I thought we needed back-up."

"It's too late to back out now, isn't it?"

"Yes, it is," says Penny with a satisfied smile.

We walk up to the desk, and Penny speaks to a perky sales girl who leads us to a private suite with a dove grey velvet lounge, three walls of floor-length mirrors and a small podium in the centre of the room.

"I can't believe you talked me into this. There's a podium here, an actual podium. I'm basically on an episode of *Say Yes to the Dress*. Have you brought a film crew along too?"

Before Penny can make a smart comment back, the door swings open and two immaculately dressed women walk into the room wheeling a garment rack full of gowns that look like they cost more than my first car, followed by a third woman carrying a bottle of champagne.

The first dress—sorry, *gown*—I try on is an Alexander McQueen black sheath dress with a built-in cape and crystal embellished neckline.

"You look fantastic," gushes the stylist.

"It's pretty amazing," Penny adds, toasting me with her champagne. In retrospect, I feel like the champagne may be the real reason Penny organised this.

"Mm. I'm not sure," I say, twirling around to see how the back of the gown falls.

"What are you concerned about, sweetie?" the stylist asks.

"I think it's a bit too much. The cape feels a tad too dramatic for a charity event. And I think I might need some colour? It's very *black*."

The stylist gives a small nod. "Okay, off it comes."

One of the stylist's assistants instantly appears at my side to help me remove the dress. I try to tell her that I can undress myself, but she insists on doing it for me. I get the impression that the assistance undressing is more because they don't trust me with dresses this expensive than because I look like I'm incapable of undoing a zip.

Next up is a very fitted gold gown with long sleeves, a deep illusion neckline and approximately one million beads on it.

"Zuhair Murad," the stylist says as I take in my reflection in the mirror. "Isn't it divine?"

"It is certainly... shiny."

I see a frown form on the stylist's face before she rearranges her face into a professional smile.

"Yes, it's hand-embellished with several thousand beads. Stunning."

"The beading is very impressive, and I do think we're getting closer with the colour. But I think it might be a bit *too* attention-grabbing."

I don't know exactly how I feel about Eddie, but I do know I don't want him to confuse me with a disco ball.

"Very well." The stylist claps, and my undressing assistant reappears.

Three gowns later, I'm in an emerald-green Jenny Packham. The pleated silk gown has a fitted waistband, a full skirt and a deep illusion neckline embellished with a more tasteful number of beads.

I stare at my reflection in the mirror and don't quite know what to say. It's the kind of dress that makes me want to spin around in front of the floor-length mirrors. And thank god there happens to be a podium here! The colour is fantastic with my dark hair and fair skin. The dress fits perfectly, making my waist look tiny and my bigger-than-I'd-like hips disappear. This might be the best I have ever looked. This is the dress.

In the mirror, I see the stylist looking at me approvingly. "This is it, my dear, isn't it?"

"It is," I whisper.

Penny lets out a whoop, and we both laugh as I launch into another twirl for good measure.

Half an hour later, I'm back on Oxford Street carrying a huge bag that contains a dress that did in fact cost more than my first car. And it feels like it's worth every penny.

CHAPTER 10

Saturday 14 August

"Is it necessary for me to have my hair and make-up done? This is technically a work event, and I've already spent a small fortune on a dress. That dress cost more than every other piece of clothing I own combined. Lucky my fancy new head of legal title came with a pay rise, otherwise we'd be sharing a bed and renting out my room."

"I don't think Aaron would be too happy about that." Penny winks.

"Aaron? Wasn't the latest a James?"

"James is last week's news. I've seen Aaron twice already. He has real potential. Although, on second thought, he may be more excited than disappointed about you sharing my bed."

I gag a little. "Maybe not future husband material, then?"

Penny sighs. "Not even short-term boyfriend material. Don't act so disgusted by the idea of having sex with me, though, please. I have a fragile ego."

"You're gorgeous, and we wear the same size clothes. If I ever decide to ditch men, you'll be at the top of my list of women to call. Happy?"

"Very, thank you," Penny declares. "Back to the point. Yes, you have to have your hair and make-up done. You're going to *Buckingham Palace,* where you were invited by *Prince Edmund.* You must be as attractive as humanly possible."

"You're not going to let me half-ass this, are you?"

"I certainly am not. I'm counting on you to marry Edmund and get me in with the royal set. I don't need a prince for myself, but you could be a good friend for once and find me an earl."

"Pen! We are not going to get married! He doesn't even like me. I'm a colleague. That's it. If you think about it, I'm not even a colleague, I'm an underling."

"Rubbish!" Penny wags her index finger at me. "I overheard quite enough of your conversation the other day to know that he either likes you or is a serial flirt."

"I'm sure he's just friendly."

"You say friendly, I say head-over-heels in love with you. Either way, you're my ticket to royal events full of eligible aristos, so you're going to have to put the effort in."

"Okay, okay, you win, I'll book appointments now. But it's not because I have a thing for Edmund, it's because I don't want that dress to be wasted on a bad hair day."

I don't know who I'm trying to convince—her or me.

Penny rolls her eyes at me. "Whatever you say, Mils, whatever you say."

THERE'S an hour to go until the gala, and I'm standing in my tiny room with a too-dim light and peeling beige wallpaper, wearing a four-thousand-pound dress and a 'natural' face of make-up that took a make-up artist over two hours to achieve. I gaze at my reflection in the mirror and feel like I'm looking at someone else. I work for the royal family every day, and have worked literally very close to Prince Edmund for the last few weeks, but the pomp and circumstance of royalty isn't part of my day-to-day life. I don't wear expensive dresses and go to parties at palaces. I'm more of a Netflix-in-pyjamas kind of girl—and not in a euphemistic way. (Give me all the long pants and fluffy slippers.) And yet, I find myself excited about tonight, not in small part because Eddie did kind of invite me. Even if it was partly for work-related reasons. Which it definitely was.

~

"Name?"

My Uber has arrived at the gates of Buckingham Palace, and a guard in a red coat and honest-to-god bearskin hat is peering down at me through the window with a guest list on a clipboard.

"Amelia Glendale," I stammer in reply. The combination of the enormous gates, the palace looming in the background, and bearskin is even more imposing than I expected.

The guard consults his list and nods at me, stony-faced.

"ID?"

I take my wallet out of my clutch and fumble for what feels like minutes, trying to pull my driver's licence out of the little pocket. I finally manage to retrieve my licence and hand it over to the guard. After studying it, the guard hands me a visitor's pass and waves my Uber through the gates.

We pull up in a drop-off line in the palace forecourt. A valet opens the door and stands, waiting for me to step out of the car. Peering up at the enormous building, I take a deep breath and remind myself that I deserve to be here. And to not trip over my hem.

My breath catches as I walk through the arched doorway into the ballroom. I've toured the palace's state rooms multiple times on the summer tours, but it did nothing to prepare me for this.

The sight of all the gilt and chandeliers glowing in the warm lights is awe-inspiring. At the far end of the room, a string quartet is playing in a raised gallery, and there's a low buzz of conversation as scores of impeccably dressed men and women congregate in small groups around the room.

Forget what I said earlier—I definitely don't belong here.

I walk into the room, trembling. I can't see anyone I know, but I can see a bar. Thank god. I'm striding across the room to get a drink when Simone from work catches my eye through the crowd and beckons me over. It's probably rude to ignore her and keep walking to the bar, isn't it?

I make my way over to Simone and the group she's deep in conversation with.

"Hi, Simone."

"Amelia, so glad you could make it. I'd like to introduce you to some people." Ugh, I hate dealing with new people. This is why I needed a drink.

Simone nods towards the man to her left. "Amelia, this is Grant, the Director of Programmes at UNICEF UK."

"Thrilled to meet you," Grant says, shaking my hand.

"And this is Kerry and Vinh from the Doctors Without Borders board, and of course Gemma, who is the COO at Save the Children."

I put on my pleasant professional face. "So nice to meet you all," I say. "Thank you so much for coming tonight and supporting our project."

"It's our pleasure," says Kerry. "We're so pleased to meet you. We've heard fantastic things about you from the team at the foundation."

"We're very excited about this project. We wanted to thank you in person for everything you've done," Vinh says.

I swallow hard. "Thank you, that's very nice of you to say. I haven't done much, though. Most of the progress is down to Simone."

"Don't be modest," Simone says, squeezing my hand. "You came up with the initial concept and have been putting in an incredible amount of work recently to make it all happen on a tight timeframe. We couldn't pull this off without you."

"That's a bit of an exaggeration," I say, bowing my head and playing with my nails.

"It's not. You've made an enormous contribution to what we're doing here."

Grant nods. "From what I've heard, you're off to a flying start in the new job. If you ever want a change of scenery, be sure to call me before someone else snaps you up!"

I smile broadly, pride swelling in my chest. Stepping out of my comfort zone into this new role has paid off.

Just then I hear my name.

"Amelia!"

I spin around and see Soph walking towards me.

"Excuse me, everyone. It's been great to meet you."

I move away from Simone's group to greet Soph. "Soph, I'm so glad you're here," I say as I lean in to kiss her on the cheek.

"So good to see you, darling. That dress is incredible on you!"

"Thanks." I laugh nervously, smoothing my skirt down with my palms. "I figured I should dress up for my night at the palace."

"Well, you've done fabulously. The colour is divine! How are you otherwise? I'm so sorry that we haven't been able to catch up since I left the foundation. Things have just been madness at Bertie's," she gushes, rolling her eyes.

"Don't apologise! I can't even imagine how busy you've been with the new job."

"Oh, it's been frantic, darling. How are you getting on?"

"Everything's going pretty well. It's a big learning curve, but I'm enjoying it."

"I'm so glad to hear it. Have you had much to do with this new Kenyan project? I don't remember hearing about it before I left."

My cheeks flush. "It was my idea, and Prince Edmund ran

with it."

"I say! Well, you're doing even better than I imagined you would then. And it sounds like you've figured out how to handle the boys."

"Mm, Prince Edmund and I get along, but I can't say the same for Prince Leo."

Soph pats me on the arm. "Don't be too harsh on poor Leo, darling. Those boys go through a lot that people don't see."

"Oh! That reminds me. I was so sorry to hear about you and Barry—I didn't realise that you'd separated."

Soph grimaces. "Thank you, dear. No need to be sorry, though. It was a long time coming."

"I had no idea. How's Isla taking it?"

"Oh, you know," Soph says with a tight smile. "She's not thrilled." She gazes off into the distance. "We're not really speaking at the moment."

"Oh, Soph," I say, wrapping my arm around her shoulder. "I'm sorry. I'm sure she'll come round."

"We'll see. She's not a child anymore—she won't be forced to forgive me because she needs me to buy her food. Anyway, have you spoken to the boys this evening?"

"No, I haven't seen them yet."

"I spy them over there in the corner. Let's go and say hello," she says.

Soph hooks her arm through mine and leads me across the room, waving and greeting dozens of people as we weave through the crowd.

I scan the room and see Eddie and Leo together in the corner of the room, speaking to a middle-aged man in a black tuxedo. Just as I spot them, Eddie catches my eye and gives a subtle half-smile. As we keep walking towards him, he gazes at me intently. Something about the way he is looking at me makes my cheeks flush and my insides feel warm and jittery.

When we finally make it over to them, Eddie looks away from

me before Soph and I sweep into curtsies, hers noticeably more graceful than mine.

"Good evening, Your Highnesses," Soph greets Eddie and Leo.

"No need for the formalities, Aunty Soph," Leo chides, leaning in to kiss her on the cheek.

"Lovely to see you, Soph," Eddie says. "Dad won't stop talking about how much you've been helping him. He can't live without you, apparently."

"Oh, I'm sure that's an exaggeration." Soph laughs.

Neither Eddie nor Leo acknowledges my presence.

Meanwhile, the man in the tuxedo greets Soph before extending his hand to me.

"Good evening. Richard Wilcroft, CFO of United Bank."

"Hi, I'm Amelia Glendale. Head of legal at the Prince's Charitable Foundation."

"Great to meet you, Amelia. Have you been involved in putting together tonight's festivities?"

"Not the party, but I've been working on the project. Ed... Prince Edmund and I came up with the idea together. Didn't we, Your Highness?"

I turn to Edmund, who shrugs noncommittally and looks at his drink.

I try again. "What's on the menu, Your Highness? I'm dying to try more royal kitchen creations. The pastries are amazing, so I can only imagine what they can do with a canape."

"I'm not sure," Eddie says coldly, before turning back to Richard.

"Prince Edmund has been bringing the most delicious pastries from Kensington into the office for me," I say to Soph.

"No work talk, please," Eddie says, wrinkling his nose in disdain.

Before I can react, Leo leans over to me.

"Hey Amy, did you bring your fit assistant along tonight? I'd like to get to know her a bit better, if you know what I mean," he says with a wink.

"Actually, *Your Highness*, it's Amelia. And no, Daisy isn't here tonight. She's also not my assistant. She's a lawyer in my team."

"Too bad. I can't stand lawyers. Always assume they know better. I'm going to check if there's anyone interesting here." Leo walks off, and I gape at Eddie. He avoids looking at me and continues talking to Richard.

I try to catch Eddie's eye, but he's studiously avoiding me. I'm not sure what's going on here, but I need to leave before things get worse.

"Excuse me," I whisper before bobbing a curtsy and turning around.

I walk as if in slow motion through groups of guests towards the door. I can feel hot tears welling up in my eyes as I cross into a large corridor, which I hope leads to the exit. Halfway down the corridor, I hear footsteps pounding towards me and then feel a hand on my shoulder.

I turn and see Eddie standing behind me, flushed from running down the hall.

"Amelia," he says urgently. "Are you leaving?"

"Oh, so now you want to talk to me?" I snap.

"Pardon?"

"Don't 'pardon?' me. I came here tonight for you, and you basically ignored me and made me look like a fool."

Eddie stares at me in silence, slack-jawed.

"You came here for me?"

"For your project, I mean. I came here for your project," I say, waving my hand. "It doesn't matter now though, because I'm done with this party."

"Right. Have a good trip home, then."

I shake my head. "I'll see you at work."

I turn my back on Eddie and walk away without looking back. This time he doesn't make any move to follow me.

CHAPTER 11

My heart pounds as I rush down the hallway. I don't realise until I get outside and let out a massive puff of air that I've been holding my breath. Leaning up against the wall of the palace, I bend over and put my hands on my hips. I'm shaking. I can't quite process what's happened—did I just yell at Eddie? And why did he act like he doesn't even know me? This is not what I was hoping for tonight.

"Move along, please, ma'am."

What *was* I hoping for? To be fair, it was a work event; I wasn't here for a private party or to hang out with Eddie. I can't blame him for having other, far more important people to talk to... can I?

"Ma'am?"

My head snaps up, and I see one of the palace guards standing in front of me.

"Who, me?"

"Yes, ma'am, you. Please move along."

"Sorry, I'm just taking a minute to collect myself."

The guard clears his throat loudly. "Ma'am, you can't touch the building. Please move. Now."

I'm about to tell him that I'm trying to process a lot right now and need a minute when I spot the glint of what I'm not sure is a purely ornamental sword on his belt. I think I'd better move.

"Of course." I step away from the wall. "Excuse me, sir," I say, gazing around the drive. "Is there an Uber pickup zone here somewhere?"

He looks at me blankly.

"A cab rank?"

The guard looks down his nose at me. "No. You're going to need to leave the grounds."

Right. I guess I'm walking out to the street, then.

Crunching across the gravel, my thoughts fly back to Eddie. I just don't understand what happened in there. Here I was thinking that we had some kind of friendship, and now he just ignores me? Have I just been imagining it? Maybe he's just being nice to me because we're stuck in an office together. Being polite and making people think that he's interested in what they're saying is a big part of his job…

Then it hits me. He's ashamed of me and doesn't want to be publicly associated with me. It's the only logical explanation. The wind whips around me, and I'm struck by how cold it suddenly feels.

Shivering as I keep wading through the gravel, I wrack my brain trying to figure out why he's so ashamed of me. Is it because I don't fit in with the palace gala crowd? Is it because he can tell this is the only nice dress I own? *Is it because I'm a commoner?*

Snap.

I stumble and fall to the ground. Perfect, my heel broke. A guard appears by my side and helps to pull me up. When I'm back on my feet, he releases my hand and disappears back into the shadows.

Standing there, gazing at the broken heel in my hand, I consider taking off my shoes, but then realise that I've still got a solid fifty metres of gravel driveway to go. Walking in broken shoes it is.

Hobbling along, my breathing becomes ragged and I feel tears start to roll down my cheek. This. This is why he's ashamed of me—I'm the kind of girl who can't even walk across a courtyard without embarrassing myself. If I were a smart, sophisticated prince, I wouldn't want to be seen with a hot mess like me either.

~

Sunday 15 August

THE NEXT MORNING I lie in bed staring at the ceiling and thinking about the gala. About Eddie. I know that I've only known him for a few weeks and that we're just colleagues, but realizing his friendly banter has all been an act or professional curtesy stings. Deep.

A sharp rap on my door breaks my train of thought.

"Mils! Are you awake? Actually, I don't care, I'm coming in!"

Penny throws the door open, bounces into the room and plops herself down next to me on the bed.

"So," she says, rolling over to face me. "Tell me everything. Spare no details."

"It was good."

"Nope, sorry. That's not going to cut it. I'm living vicariously through you, here. I need more than that."

"OK. So, the party was in the ballroom, which is about as opulent and intimidating as you'd expect—enormous chandeliers and paintings, gold everywhere, thrones, the whole shebang."

"How many people were there?"

"I'm not sure, maybe three hundred?"

"Anyone interesting?"

"I didn't talk to many people, mainly Soph and some charity execs."

"And Edmund? You spoke to Edmund, didn't you? You didn't spend my monthly income on a dress to not talk to him."

I let out a deep sigh and close my eyes.

"Yes, I spoke to him."

"I'm sensing a story," Penny responds, her eyes sparkling.

"There is a story, but I'm not sure if it's a good one. Soph and I went to speak to Leo and Eddie. Leo was rude and arrogant as usual. Eddie was... cold and weird. To be honest, he was pretty rude to me, too. He gave off the vibe that he didn't want to be seen with me."

"Well, that's not ideal. What did you do?"

"I left. It was all a bit much."

"So, that's it?"

"Not quite," I say carefully.

"Go on..."

"After I left the ballroom, Eddie came to find me."

"And?"

"And nothing. He came to ask if I was leaving, I said something snarky to him and then I left."

"You left, just like that? You didn't ask him what was going on?"

"Honestly, I was pretty hurt. I wasn't interested in talking to him about it. I just wanted to curl up in bed with a book and forget all about it."

"How did that work out for you?"

I laugh. "Not super well. I was in bed, but I spent all night obsessing over why he thinks I'm not good enough for him."

"Oh, love, I'm sorry. I'm sure there's an explanation, though. Maybe he was just having a bad day."

"Maybe. All I know is that it's going to be pretty darn awkward in the office tomorrow."

$\sim$

Monday 16 August

I GET into the office extra early to make sure that I'll be busily ensconced in work by the time Eddie arrives. Anything that will help me feel like I have even the tiniest hint of an upper hand.

A bit after nine, Eddie walks into the room.

"Good morning, Amelia. How was the rest of your weekend?"

I keep my eyes trained on my keyboard and say nothing.

"Hello, Amelia? Have you recently lost your hearing in some kind of tragic earwax removal-related incident? Or taken a vow of silence to discover your inner zen perhaps?"

I glare at Eddie.

"Really? We're joking around now like nothing happened?"

"Er, yes?" Eddie's brow creases. "Did something happen?"

"We were at a party at your parents' palace on the weekend, your brother was rude to me and then you completely blanked me. I don't get it."

Eddie puffs out his cheeks.

"I'm sorry."

"For which part of it? For pretending to be nice to me for the last three weeks?"

"No, not for that. That's not what's going on here. I'm sorry for acting strangely at the gala, and for Leo. He can be an utter arse sometimes."

"You don't need to apologise for Leo. I expected him to behave like a child. *You* surprised me. I thought we were friends, and then you act like you don't even know me and have no interest in what I have to say?"

Eddie's shoulders droop. "I know. I'm sorry I did that to you."

"I appreciate your apology, but I don't understand why you did it. Are you embarrassed to be seen with your commoner employees?"

"No!" he exclaims, rubbing his temples. "It's nothing like that."

"Then what *is* it like?"

"I've never enjoyed public appearances. There's so much pressure to be perfect, and so many eyes on me. I find them incredibly stressful."

"That sounds tough, but it still doesn't explain why you treated me like that."

"Ah, but it does." Eddie looks into my eyes, his face drawn and tired. "It's my defence mechanism, you see. Over the years, I've learnt to compartmentalise for my own sanity. I've found that the easiest way for me to deal with the attention is to share as little as possible about me and my life. The public doesn't get to be involved in everything."

"What does being rude to me have to do with keeping the public out of your life?"

Eddie flexes his fingers and turns to look out the window.

"I didn't want people to notice us talking because I enjoy spending time with you and I want us..." he trails off. "I want us to be friends. I don't want anything getting in the way of that."

Ugh, can I be mad at that?

"Thank you for telling me all this," I say. "I'm not going to pretend that I understand it all, because I don't. But I believe you that you didn't intend to offend me, and I can relate to you wanting to project a certain image at work."

Eddie turns to face me. "Friends?"

My heart squeezes, and I pause for a beat before giving a small nod. "Friends."

Eddie flashes me a dazzling smile, dimple out in full force.

CRAMMED up against the wall of a train carriage on my way home after work, I stare out the window and think about Eddie. Over the last month, I've learnt a lot about him, and I've realised that the man I thought I knew from years of following royal news and gossip bears very little resemblance to the real Eddie. That man is *Prince Edmund, heir to the throne*, a carefully constructed (and not always endearing) public persona. Edmund, the *real* Edmund, is an entirely different beast. Things I've learnt about *Real Edmund* in the last few weeks include the following:

- When he concentrates, he chews on the ends of his very fancy pens.

- He consistently makes himself a cup of tea, forgets to drink it and then makes another one so that by the end of the day his desk looks more like a teacup graveyard than a place of work.

- He genuinely wants to use his position to help people and make a difference in the world.

- He has one dimple, but you'll only see it when he gives you a proper, genuine smile. You'll never see it in public.

- His taste in reality TV is almost as bad as mine.

- He's terrified of cutting himself with ceremonial scissors.

- I have a huge crush on him.

Shit. Penny was right.

How am I going to sit across from him tomorrow morning knowing how much I like him and that he wants to be *friends*? Being friends with someone has never sounded so unappealing. He may as well have said he wants to coat me in honey, dump me on a mountain and watch bears tear the flesh from my limbs. At this point, I'd almost take being eaten by bears over being friends.

"So, how was the chill factor in your office today?" Penny asks as I walk into the flat.

"It actually wasn't as awkward as I expected. Eddie apologised."

"What did he say?"

"He said he didn't mean to offend me, he was just stressed out and was very sorry that he upset me." I'm careful not to share too much about what Eddie said. I feel that telling Penny everything would be a betrayal of his trust.

"I knew he liked you! I can't wait to be a bridesmaid at a royal wedding. It'll be the start of my career as an Instagram influencer. I can give up my day job and post swipe-ups and affiliate links all day. People will even pay me to go to their bars!"

"Don't get too excited. He said he wants to be friends."

Penny winces. "Ouch. *Friends.*"

"Yeah."

"How do you feel about that?"

"Well... it's better than him hating me."

"But?"

"But it's not what I want."

"I knew it! Good job finally admitting it, Mils. So, what's the plan? How are we going to get you your man?"

I shrug. "I don't think there's anything I can do. He made it very clear that we have a purely professional relationship, and I want to respect that. Besides, as you may have noticed, he's a literal prince, and I'm, well... me. He's so far out of my league I basically need binoculars to see him."

"We'll see. Based on what you've told me, I don't think you should rule yourself out just yet."

"I'm not sure that I should be trying to go after him anyway. I spent years thinking that Leo was Prince Charming, and look how that turned out. What if Eddie has me fooled too? Maybe I've just been sucked into the fairy-tale mystique of another prince."

Penny purses her lips. "Is that what you really think?"

"Honestly," I say, sighing, "I have no idea. I don't trust my judgment when it comes to this family."

"The thing is, Mils, in all those years that you had a thing for Leo, you never *knew* him. You only knew what you read about him. This is different. You know this guy—like, really know him."

"Do I, though?"

"The Edmund that you've told me about, the Edmund you know... he's not the same person that I know from reading the papers and watching documentaries."

"But how do I know that the Eddie I know is the real deal, and not an act?"

Penny shakes her head. "You don't, babe. You've just got to trust your gut."

It's a shame my gut has no freaking idea what's going on.

CHAPTER 12

Tuesday 17 August

TUESDAY MORNING I walk into work determined to maintain a strictly professional relationship with Eddie despite my recent epiphany regarding my not-entirely-platonic feelings for him. To protect my poor heart, I am going to keep my distance. I am not going to let myself be taken in by the charms of another prince or fall into the trap of assuming I have some kind of special relationship with him. He may be funny and sweet, but he is also the future king of England and there's no world outside of a romance novel where he ends up with someone like me.

When I open my door, I see Eddie perched on the edge of my desk holding coffee and a brown paper bag.

"Pear and raspberry muffin? I'm determined to convert you to the joys of eating breakfast. If fresh pastries are the only thing that will convince you, so be it."

My stomach rumbles at the sight of the bag which I reach out and grab hungrily. "You're the best, you know that, right? How did I ever live without you?"

Eddie grins at me, and my stomach swoops. It may as well be a butterfly enclosure in there right now.

So much for maintaining a professional relationship.

AFTER A LONG DAY of trying not to stare at Eddie across the room, I've packed up my desk and am putting on my coat when he looks over at me.

"Amelia," he says questioningly, "what are you doing this evening?"

"Nothing much, just hanging out at home."

"Would you like to come over for dinner?"

I blink rapidly. "Come over? To your apartment at the palace?"

"Yes. Well, no. Technically you'd be having dinner at my cousins Lucy and Emma's place. They came back from Antigua last night, so we're planning to meet for dinner and a TV binge tonight."

"Oh," I say, not quite sure how to respond. Is he overcompensating for being rude the other night and expecting me to say no? Or does he want me to come and hang out with him and his cousins? Who are princesses. And go on holidays to places with names like Antigua, probably on super-yachts.

"As I said the other day"—he clears his throat—"I want us to be friends, and I thought this was something you'd enjoy. But don't feel you have to say yes."

Huh, maybe it's not a token invitation that I'm meant to reject. I guess there's only one way to find out.

"Sounds good," I say, trying to act cool.

Eddie breaks into a big, goofy grin. "Fantastic!"

"So where exactly am I going? And how do I get in?"

"I'm about ready to head off, so if you can wait five minutes, you can come with me."

"I don't need to get changed into something more... palace-appropriate?"

He tosses his head back and laughs. "Trust me, formal dress is not required."

"Okay, great. I'll just hang out here until you're ready to go."

I pull out my phone and try to look casual as I text Penny.

Me: *So... Edmund asked me to come and have dinner with his cousins.*

Me: *At KP.*

Three little dots appear on my screen.

Penny: *OMG!*

Penny: *He invited you to KP to meet his family?!*

Penny: *When is it? You said yes, right?!*

I glance over and check that Eddie is still safely distracted before I reply.

Me: *Going now.*

Penny's reply appears straight away.

Penny: *OMG! Tell me everything. I need a live stream here! Don't you dare put your phone away!*

With that, Eddie logs off his computer and stands up. I take that as my cue to throw my phone back into my handbag and smile. "Ready to go?"

"I am. Shall we?"

"Let's do it."

We walk out into the corridor, and Walters and another PPO I haven't seen before appear, trailing a respectful distance behind us to the lift.

We all head down to the basement in silence. As the lift opens, a Range Rover SUV with dark tinted windows pulls up. Walters hops up into the front passenger seat while the other PPO opens a door for Eddie and me. When we're seated, the PPO closes the door and taps on the side of the car, signalling for the driver that we're clear to leave. The entire process makes me feel like I'm some kind of celebrity. I could get used to this.

"So what have I gotten myself into here? Is it just going to be us and your cousins?"

Eddie chuckles. "Yes, it should be. They might have invited Leo too, but I don't think he's around tonight. You'll love Lucy and Emma. They're very casual and always good for a laugh."

"It must be nice having family around all the time," I say wistfully. "My family is all back in Australia, so I don't get to see them often. I've only been back once since I moved here."

"I didn't know that. How long have you been in London for?"

"About four years now."

"That's a long time to go with only seeing your parents once," Eddie says, his eyes crinkled.

"It is. I miss them. I try not to think about it too much, though, I guess. I know I'll probably move back one day and make up for lost time."

"Have you got any trips home planned?"

"Not at the moment. I might be able to go for Christmas. It's hard with the new job—there's so much to do. If I'm going to visit, I need to find a time when I can take at least a few weeks off, given it's such a long flight to get there. A quick trip isn't really worth it." My eyes start to get misty as I think about my parents, sister and dog back home.

"Do most of your family live at Kensington?" I ask, shifting the conversation back to Edmund and away from things that might make me cry if I think about them for too long. As a long-term royal fan, I know exactly who lives at Kensington Palace, but I can't exactly tell Edmund that. It's like when you meet someone for the first time and already know who they are from having stalked them online, but have to play dumb so you don't come across as super creepy.

"A lot of them do. It's a bit of a family compound, really. The main building has several apartments in it. Aunt Helena lives in Apartment 1, and Mum and Dad were next door in Apartment 1A until they moved to Buckingham Palace after the coronation.

Some of Gran and Dad's cousins live in the smaller apartments. Then there are cottages outside the main building. They're where Lucy, Emma, Leo and I live."

"That's so nice."

"It is. Although it's not as cosy and happy families as all that. Most of them have residences elsewhere as well, so they're not around all the time. There are also dozens of courtier offices and some privately rented apartments around."

"Well, still sounds pretty nice to me," I say, smiling. "Why doesn't Caroline live there too?"

"She used to. But she convinced our parents to let her move up to Inverness a few years ago now."

"She did her uni degree up in Scotland too, didn't she?"

"Yes, she studied at the University of Edinburgh, then came back and put in two years of face-time here before she moved back."

"Why Scotland?"

"She's never been one for the city—she feels trapped here. She likes being out in the country, riding every day and being able to walk for miles without coming across anyone. Growing up, she used to pretend that she was a farmer's daughter. Palace life with the social commitments and people buzzing around everywhere is her nightmare."

"Country life does sound pretty relaxing. Doesn't she miss you all, though? You and Caroline have always seemed very close."

"We were. We still are, really. I don't see her in person as often as I used to, but we keep in touch. She FaceTimes in to my dinners with Leo and Lucy and Emma quite often to check in on us all."

"How do your parents feel about her abandoning them for Scotland?"

"They don't particularly mind. They spend a lot of time up at Balmoral in any case, so they see a lot of her there. They'd never let me do it, of course. As the oldest, I'm expected to stay here and do my bit. Caro and Leo have never had the same kind of pressure."

Eddie's face is drawn, and I don't quite know what to say. After a moment, he shakes his sombre expression off and turns to look at me.

"Amelia, can I ask you something?" Eddie asks, his eyes searching mine.

"Sure, anything."

He clears his throat loudly. "It's about Leo."

"What about him?"

"Do you… are you interested in him?"

I scoff. "You've met him, right? Trust me, nothing about that ego is appealing to me."

"Are you sure? I know he's a bit of a prat sometimes, but he's not all bad. Women normally love him."

"I'm positive."

A small smile appears on his lips.

Before I can get carried away reading into why he's asking me about my interest in Leo, we arrive at the gates and a pair of guards approach the car. They verify that it is in fact Eddie in the car and wave us through.

"Do I have to sign in or anything?" I ask Eddie as we drive through the grounds. "I'm not sure security should let random people in like that."

"Well, you are in the car with me, so the risk of you being a burglar or serial killer is likely to be fairly low."

"How do they know that I'm not holding you at gunpoint in here? I could have kidnapped you."

"I'd like to see you try. Just quietly, Amelia, while I'm sure you're quite strong, I think I could take you."

Eddie pokes at my bony arm, and I burst into giggles.

"Also, I put you on the guest list at the gate."

"But you didn't ask me until the last minute. What made you think I'd say yes?"

"Well," Eddie smirks. "I've been told that I can be quite charming."

He grins at me, and my heart melts a little. Okay, a lot. It melts a lot.

"Here we are," Eddie declares a moment later as the car pulls up in front of a two-storey red brick house covered in ivy. "Ivy Cottage," he says as I gawp out the window. "I'm next door at Wren House, and Leo is over there at Nottingham Cottage." He points towards the neighbouring red brick houses.

"I think that you and I may have *slightly* different ideas of what a 'cottage' is," I say, looking up at the house. While it looks cosy and surprisingly modest for the home of the fifth and sixth in line to the throne, it's not exactly a two-room country shack.

Eddie shrugs. "Our places aren't all that over the top. The girls and I have three bedrooms each, and Leo has two. I'll readily admit though that these houses are far nicer than anything I could afford if I'd been born into a different family."

"So you admit that there *are* some perks to being a prince."

"I concede," he says, putting his hand on his heart. "It's not all pressure and paparazzi packs."

"Good, I was starting to worry that royal life was wasted on you."

CHAPTER 13

Eddie rings the doorbell, and the heavy wooden door with diamond-shaped panes of glass up the top soon swings open to reveal Princess Emma in a fluffy robe holding a cocktail.

"Edmund, finally!" She throws her non-cocktail holding arm around Eddie and then stands back and looks at me appraisingly. "And this," she says dramatically, "must be Amelia. Pleasure to meet you, darling."

"Was I the last person in London to find out I was coming here tonight?"

Emma lets out a peal of laughter.

"Oh, I like you already," she says. "Come in, come in."

We pass through the modest entryway and into a cosy sitting room with a very Hamptons-meets-English-countryside vibe. There are plump linen sofas, drowning in throw cushions, arranged around a whitewashed brick fireplace. Big vases of fresh flowers and greenery are perched on almost every available surface.

In the corner, there's a navy-painted sideboard inlaid with an intricate pattern of what I suspect may be genuine ivory. I suppose you can get away with that if it's a family heirloom. The sideboard is set up with a buffet of nachos, tacos and margaritas. Not what I expected from palace catering. The margarita jug is almost empty.

Emma must see me eyeing it off because she says, "You were meant to be here half an hour ago. We held off on food but couldn't bring ourselves to wait for drinks."

"Eddie, you didn't invite me until half an hour ago. When exactly did you tell your cousin here that I was going to come with you?"

Eddie's ears turn pink, and he loads up his plate, ignoring the question.

"Friday, darling. He told us on Friday that he was going to ask you along tonight."

He'd had this planned even before the gala? Interesting, very interesting. If I was prone to fantasising, I might think that means Penny is right about him being interested too. Best to keep my thoughts firmly planted in reality, though. I'm sure there's another explanation.

"Grab a plate! The reality shows we missed this week aren't going to watch themselves."

I take a plate from the sideboard and start serving myself some food as Princess Lucy emerges from the kitchen wearing a matching fluffy robe.

"Hi!" she says with a grin. "You must be the lovely lawyer we keep hearing about. I'm so glad you could make it." She leans in to give me a kiss on the cheek and then looks over at Eddie. "Cousin, tolerable to see you as always."

"Love you too, Luce," Eddie shoots back.

Once we have our food, we all plant ourselves on the large sofas by the fireplace and rest our plates on our laps. I can see now what Eddie meant about the lack of formalities.

Lucy rummages around through the sofa cushions before pulling out the remote and thrusting it triumphantly into the air.

She hits a button, and the painting over the fireplace rises up to reveal an enormous TV.

"What are we watching, kids?" she asks, brandishing the remote.

"I vote for *Love Island*," Emma calls out.

"I'm too far behind," Eddie complains. "There are just so many episodes, I can't keep up with it. Watching it is essentially a full-time job. Do you think Dad would let me do that instead of charity luncheons?"

"Unlikely, my dear," Lucy replies.

"Don't let too many of your future subjects hear you say that, Eddie," I say. "It might give them the impression that you're scared of hard work."

"She's got a point there, Eddie," Lucy muses. "Luckily, everyone already thinks you're a ponce, so it wouldn't do too much more damage. Oh, there's a new season of *Below Deck*!"

"That I could watch," Eddie says, nodding heartily.

"Your wish is my command, Your Highness," she says with a flourish.

Soon the fantastically grumpy Captain Lee is on screen having an awkward dinner with a hideously drunk forty-something stockbroker and his group of young female "friends."

"Why do these guests always insist on having the captain have dinner with them?" I ask. "Is that a real thing or a reality TV thing?"

"Excuse me, are you asking us because we look like the kind of people who spend a lot of time lolling around on yachts?" Emma asks, lips pursed.

"Um." I glance at Eddie nervously, but it doesn't appear that he's going to dig me out of this one. "No. Well, maybe?"

Emma and Lucy both laugh raucously. "Don't worry, love," replies Lucy. "She's just playing with you. We do in fact spend *quite* a bit of time on yachts."

"In our defence, we've never made a captain sit through a sloppy drunk dinner with us, though."

"Not that we recall, anyway. Speaking of yachts, Em, why do the deckhands on the yachts we stay on never look like this?"

"Good question! We pay enough for the bloody things. Surely they could throw in the occasional deckhand-slash-underwear model or former stripper."

Sounds like I was right about the super-yachts.

"You two are terrible," Eddie declares. "Tripping around the world on boats crewed by not-quite-attractive-enough men while the rest of us stay here doing all the work."

"I'm sorry, *Your Highness*." Lucy leans across and kicks Eddie in the shin. "I'll have you know I did over seventy appearances last year. That is quite enough hand-shaking to earn me a holiday or two."

The three cousins are busy teasing each other when the doorbell rings.

"That'll be Leo," Emma says.

Eddie jumps up to open the door. "Perfect timing to get me out of this conversation."

When he reappears he's being followed by Leo and... wait, is that... Kayla Monroe?

"Leo, great to see you!" gushes Lucy. "Kayla." She nods.

Leo sees me on the sofa and says hello before shooting Eddie a curious look.

Eddie sits back down next to me, closer now than he was before. Close enough that I could let my leg rest against his and have it almost look like an accident. It's torture.

I check over my shoulder and see that Leo is busy helping himself to nachos while Kayla hovers nearby, not eating.

"Are Leo and Kayla... *together*?" I whisper to Edmund.

He leans in to whisper a response. He's so close that I can feel his warm breath on my neck as he talks. A tingle runs down my spine. "For about six months now. Dad's furious. Won't let them go public."

"Who can make me some lemon water?" I hear Kayla ask. "I'm on a cleanse."

"Kayla." Emma sighs, exasperated. "We don't have full-time staff here. You can call over to Mummy's and see if anyone is still in the kitchen, or you can make it yourself."

"Make it myself?" Kayla lets out a little snort and pours herself a plain water instead.

"What's on tonight?" Leo asks as he launches himself into the corner of the sofa.

"*Below Deck* marathon," I say. "One of the deckhands is trying to crack on with two stewardesses and a guest in the same night."

"Fair play to him."

"Why do we always have to watch this rubbish?" Kayla moans. "It's so mindless."

Emma makes a noise that sounds suspiciously like a snort covered by a cough. Leo glares at her, and everyone falls silent until Kayla looks at me.

"Who are you by the way?"

"Amelia, Amelia Glendale. I work at the princes' foundation."

"I invited her," Eddie chimes in.

Kayla casts her eyes over my hair and outfit and then goes back to making doe eyes at Leo, clearly deciding that I'm not worth any more attention.

On screen, a deckhand—one of the former stripper variety—gives a guest a lap dance.

Kayla wrinkles her nose. "These shows are such a poor excuse for film. Where's the artistic merit?"

I lean over to Eddie and whisper, "She's a reality star, right? She's not a classically trained Shakespearean actress I'm confusing with someone else?"

He nods and rolls his eyes.

Two hours and at least four crew member hook-ups and break-ups later, I start yawning.

"I'm going to call it a night. I've got an early meeting tomorrow."

"No! Don't go!" Emma urges.

"I have to go sorry. I'll never make it into the office by eight if I stay."

"Eight in the morning? Ghastly! If I were in charge of things around here, first order of business would be to ban meetings that start before nine thirty."

"Take note, Eddie, might want to add that one to your 'to do as king' list," Lucy calls out.

Eddie nods. "Will make it a top priority."

"I appreciate that. But in the meantime, I need to get some sleep before tomorrow."

"We understand, dear," Lucy says. "Let me walk you out."

Eddie stands quickly. "Don't worry about it, Luce. I should get home too, so I'll show her out."

"Very well. Make sure you don't come back. We're going to switch to *Love Island*."

Eddie and I walk towards the door. I turn back and address Lucy and Emma. "Thanks so much for having me. This was great."

"Anytime! Make sure Eddie brings you back soon," Emma replies.

Edmund ignores his cousin and opens the door, gesturing for me to walk ahead of him.

"Walk next door with me, and I'll ask one of the PPOs to take you home?"

"Sure, that would be great, thanks. And thank you for inviting me tonight. It was fun. It felt a bit like being back home with my sister."

"Did you really enjoy this, or are you just saying that? I'm aware that my family can be a bit... difficult for outsiders to deal with."

"I did. I'm not normally that good with talking to new people, but I really like Lucy and Emma. It was fun."

"But?" Eddie asks, sensing my reluctance.

Should I say something about Leo and risk offending him and the entire royal family when they could have me fired instantly? No, probably not.

"But nothing. I don't want to cause any trouble."

"If it could cause trouble, I need to hear about it. Was it Kayla? She doesn't get along with anyone here. I can't for the life of me figure out what Leo sees in her. Other than... you know."

"The stunning model-slash-TV-star thing?"

"Er, yes. That's the one."

"It's not Kayla. I mean, she wasn't particularly nice to me, but I don't mind. It's Leo. I just can't seem to get on his good side."

"Don't worry about Leo. We all love him to bits, but he can be a bit of an arse. Especially at the moment."

"Since he started seeing Kayla?"

"There seems to be quite a strong correlation, yes. It's not entirely her fault, but she indulges it. I'm sure he'll come good when they split up."

"You don't think they'll last?"

"Ha! No chance."

"Because she's a commoner?" I ask, wrinkling my nose.

"What? No, nothing like that. The family is keen on tradition, but we still live in the twenty-first century. No one would object these days to one of us marrying a 'normal' person."

Huh, good to know. Definitely filing that nugget of information away for future reference.

"They won't last because fundamentally she's rather unpleasant. I'd be shocked if she's interested in Leo for his personality. I assume she's only interested in what being with him can do for her. He'll see through it eventually."

"Well, for your sake, I hope so. Can you imagine the low-carb, raw vegan Christmas lunches?"

Eddie pulls a face. "I'd rather not. Let's hope it doesn't come to that." He checks his watch. "It is getting quite late. I should let you get home. Thank you for coming. As much as I don't want to give Emma the satisfaction of thinking she's successfully told me what to do, I would like you to come back again."

"I'd love to."

A Range Rover pulls up next to us. I can't tell if it's the same one we arrived in or a different one. They probably breed them on the property like horses and keep them in a stable.

Edmund and I stand in silence, staring at each other. He moves almost imperceptibly, and for a moment, I think he's going to lean in and kiss me.

I bite my lip and gaze at the flecks of green in his eyes. He's so close it would take nothing for me to close the gap.

Suddenly, Edmund breaks eye contact and shoves his hands deep in his pockets.

"Well, I should let you go."

He lingers, looking like he has something else he wants to say.

"Amelia?"

"Yes, Edmund?"

He pauses before speaking slowly. "Have a good night."

CHAPTER 14

My mind is racing as the protection officer drives me home. Did I just spend hours eating nachos with my hands and watching trashy reality shows with not one, but four members of the royal family? I don't remember taking anything, but it may have all been an elaborate hallucination. It feels a million miles away from sitting in my lounge room back home, watching Queen Alice's annual Christmas message on TV with my grandmother.

Most importantly, though, am I really going to let myself have a crush on a way-out-of-my-league prince after how my affection for Leo turned out? This isn't a fairy tale or a fantasy—it's real life, and falling for another prince can only lead to soul-crushing disappointment.

Argh, I didn't give Penny any updates, and now my phone battery is dead. I'm going to be lucky if she doesn't kill me as soon as I walk in the door.

Sure enough, I let myself into the flat, and she's waiting on the sofa.

"Amelia Marie Glendale! Have you got any idea how worried I've been about you?"

"Pen, I know you were dying for updates, but don't try to tell me you were worried about me. I was at one of the most heavily guarded places in the city. Nothing was going to happen to me."

"Okay, okay. I wasn't worried about you, but you should have been worried about me. Your lack of updates could have literally killed me."

"I'm sorry. I couldn't pull out my phone without him noticing, and then my battery died."

"I don't want excuses, missy, I want deets. Were you at his apartment?"

"No, we went to Lucy and Emma's house."

"What was it like?"

"Not as big as you might expect, and quite homey. But they've obviously renovated recently. It looks like a page from a Pottery Barn catalogue, but a much, much more expensive version. It's all the sort of furniture where you're not meant to be able to tell how expensive it is unless you already know who made it."

"So they don't have mismatched hand-me-down dining chairs like us?"

"They do not."

"Was it just the four of you?"

"At first it was, but then Leo came along too."

"Bad luck."

"I know right? Oh! And you'll never guess who he brought with him. Kayla Monroe."

"No! Wow, his standards are falling. She's hot, but she's not that successful and a bit low-rent for him."

"It was so strange. Apparently they've been dating for months, and the palace does not approve. I can see why—she's a piece of work. Absolutely her own number one fan."

"At least that explains how she scored an invitation to Edmund's non-wedding."

I stretch out and yawn. "It does. I'm pretty tired, so I'm going to head to bed."

"Not so fast! We haven't even gotten to the good bits yet. How was Edmund?"

"He was good, much more relaxed than I've seen him before. He and the princesses seem super close. They treat him like a normal person. He doesn't have many people in his life who will tease him or call him out on things."

"No, I can't imagine many people are willing to risk offending him."

I make a show of yawning again and close my eyes sleepily.

Penny watches impatiently. "Last question, and then I'll let you go to bed, I swear."

"Okay, one more question."

"Did he profess his undying love for you?"

"Pen!" I throw a pillow at her head. It misses and hits the wall, shaking the framed Ikea poster of the London Bridge that hangs above the sofa.

"That's not an answer, Amelia."

"He did not. He was friendly, that's it. It was nice, though."

"Lame!"

"I'm done! We can talk tomorrow," I say, getting up and hauling myself to bed.

∾

Thursday 19 August

THE REST of the week we're busy working on final preparations for the Kenya trip.

As I'm flipping through my Outlook calendar on Thursday, I look over to Eddie. "I can't believe that there's only a week left until the trip. Are you excited?"

"Yes and no," he says circumspectly. "I'm looking forward to getting out of London and seeing how everything is shaping up in Kenya."

"What's the part you're not looking forward to? Do you have a phobia of wildebeest?"

Eddie shakes his head.

"Zebras? It's zebras, isn't it? Just think of them like striped polo ponies. Although best not to try to ride them."

Eddie looks at me. "It's not animal-related. Although I did once have a fairly unpleasant experience with a warthog."

"Well, that's a story I need to hear."

"Amelia," he says, wringing his hands. "There's something I've been meaning to tell you, but I never quite found the right time."

"What is it?"

"Dad has decided that it's time for me to come back to the palace offices so that his team can keep a closer eye on me. He wants me back there as soon as the trip is over."

"Oh."

I stare blankly at Eddie, not sure what else to say.

"I... I knew you'd go back eventually, but I thought you were going to be here for a while longer."

"I hoped I would be. I've enjoyed my time here. It's made me feel refreshingly normal. And productive. It's very different than having the whole palace team watching my every move."

"You can't ask to stay longer?"

"I'm afraid not," Eddie says, shaking his head. "Dad is quite literally the boss. What he says goes. More fool he who dare question one of his decrees."

"Has he always been like that?"

"Sort of. He's always been fairly, shall we say, *robust* in his suggestions about what we do and how we behave, but it's been a whole new game since he took the top job. He thought Gran was too soft on the family and is going out of his way now to make it clear that he won't be taking the same approach. He's going to run a tight ship whether people like it or not."

Eddie's shoulders slump, and he gives me a weak smile.

"I'll need you to bring me croissants at least twice before you leave for the trip then," I say, flashing him a bright smile, trying to lighten the mood.

"Before we leave for the trip, you mean."

"No, before *you* leave for the trip. I'm not going."

"Pardon?"

"I'm not going on the trip."

"Why ever not?"

"I never go on these trips. I can do my bit from here. The whole point of you and Leo going is for the publicity and photo ops. No one needs a photo of me petting an elephant."

He gazes at me. "You should come. This project is as much yours as it is mine."

"I appreciate you saying that, but it's not really my project. I had an idea, but you and the team are the ones who've made it happen. Besides"—I shrug—"I'm a behind-the-scenes kind of girl. You're welcome to the attention."

"I don't really want the attention either, you know."

"You may not enjoy the attention, but it's part of your job description. It's not part of mine."

"It's the worst part by far. That's why I want you there to help me through it."

He wants me to help him through it. My mind fills with cosy images of us sitting and laughing together on a tour bus. It's very tempting.

"I'll consider it, I promise."

"Make sure you decide fast. We leave in a week. And keep in mind I can always pull rank and just order you to attend. Don't think I won't do it."

PENNY and I are at another bar near my office for an after-work drink.

"Are you going to go?"

"I'm not sure. It's so hard to decide."

"Why exactly is it hard to decide if you're going to go on a free overseas trip with a prince?"

"Pen! Shh!" I scan the room, looking for any sign of paparazzi or reporters, not that I'd recognise any even if I did see them.

"Okay, okay. Why don't you want to go away with 'Frank'?"

"It's not that I don't want to go."

"Then what is it?"

"If I'm honest, it's actually that I want it too much. In less than two weeks, he'll be back from Kenya, back to his other 'office' and I'll never see him again. I don't know if my poor, battered heart can take spending even more time with him before he disappears."

"Oh, love, I get that, I do. But are you *sure* you'll never see him again? I don't know him at all, but based on what you've told me, I'd put money on him genuinely wanting to be friends."

"You might be right. But him wanting to stay friends doesn't help me here. If anything, it makes things worse. Staying in contact after he leaves will only make me fantasize about him deciding he wants to be more than friends, and that's how I'm going to end up with a broken heart and a very large drinks bill."

"Well, as an objective outsider, I think you'd be barking mad not to go."

"Thanks, Pen, that's super helpful."

"I'm being serious. It'd be an amazing experience even if nothing happens with him. Besides, I need to live through you here. Even you being just friends with 'Frank' is far more exciting than anything going on in my life."

"I'm sure that's not true, Pen. You're always doing something interesting. Seen anyone with any potential lately?"

"No. Ugh, maybe, I don't know. I was chatting to a guy last night who seemed cool. I haven't met up with him yet though, so he could still turn out to be a serial killer or have a foot fetish."

"Ooh, would you rather—date a serial killer or someone with a foot fetish?"

"The serial killer, for sure. At least I'd be able to write a memoir that could be adapted into a made-for-TV movie. There are no upsides to a foot fetish."

"Totally agree. If you're going to date someone with a weird fetish, at least choose a feeder so you get cake out of the deal."

∽

Friday 20 August

AT MIDDAY the next day I'm alone in the office, proofreading a contract when there's a knock on the door. I look up and see Lucy and Emma standing in the hall.

"Hey! Good to see you."

"You too, dear," Lucy says as she and her sister walk into the room.

"Are you here to have lunch with Eddie? He's in a meeting at the moment, but he should be back in about fifteen minutes. You're welcome to wait here until he gets back."

"Actually..." Emma says with a mischievous grin, "we're here to have lunch with you."

"Why?"

The princesses laugh.

"Do we need a reason?" Lucy asks.

"Kind of. I mean, you're *you,* and I'm a nobody you barely know."

"You're not nobody, you're the head of legal for our cousins' charity. At least that's what it says on your door, so I assume it's true."

"And we *do* know you," Emma adds. "We've shared melted cheese and watched TV together. Those bonds run deep."

"Well, when you put it that way, how can I refuse?"

"You can't." Emma responds. "And if you tried, I'm sure we could have you locked up in a tower somewhere."

"Shall we go?" Lucy asks, nodding towards the door.

I have hours of urgent work piling up on my desk, but I can't exactly say no to two princesses.

"Why not."

We walk down the street until we come to a Japanese cafe.

"Does sushi suit you?" Lucy asks.

"Sure. Are we okay to just go in? Don't you need security to clear the place first?"

"I wish!" Emma exclaims with a chuckle. "We're not that important."

"Eddie and Leo have much more security than we do. We have protection officers assigned to us, but they don't follow us everywhere like they do the boys. We can largely go where we like," Lucy explains.

"As long as we don't do anything too daft," Emma says.

"Right. I guess I'd just assumed that you were all treated pretty much the same from a security perspective."

"No, no. A lot of things are different for us. Some things are a lot easier being further down the food chain."

"And thank the lord for that!" Lucy says. "I couldn't stand living like Edmund. Everything is far too controlled for my liking. I have no idea how he manages it."

I nod. "It seems pretty tough."

"There are advantages, but sometimes it's not all it's cracked up to be. Unlike Caroline who has managed to largely escape, there's no way out for Edmund," Lucy says.

"Lucky for us, we get most of the perks and not many of the downsides," Emma says as she sweeps the door open.

We find a table and order some sushi rolls.

Lucy looks me in the eye. "So," she says, tapping her fingers on the table, "Eddie told us he asked you to go on the Kenya trip."

"He did." Where is she going with this?

"Are you planning to go?"

"Probably not. I've got plenty of work to get on with here."

"You should reconsider."

"You think I should go? There's no real reason for me to be there. It's effectively a publicity trip, and that's not part of my role."

"Mm, be that as it may," Emma says, "we think you should go."

"Why?"

"For Eddie," she says simply.

"I'm not sure I understand."

Emma fixes me with a determined stare. "Look, poor Eddie's had a tough run this year. He was torn up about Gran, and then the wedding fiasco took a big toll on him. The press attention afterwards didn't help."

Lucy clucks before Emma continues speaking.

"We don't know what's going on between you and Eddie. He hasn't told us anything. But what we do know is that he's been much happier since he started working with you."

"Happier than he's been in a long time," Lucy adds. "We also know that he's a bit nervous about going out and courting public attention after what happened, so he could use some moral support on the ground."

My face is burning when I reply. "I'm glad that you want the best for him, and I do too. But I'm sure his happiness at the moment has nothing to do with me. He's probably just pleased to be spending time away from KP. Besides, he'll have Leo there for support."

Emma rolls her eyes. "Amelia, the bottom line is we want what's best for him, and it appears what's best for him is spending time with you."

"Also," Lucy says, "do you *really* expect Leo to be provide top-notch emotional support?"

I laugh. "Not a chance."

"Edmund needs someone on his side for this."

"He does," Emma agrees. "And you're much more fun than Sibella ever was, so we'd like it to be you."

"She was such a bore. You know she wouldn't even eat on the sofa? She thought it was 'common.' As members of the royal family, I believe we are the ones entitled to determine what is or isn't common."

"Will you at least consider it?" Emma pleads.

"I will, I promise."

"Good," she nods. "Enough about that. We have much more important things to talk about. Have you been watching *The Bachelor*?"

CHAPTER 15

Monday 23 August

"You're really going to come?" Eddie asks with a gleeful, puppy dog expression that is very unbecoming of royalty.

"Why not? It'll be a pleasant change to see something I've worked on in real life."

Eddie claps his hands together. "Fantastic! I can't wait to show you Kenya."

"You've been before haven't you?"

"Quite a few times. Caroline, Leo and I have all spent a lot of time in Africa. We went on a couple of trips with our parents when we were younger, but we started going by ourselves about ten years ago."

"What's the appeal—the fine colonial history, the big-game hunting?"

Eddie smiles coyly.

"That was a joke! Please tell me it's not big-game hunting. I don't think I want to know if you've shot an elephant."

"Don't worry, I'm not much of a hunter. I've never shot anything bigger than a fox."

"I don't even know how you can do that. It may just be because I didn't grow up here, but the idea of shooting at animals for fun has never made any sense to me."

"Can I tell you a secret?"

I lean in closer. "Always."

"To be perfectly honest, I don't enjoy the idea of killing anything. Gran was always incredibly keen on hunting, but I've never enjoyed it. I go out on shoots to keep the family happy, but I try not to hit anything. Luckily for me, I have truly horrendous aim, so I don't need to try very hard to miss. I've shot a fox exactly once, and it was more of an accident than anything. I'd been aiming at a tree."

I laugh. "Oh dear, that must have been a bit of a shock for you."

"You have no idea. Dad was thrilled that I finally hit something, but I was so upset I shook for an hour. I still think about poor Socks sometimes."

"Socks?"

"Yes, I named the wretched thing Socks because it had little white paws," Eddie says, looking wistfully out the window.

"You named a fox *after* you shot it?"

"Indeed. Didn't help assuage the guilt."

"No, I don't imagine it did. I think we can safely say that the repeat visits to Africa aren't about shooting Simba."

"I love the landscape and the people, but to be frank, the chief appeal for me has always been anonymity. I'm not completely anonymous on trips there, of course, and I still have security and other constraints, but for the most part, people there either don't know who I am or don't care. Either way, they treat me like a normal person."

"That must be very different to being here," I say.

"It is. It gives me a glimpse of a different life. Something slower, with less pressure and fewer people to disappoint."

"I know it's completely different, but I can relate. I've spent my whole life convinced that I'm not good enough and that I'm going to let everyone down. Perils of an A-type personality. I can't imagine you disappointing anyone, though."

"Oh?" Eddie looks at me, eyebrow raised. "Are you saying you find me 'not disappointing'?"

The butterfly swarm in my stomach darts around. "I, uh..."

"Yes?"

Pull it together, Amelia, pull it together.

"All I mean is that, objectively speaking, you do a good job. You're dedicated and reliable. And you never do anything offensive that causes a scandal. Other than the whole wedding disaster, I guess, but that was more Sibella than you."

Phew, good save.

"We've spent a month together, and the most flattering thing you can say about me is that I'm inoffensive? I've made quite the impression, haven't I?" Eddie asks, amused.

I slap his arm playfully, hoping to defuse the tension. "Stop fishing for compliments, Your Highness. I'm not going to tell you how great you are. You've got more than enough people to do that."

"Ah, that's a shame," says Eddie, grinning. "I was rather hoping to hear it from you."

There's that dimple again. I swear, it's going to be the death of me.

∽

Thursday 26 August

THREE DAYS LATER, I'm throwing the last few things into my suitcase as a car horn blares outside the flat.

"Your car's here!" Penny calls out from the lounge room.

"Almost ready!"

"Have an amazing time, lady. Send lots of photos. You won't be welcome back if I don't get regular updates."

"Understood. I'll see you in five days."

"Can't wait."

The car horn beeps impatiently outside. I lean over and open the window. "I'm coming down now," I call out to the driver.

I grab my suitcase and head down to the street.

"Ms. Glendale?" the driver asks through the open window of a dark sedan.

"Yes, that's me," I say, hopping into the back seat.

"Where are you off to, love?"

"Kenya."

"That's a bit exotic. Going on a safari, are you?"

"No, I'm going on a work trip, actually."

"Too bad."

We fall into silence, and I'm checking my emails when I look out the window and notice something doesn't look quite right.

"Excuse me, shouldn't we have turned the other way for Heathrow?"

"Heathrow? Details I got said London City. Private terminal."

"Right, of course."

Private terminal? Did the foundation charter a jet for the team? It feels a bit excessive for a charity trip, but I'm not going to say no.

Half an hour later, we pull up at the small private terminal, and I'm ushered into a room that's more like a boutique hotel lobby than an airport lounge. The walls of the small room are covered in sea grass wallpaper and oversized paintings, and there are eight plush leather armchairs arranged around the room together with a collection of velvet cushions and ottomans.

I'm the only person in the lounge, so after an attendant takes my luggage, passport and drinks order, I plant myself in an armchair and find a magazine to read while I wait for my coffee.

I'm reading an article in *OK! Magazine* about Gwyneth

Paltrow's latest vagina cleansing method—something involving power crystals and burnt sage, which sounds both unpleasant and unsanitary—when the door opens. Eddie, Leo, Henry and Charli walk with a couple of PPOs following behind them.

"Found the place all right, I see, Amelia?" Eddie asks pleasantly. "I normally fly commercial, but Leo here insisted on chartering a jet."

"I can see why. This lounge is fantastic. Hands down the best airport experience I've ever had."

Eddie takes a seat in the chair next to me and smiles.

Meanwhile, Leo laughs derisively. "Never flown private before? How quaint."

Eddie rolls his eyes. "Give it a break, Leo. You don't have to be rude."

Leo comes to sit opposite us while Henry, Charli and the PPOs try to make themselves invisible in the corner.

"I'm not being rude. I'm just pointing out that Amelia here isn't exactly used to our lifestyle. She doesn't fit in."

Wow, clearly Leo is about as fond of me as I am of him. He's got a point though—this is about as far from my normal Thursday morning as you can get. Luxury for me is paying the extra for a fancy Uber—and I've only done that once.

"Leo," snaps Eddie. "What's gotten into you?"

"Nothing's 'gotten into' me. I just don't think it's very fair that you get to bring your girlfriend along on this trip while I'm expected to pretend I'm single just because you and Dad think Kayla is beneath you because she's been on reality TV shows."

Eddie stares at Leo in stunned silence. He glances over at me awkwardly before turning back to Leo.

"I think we need to clear up a few things, brother. First, it's Dad who decided that he didn't want your relationship with Kayla to be public. Don't blame me for that one. Second, Amelia is *not* my girlfriend. She's here because this is her project too, and she deserves some credit. That's the only reason I asked her to come. Period."

My stomach sinks. I don't know what I was hoping for out of this trip, but I need to remember that for Eddie this is about work. For him, it's just another in a string of these trips. It doesn't mean as much to him as it does to me. *I* don't mean as much to him as he does to me.

~

ONCE WE'RE SEATED on the plane and waiting to take off, I pull out my phone and text Penny.

Me: *Eddie and Leo had a fight in the airport lounge about me being here, super awkward.*

Penny: *A fight about you? Why?*

Me: *Leo is annoyed that he wasn't allowed to bring Kayla.*

Penny: *Well, I don't see how that's your problem or Eddie's problem. I vote to just ignore him.*

Me: *Ugh, I will. I just hate the tension.*

Penny: *Ignore it and focus on the sexual tension, kiddo. Much more exciting.*

Me: *Penny! This is a work trip where I will be entirely professional.*

Penny: *Whatever you say...*

Penny: *I have to get going for dinner. Second in-person date with Jack. I know I say this a lot, but I think he's a keeper.*

Me: *OK, enjoy. Text me later if you can xx*

After take-off, I put on my headphones and try to avoid eye contact with Eddie and Leo. Leo is easy to avoid, given that he appears to be pretending that I don't exist. Eddie is not as easy. The jet seats about a dozen people in a combination of oversized leather seats and sofas. Eddie has chosen to sit in the seat facing mine and seems intent on making it very difficult for me to ignore him.

"What are you listening to?" he asks, peering over at my phone.

"Just music."

"What kind of music?"

"Just a random Spotify playlist," I deflect.

Eddie gets a dangerous glint in his eye. "It's something deeply embarrassing, isn't it?"

Before I can answer, Eddie leans over and grabs my phone out of my lap. He looks at the screen and laughs.

"You're listening to late-nineties Britney? Are you listening to this seriously or ironically?"

I look away and say nothing.

"Of all the music in the world, this is what you choose to listen to while flying on a private jet? I'm sorry, Amelia, but I'm not sure if we can be friends anymore."

I peek back towards Eddie and see him watching me, highly amused.

"In my defence, I maintain that it's less embarrassing to be listening to nineties Britney than recent Britney."

"You have a point there. Anything post-head shaving era would be truly unforgivable."

"Agreed. Remind me to never let my children be child or teen stars of any kind."

"Why?"

"I don't want successful children who turn into train wrecks. Almost no one who grows up in the spotlight like that ends up being a well-adjusted adult. Have you *seen* Amanda Bynes or Aaron Carter in the last five years? When a person gets to the point where they think multiple facial tattoos are a good idea, you know something is very wrong."

An uncomfortable silence settles between Eddie and me, the jovial atmosphere of minutes earlier has evaporated.

I slap my forehead. "I'm so sorry," I say. "That was a stupid thing to say. I didn't mean you."

"It's fine," Eddie says, gazing out the window.

"No, it's not. Honestly, you're surprisingly normal for someone who grew up with so much attention. You're by far the most normal royal I know. Although to be fair, the only other royals I know are your brother and cousins, so it's a low bar."

"That *is* a low bar," Eddie deadpans.

CHAPTER 16

WE LAND LATE at night at a small airfield outside Kibwezi, a town a few hours south of Nairobi. When we disembark, there's a small fleet of jeeps waiting to take us to the lodge where we're staying in the Tsavo West National Park.

Simone and Francis are there to greet us.

"Welcome, Your Highnesses," Simone says as we enter the lobby. "Glad you finally made it."

"Thanks, Simone. It's good to be back," Eddie replies.

Charli returns from reception with a stack of key cards. "Now, I've got all your room keys here. We're all up on the first floor—up the stairs so that we can secure the floor. Prince Edmund, Prince Leo and the security team are to the left, everyone else to the right."

I take the key Charli is thrusting at me. "Great, thanks."

"Any chance of a welcome drink?" Leo asks.

Charli winks. "A few of the others are in the bar waiting for you."

"Right, I'm off then," Leo says, rubbing his hands together.

"Will you come for a drink, Amelia?" Eddie asks.

Will I go drinking with Eddie at a hotel where we're both

staying? Not the best idea. I was hoping to get through at least the first twenty-four hours without throwing myself at him. Repeat after me, Amelia: *I will not embarrass myself by drooling over a man who is so far out of my league that he may as well be on the moon.*

"I think I'd better head to bed. I'm exhausted after the flight," I say.

Eddie's face falls briefly before recovering his passive expression. "Eminently sensible of you, as always. Have a good night."

Eddie walks off to the bar with Charli. I'd better get to my room ASAP before I change my mind.

I WAKE UP, tossing and turning around in my bed. The temperature in this room is way warmer than I'm used to sleeping in, and it's not working for me. I get up and search around the room for water, but all I can find is the empty bottle that I drank before bed. Do I go down to the lobby and find more water, or stay here and try to sleep? I don't want to leave the room because I'm lazy and don't want to have to get dressed, but I'm also very thirsty. I could just drink tap water from the bathroom, but I don't know what the water situation is here. I refuse to put on proper clothes, though. Hotel robe over my shorts and tank top is as far as I'm willing to go.

I grab a robe and slippers from the bathroom and then open the door and pad down the hall. As I get closer to the central staircase, I can hear footsteps. A security guard on patrols maybe? But when I get to the stairs, I see it's not a security guard —it's Eddie, pacing up and down the hall. In plaid pyjama pants and nothing else. I catch a view of his toned chest—I guess he was in the army after all—and audibly gasp. As I clap my hand over my mouth, Eddie stops pacing and looks up. Bollocks, I think he heard me.

"Amelia," Eddie says, walking over to me. "What are you doing up?"

"Just going for a walk," I say.

He cocks his head and smirks. "At three in the morning, in a hotel that has lions living on the premises?"

"For water. I was going for a walk down to the lobby to find some water. It's pretty hot in here."

"It is, isn't it?"

Suddenly I realise that I'm staring at Eddie's chest again. Oops. I'm also very aware of how thin this robe is. Keep it together, Amelia—you're keeping this professional, remember? I drag my eyes back up to Eddie's—also quite attractive—face.

"What are you doing out here in the middle of the night?" I ask.

"Couldn't sleep," Eddie shrugs. "I always get so nervous the night before big engagements. I end up spending half the night pacing around, rehearsing speeches in my head."

I'm feeling incredibly nervous right now too, and it's got nothing to do with public speaking.

"I'm sure you don't need to be nervous. You always sound very professional in public."

"That's most likely thanks to all the late-night pacing."

I laugh. "I'll admit, I hadn't considered that possibility."

"We may never know for sure."

We stand looking at each other for a moment. Danger, Amelia, danger. Please extract yourself from this situation immediately.

"I should find that water and then try to get back to sleep. We're scheduled to leave for our breakfast engagement in less than four hours."

"Always the sensible one, aren't you?"

"I'm your lawyer. You pay me to be boring and sensible."

"Fair point. Hopefully we meet like this again one night when you're not on the clock."

Okay, definitely time to leave before I do something stupid. "Goodnight, Edmund," I say, turning to walk down the stairs. "Goodnight, Amelia."

~

Friday 27 August

IN THE MORNING, we all pile into the jeeps and drive further into the national park for a breakfast reception with members of the local Maasai tribe on the banks of a large mineral spring. The sight of the reflective waters and surrounding greenery amid so much red dirt is stunning.

A Maasai guide gives us a tour around the springs.

"Oh!" I gasp as we round a bend. Right near the edge of the water is a group of four giraffes—a family of two adults and two young. Members of the Maasai tribe are assembled next to the tower, equipped with buckets of leaves and carrots. Yup, a group of giraffes is called a tower. How apt.

"Your Highnesses," one of the Maasai welcomes Eddie and Leo with a deep bow. "Welcome back to Kenya. Would you care to feed the giraffes?"

"Brilliant," Leo replies.

The guide leads Edmund and Leo towards the animals.

"Amelia," Edmund says. "Would you like to have a crack at this, too?"

"Sure!"

We're each handed a carrot and told to hold it out away from our bodies. We walk up to the giraffes and hold out our hands. After a big sniff, one of the young giraffes cranes its neck down and wraps the carrot in its long, blue tongue and draws it back into its mouth, leaving not an insubstantial amount of giraffe drool on my hand. Yuck.

I'm hunting around for something to wipe my hand on when

I hear a strange yelp that sounds like a cat after someone's stood on its tail. I whip around to find the source of the noise: Eddie, about a metre away, with a giraffe licking his face. I never thought I'd be so grateful to have wild animal drool only on my hand.

When our tour finishes, we load back into the jeeps for the drive to a lunch reception in Kibwezi. Eddie furiously tries to clean the drool from his face with a packet of baby wipes and then drenches himself in hand sanitiser.

"Eddie, I'm going to have to confiscate the sanitiser before you start drinking it."

"Please don't take it away, Amelia. I need it. My face is never going to be clean again without it."

I narrow my eyes. "I'll let you keep it, but I'll be watching you, Your Highness. The minute you take a swig, I'm telling Charli you need a trip to rehab."

"Can you please?" Eddie says, laughing. "I could really do with a thirty-day rest. I've heard they don't even let you keep your phone. What a dream."

"Let's get through the next two days before you fake an alcohol addiction to get a break, please."

"As you wish, madam," Eddie says with a flourish.

~

Saturday 28 August

THE NEXT DAY, we're off to tour the new school. When we arrive, the school is a jubilant explosion of colour, and all the children are gathered outside to greet us with a song and dance. The excitement is infectious. Everyone is grinning other than Eddie, who seems more preoccupied with the small contingent of local press standing to the side of the yard.

The head teacher and head nurse take us on a tour of the

school and attached medical clinic, giving us an overview of the amazing facilities and programs they're offering the community. I'm getting a bit choked up. I always know what we're working on and see reports about the impacts of programs, but there's nothing quite like seeing something in real life and shaking the hands of people whose lives might change for the better—even just a tiny bit—because of work you've done. Real talk, it's totally overwhelming. I've always liked my job, but it's never felt as fulfilling as this.

After the tour, Eddie and Leo are scheduled to do interviews outside the school. Eddie hangs back in the foyer, pacing in small circles. I wait awkwardly in the corner, not sure if he wants to talk to me. Charli frowns and walks over to him. I can hear her talking to him quietly.

"Okay there, Your Highness?"

"Yes," says Eddie. "I'm fine. Fine."

"Don't worry—we've thoroughly briefed everyone. If anyone so much as thinks about asking you a question about the wedding, they'll be out of here."

Edmund puffs out his cheeks.

"Promise?"

"I promise," Charli says, smiling.

"Shall we get on with it then?"

"Yes, Your Highness. Right this way."

Eddie and Leo stand, side-by-side, in front of the school building while I stand with Charli, Henry and the rest of the team off behind the press pack. Eddie stands, stiff back and drawn face as the men pose for photos together, with the staff and with the children. Then the questions start.

"This is your sixth school in Africa. What draws you to support education?"

"The value of education can't be understated," Eddie says.

"Care to elaborate, Your Highness?"

"No."

Right, so he wasn't kidding when he told me he's uncomfortable with interviews.

Leo laughs gregariously. "Education is the start of everything. I can't say I was ever much one for school," he says, winking. "But you can't beat the impact it has on lives. Every kid we send to school is a kid with a better future."

The reporters lob more softball questions at the pair. Leo answers most of them, grinning and personable. Describing Eddie as aloof would be generous.

"Alright, last questions, please," Charli says.

"Why did you choose to include a medical clinic here? Will you be doing the same in future projects?" a reporter asks.

Leo grins broadly. "We figured we're already here, so why not?"

Some reporters titter appreciatively.

"We're all about doing as much as we can for the community. Can't go to school if you're sick and don't have access to a doctor, so from here on in, we'll be teaming up with Doctors Without Borders to provide high-quality medical care wherever we build schools." When Leo finishes talking, members of the team and press applaud.

"It makes sense to exploit the efficiencies of co-location," Eddie adds. His comment is met by silence. He shuffles awkwardly and looks across the yard to where I'm standing with the rest of the palace team. As he does, I manage to catch his eye and give him a quick thumbs-up and what I hope is an encouraging smile. Instantly, his shoulders drop and he looks more relaxed.

He breaks the silence. "We want to do everything we can to make sure that these kids get to be kids and don't have to worry about where their next meal is coming from or catching a preventable disease." He grins as he reaches out and ruffles the hair of a conveniently located child. That's the Eddie I know.

"It's been great to talk to you," Leo says. "But I think we're going to have to leave it there—we've got a game to play." He nods towards a group of school children waiting patiently in the wings with a football and waves to the reporters. "We'll see you all next time."

Before I can say anything to Eddie, the princes have been assigned to opposing teams and are taking to the makeshift football field.

As they kick the ball around, the uncomfortable Edmund of earlier melts away. When he's playing with the children, he's back to smiling and laughing. Halfway through the game, a little boy picks up the ball. Edmund runs up behind him, pulls him up onto his shoulders and dashes towards the imaginary net.

"Goal!" he cries. "We win, we win!" He runs laps around the field, giving everyone high-fives with the boy still riding high on his shoulders.

"Oi!" Leo says, red-faced. "That was cheating."

"What?" Eddie asks.

"You were cheating. You can't win like that."

Eddie laughs. Leo storms across the field and shoves him in the chest. "I'm serious. You can't cheat and then claim you won."

"Leo, it's a game," Eddie says, smiling.

"It's not just a game! It's your whole life!"

Eddie stops in his tracks and places the boy back on the ground. He's not smiling anymore.

"You go through your life doing whatever you want and expecting everyone to praise you. No one ever pulls you up on anything. You think you're so special. But you know what, brother? No one likes you. People put up with you because you're the firstborn, but they'd prefer me. Ask anyone."

"Calm down, Leo, there are still some reporters milling around. Let's talk later in private."

"You'd like that, wouldn't you? You're always trying to maintain your drama-free image. Well, I'm done with it. I'm leaving."

"You're heading back to the lodge?" Eddie asks.

"No, I'm flying back to London. I'll come back for the rest of my tour once you've gone. I can't stand to be in the same country as you for another minute."

Eddie looks like someone has slapped him in the face. "Okay," he says. "I'll see you at home then."

Leo stalks off, leaving the rest of us in shock.

CHAPTER 17

THE MOOD IS sombre when we convene in the lodge's dining room for lunch. Charli is in damage control mode, tapping away at her phone—presumably trying to avoid the story of Leo's meltdown making the news. Henry and the rest of the team sit, studiously avoiding Eddie's gaze.

Halfway through lunch, Eddie claps. One of the poor PR underlings is so shocked that she actually jumps in her seat and spills coffee everywhere.

"Sorry, didn't mean to startle anyone," Eddie says. "I want to say thank you so much to all of you for helping to make *most* of this trip such a success. We don't have any events scheduled for this afternoon or tomorrow morning now that Leo is *unavailable*, so I thought we should all have a bit of a break before I fly home."

"That sounds nice," I say to fill the silence that meets Eddie's announcement.

"I've booked a villa down on the coast. We'll leave after lunch."

A few people smile while the others give each other sceptical looks across the table.

"Where are we going?" I ask Eddie as the rest of the team finish their lunches and drift away to pack.

"Diani Beach, on the coast near Mombasa. It's one of my favourite places in Kenya. You're going to love it."

"I'm sure I will. I assume this will sound super ignorant of me, but I've never imagined Kenya as a beachy place."

"When most people think of visiting Africa, they think of the safaris and savanna, but the beaches are incredible too. We should get ready to leave. It will take a few hours to get there."

Late in the afternoon, we arrive at Diani Beach. I'm not sure what I was expecting, but this isn't it. We park in front of a sprawling white building. The two-storey, colonial-style villa is punctuated by columns and iron lacework. The opulence of it sits in sharp contrast to most of what we've seen over the last couple of days.

"It's quite something, isn't it? Not exactly traditional architecture," Eddie muses as he watches me take in the scene.

"I assume this was a British creation?"

"Yes, it was built as a coastal residence for the governor back in the late 1890s when Kenya was a British colony. He stayed here while he supervised completion of the Mombasa railway. After that, it was the governor's summer home. It was donated to a local social enterprise about ten years ago now, and they've been running it as a hotel and using it to run hospitality training programs to people from surrounding towns."

"I love that. Reclaim history."

"It is great. It's the kind of thing I hope I can do more to support now that I'm higher up the chain. But enough history. You need to see the beach."

After we drop off our bags inside, Eddie and I walk down the path to the beach. Sitting on the pure white sand, surrounded by palm trees and looking out at the crystal clear, aquamarine ocean, I can't quite believe this place exists.

I glance over and see Eddie leaning back in the sun, a blissful smile on his face. This beach feels magical. And incredibly romantic. Or it would be if I were here with someone who was interested in me instead of someone still reeling from being dumped on live television.

"You were right, Eddie. This is incredible."

"Isn't it?"

"It's so different to everything else we've seen over the last few days. It's like we're on a Pacific island."

"I wanted to come here on my honeymoon, but Sib insisted on Bora Bora." Eddie stretches back and closes his eyes. "Not that it mattered in the end."

Hello there, heartbreak, thanks for crashing my perfect day.

"Her loss."

"Thanks. You don't have to say that, but I appreciate it."

"I'm not saying it because I have to, I'm saying it because I think she was crazy to leave."

Seriously. Who on earth would break up with Eddie? Funny, kind, hot *and* lives in a palace? There's no way I'd be leaving that.

Eddie opens his eyes and gives a wan smile. "Some people might think so, but she had her reasons."

"You don't have to tell me if you don't want to, but what happened? Why did she leave?"

"It's a long story."

"I'm sorry, I shouldn't have asked. It's none of my business."

I really want to know though. Obviously.

"No," he says, laughing. "It's not. But I'll tell you anyway. After all, you did fly to another continent because I asked you to."

"Excuse me, I came here for work!" I exclaim. "But also because you asked me to," I admit.

"And for that you're going to be rewarded with the woeful tale of my almost-wedding."

"Worth flying half way around the world just for that."

"Things with Sib were always complicated. You know that she grew up down the road from our country estate?"

"Yes, I think I'd read that."

I had definitely read it. Many times, in the countless articles I read over the years about Eddie and his family. But best not to let him know that and come across as too much of a stalker.

"Well, her family has been involved with my family for generations. Her grandmother was one of Gran's ladies-in-waiting back before they both got married, and our mothers are old school friends. We spent quite a bit of time together growing up. We always got along well enough and dated for a little while when we were teenagers. It became clear almost immediately though that we were not meant to be."

"So how did you end up together for twelve years and engaged?"

"Yes, well, we were never in love, but when we started university, we had an... arrangement. Officially we would say that we were together, but privately we were single."

Well, this is a story I've genuinely never read about. It does explain why he hasn't seemed as devastated by the break-up as you'd expect though.

"Why would you do that?"

"It gave me an excellent cover. It meant the press weren't digging around to find out who I was dating, and girls who were just after the social status weren't throwing themselves at me. Not as many as might have been otherwise, anyway. It took a lot of pressure off me."

"That makes sense, I guess, but why would Sibella go along with it?"

"Simple, because her parents' greatest dream in life is for her to marry me and eventually become queen."

"So she just let her parents think you were actually together?"

"She did. In fact, so did I. My parents always approved of Sib, so us ostensibly being a couple also avoided any pressure from the family to find a 'suitable' bride."

"Makes sense. But how did you go from pretending to date while you were studying to standing at the front of Westminster Abbey?"

"Ah, one flaw of this grand plan was that it worked a bit too well. Whenever I considered calling it off, I thought about the feeding frenzy that it would cause in the press and with my family, and it just... it all seemed too hard."

"And Sibella was okay with that?"

"She never pushed me to end the charade. In retrospect, at some point I think she decided she wanted us to get married. She was never in love with me, but she enjoyed the privileges and attention. Ultimately, she liked the idea of being a princess."

"So why did you propose? Didn't you ever want to have a real relationship?"

"That's where my parents come in. They were happy thinking that Sib and I were a solid couple, so they never tried to rush me into marriage. Not until a year ago when Gran started getting sick. The reality of Gran not being around forever hit them, and they decided it was time for me to have a more settled life and produce some heirs."

"You proposed to make your parents happy?"

"Yes and no. It was more about making Gran happy than making my parents happy. And I didn't hate the idea. Sib isn't who I might choose to marry if things were different, but we've known each other a long time and were very close friends. She knew what she was getting into and would have been able to take on the role my family expected her to."

Not exactly a romance for the ages.

"But she decided she couldn't go through with it?"

"She did. Maybe not for the reasons you'd expect, though. It turns out she met someone not long after we became engaged. She didn't tell me about it until the day after the wedding. When it came down to it, she wanted love more than a better title."

"That must have been incredibly hard for you."

"It was. The press was a nightmare, and my parents were even worse. The hardest part though was having to go through it without Sib. I was so used to her having my back when it came to dealing with all of that."

"Do you miss her?"

"Despite everything, I think I do. When you're in a position like mine, it's hard to trust people. There aren't many people at all who truly know me, so losing one is an enormous blow."

"I'm sorry."

"Thank you. I'll be fine, though. It hasn't been an enjoyable experience, but in a way I'm grateful for it because it gives me another chance at having a real life, and a real relationship."

He gazes into my eyes, and my spine tingles. Call me crazy, but maybe I have a chance with Eddie after all.

AFTER AN AFTERNOON SWIM in the ocean, I'm back in my room lying on the bed and reading a book when there's a knock on the door. Padding over to answer the knock, I half expect to find Eddie standing in the hall. That's me, ever the optimist.

Holding my breath, I open the door and find a hotel employee, not Eddie, waiting for me. Damn.

"Good evening, ma'am," he greets me. "Dinner will be on the beach at seven p.m."

"Thank you."

The man nods and disappears down the hallway, presumably to deliver the message to the rest of the team.

I check the time on my phone: six thirty. I'd better have a shower and get dressed if I'm going to have any chance of making it to dinner on time.

Half an hour later, I'm making my way down to the beach in one of the bright geometric print summer dresses that moved to London with me. Yes, I moved to London with a suitcase full of summer dresses. Clearly I didn't understand what I was getting myself into. London weather means that my dress collection sees far more of the inside of my wardrobe than the sun.

I scan the beach looking for the group, but can't see them. I walk a little way further out towards the ocean before I spot it. At the end of a small jetty is a white linen tent and a small table set for two, lit by torches and candles.

"Amelia!"

I whip around, and my heart skips a beat when I see Eddie walking down the beach towards me.

"I see you found our table."

"Did you organise this?"

"I did."

"Just for you and me?"

"Just for you and me."

As I start to feel weak at the knees, Edmund holds out his arm, and I hook mine through it and let him lead me down the jetty.

I may need to find a way to subtly pinch myself and make sure I'm not dreaming. Then again, even in my wildest Eddie daydreams, I never imagined something like this.

When we reach the end of the pier, we find the small table weighed down with platters of seafood and candles. There are two chairs next to each other, both facing the ocean. Eddie pulls out a chair and gestures for me to take a seat. As I do, my arm brushes against him, and my skin tingles.

"Now, when you say you organised this... do you mean that you actually organised it yourself, or did you 'organise' it in the way that the Bachelor 'organises' his dates with contestants by turning up after a production team spends a week making them happen?"

Eddie laughs, and his eyes crinkle at the edges. Is it possible that he's even more attractive in candlelight?

"I called reception and asked them to set up our dinner on the pier here. Is that sufficient organisation for you?"

"Hmm, I'll give you some credit. Disappointed that you weren't out catching the lobsters yourself, though."

"Noted. I'll try harder next time, I promise."

"I'm looking forward to it." I smirk.

"Have you enjoyed your introduction to Kenya?" Eddie asks over scallops.

"Much more than I imagined I would. It's been great to see our work come to life."

"If only you'd had better company."

"Shush, you. The company has been... satisfactory."

Eddie chuckles and tips his glass of champagne towards me. "To satisfactory company."

I linger over my oysters. How far can I push this? What do I have to lose if I might never see him again after this week?

"Eddie." I hesitate, my stomach full of a giant bundle of nerves. "Can I be serious for a minute?"

"Always."

"I know that you're going back to working from KP and your usual engagements next week and we might not see each other again, so I wanted to take my chance to say that I've loved spending time with you."

"Have you now?"

"I have. I'm sure you hear this all the time, but you're so thoughtful and funny and easy to talk to. I'm going to miss you."

Eddie reaches over and takes my hand in his. He looks up and locks his eyes on mine.

"I'm going to miss you, too. I've gotten used to seeing your face all day."

He's going to miss me. *Me*, a hot mess of a girl who has no idea what a salad fork is and doesn't remember to do laundry until I run out of underwear. Now I really need to pinch myself.

We sit in silence, Eddie's thumb tracing gentle circles on my hand. Is this really happening? I suppose there's only one way to find out. We've come too far for me to wimp out now. I lean my head on his shoulder and can feel the rise and fall of his chest as he breathes.

"Amelia?"

"Mm?"

"I don't want to stop spending time with you."

When I look up at Eddie, he brushes my cheek with his thumb before tracing it down to my chin. He hesitates for what feels like hours before inching ever so slightly closer.

Just when I think I can't bear the tension any longer, his mouth meets mine with a jolt of electricity. He kisses me for hours. Or minutes. Or days. It's hard to say—time seems to lose all meaning when I realise that I'm sitting on a beach in Africa at sunset kissing a prince. If this is all a dream, I'm going to be pretty damn disappointed when I wake up.

When we finally break apart, Eddie stares into my eyes.

"Are you okay? Is this okay?" he asks, furrowing his brow.

"Only if you promise that there's a lot more of this in our future."

He grins and wraps his arm around me.

"I guarantee it."

CHAPTER 18

Sunday 29 August

"Are you sure we have to leave?" I whine, laying back on a sun lounger on the beach. The cabana's white linen curtains billow around me in the wind.

"Amelia," Eddie says, rolling over on his lounge to face me. "Are you asking me to renounce my right to the throne, run away with you and sell seashell crafts on a beach somewhere?"

"I hadn't been planning to, but now that you suggest it, it sounds pretty tempting."

"I think we could make a real go of it. I expect you'd make fantastic shell necklaces."

"Oh, I would. You can't even imagine what I can do with a glue gun and fishing wire."

"It might just be worth giving up the crown to find out. You're a terrible influence, Amelia. Were you aware of that?"

"Me? If anyone's a bad influence here, it's you. I am a dedicated, hard-working employee and all-round upstanding citizen."

"Hard-working, eh? All I see is someone who goes on

completely unnecessary international junkets and lazes around on the beach."

I punch Eddie in the arm. "Do I need to remind you that you're the one who brought me here?" I stretch my arms out above my head. "Seriously though, Eddie, I just wish we could stay a few days longer. This trip has been amazing. I don't want to go back to real life. Not yet anyway."

Eddie breathes in and closes his eyes before exhaling slowly.

"Trust me. There is nothing I'd enjoy more than staying here longer with you. Preferably without the security and palace aids. No interruptions, just you and me."

A tingle runs down my spine. "Sounds like a dream."

"I can't, though. As much as I want to, reality and my father are both waiting for me back in London."

"What's he going to do if you come back a few days late—put you in the gallows, lock you up in the Tower of London, make you cut a ceremonial ribbon every day for a year?"

"All entirely realistic possibilities. My preference would be for the Tower. At least I could catch up on my Netflix queue while I was there."

Eddie laughs at his own joke. God, he's adorable when he thinks that he's said something funny, he always looks so proud of himself.

"Hey," I whisper, interrupting his laughter. "What's going to happen when we get back? With us, I mean."

The laughter stops, and Eddie looks at me. "Amelia, when we get home, I'd like to take you on a proper date. I know that my position and everything that comes with it is a lot to handle, but I think there's something here, and I want to see where it goes. If you don't want to get involved with me because of all the complications, though, I'll understand." He takes my hand. "I won't like it, but I will understand."

I squeeze his hand. "Yes, I will go on a date with you. But only if you promise to bring me pastries."

"It's a deal."

I'm still giggling when I notice that his smile has faded.

"Amelia, have you really thought about what you're getting into here?"

"I obviously don't know exactly what your life is like, but I've worked for your family for a while now and have spent a bit of time around KP, so I think I have a pretty good idea."

He sighs and shakes his head. "Dealing with the family and the palace machine is one thing, but my greater concern is the press and the public. As far as the world knows, I'm completely heartbroken over Sibella. When people find out that I have moved on so quickly, there will be significant interest."

I snort. "You've met me, right? I'm not nearly interesting enough to attract media attention."

"You will, though. Anyone involved in my life is seen as fair game. Sibella was constantly in the press, photographed everywhere she went."

"Sure. But she was always part of your world—people were taking photos of her way before you ever dated. Also, let's be honest, from what I've seen, she didn't exactly try to avoid the attention."

"That is true. She was fairly comfortable with the attention and tended to use it to her advantage."

"Eddie, I'm not interested in being famous. I never have been. I'm sure that if we were to ever go to a public event together, there would be stories, but I'm not planning to engage in the whole celebrity thing. I like my life, and I'm not going to let it change."

"I admire the purity of your intentions, Amelia, and trust me, I am one hundred percent aligned with your lack of interest in courting fame. I am not at all convinced that it's as easy as just choosing not to pose for photographers, though. The press can be ruthless."

I chew on my lip. Maybe he's right, maybe this isn't a good

idea. I can't imagine being of any real interest to the public, but I've never been in this situation before.

Eddie strokes my cheek.

"Perhaps when we return home, we should stay out of the spotlight. Not forever, just for the next few months."

"You want to hide me?"

He smiles. "That's not exactly how I'd describe it. I want to give both of us an opportunity to explore this relationship privately and give you a chance to adjust slowly. I also want to avoid landing myself in another media feeding frenzy."

Did I hear that right—did he just use the word *relationship* to describe what's going on here?

"If you think that's best, I'm happy to fly under the radar. But, uh… just to clarify, when you say relationship…" I trail off, unsure how to finish my question. I'm not sure that asking him to define our relationship after one date is a great move. He's the one who used the "R" word though.

"Amelia, I don't want to scare you off, but I need you to know that I'm not interested in casually dating someone. My position and my heart won't allow it. I don't let people into my life easily, but once you're in, you're in for the long haul."

He presses his lips against mine and then pulls back and grips my shoulders. "I want you to know that I wouldn't be starting something with you if I didn't think it could go somewhere." He brushes the hair from my face. "If this isn't what you want or if you feel that it's all too complicated, I need to know now. I can't stand the thought of losing you as a friend. So if we start this, I need to know that you're going to give it a real shot. Because I certainly plan to."

Swoon.

"Eddie, I've never met someone who understands me, respects me and makes me laugh like you do. You being a prince may complicate things, but you're worth complicated. I'm in."

~

THE FLIGHT ATTENDANT is making final preparations for take-off when my phone buzzes in my pocket. I pull it out and see a new message from Penny

Something to tell me???

Before I can figure out what she's talking about, my phone buzzes again and a link to an article from *The Sun* appears in the chat. My jaw drops when I click on the link and see a photo of Eddie walking away from the altar at his wedding next to a photo of me taken at Penny's birthday party last year.

EXCLUSIVE! Edmund moves on!

The Sun can exclusively confirm that Prince Edmund has wasted no time in moving on from Lady Sibella.

Edmund's new lady love is Amelia Glendale, a lawyer working for the Princes' Charitable Foundation. There are rumours that Amelia, who has worked for the foundation for three years, and the prince became involved well before his ill-fated wedding. Is Amelia the reason Sibella left? Some say that Sibella discovered Edmund's cheating mere days before the wedding and tried to put it behind her, but fled at the last minute after discovering that Edmund spent the night before the wedding holed up with his lover.

The prince is clearly obsessed with Amelia and unable to be apart from her for long. A source close to the couple confirmed to The Sun *that the prince insisted on Amelia accompanying him on his current charity trip to Africa. The source has revealed that he went as far as flying a private jet to Kenya to avoid the couple being spotted en route. The prince's team is desperately trying to cover up the affair, with Amelia being notably kept out of all press photos of the trip.*

. . .

I'm still reading the so-called exclusive when Charli appears next to Eddie. Her face is like thunder. This is not good.

"We need to talk. Now."

Eddie looks up from his book, startled to find Charli glaring at him.

"What's going on, Charli?"

"I could ask you the same thing, Your Highness."

"Pardon? I haven't the foggiest what you're talking about."

"I assume you haven't checked the news today then."

"Not in the last hour, no."

Charli looks at me, and I let out a little gulp before quickly turning my head away from her.

"You! You know what's going on. Did you leak it?"

I spin back around. "You think this was me?"

Eddie looks from Charli to me and back again. "I'm confused. What are we talking about here?"

"Are you going to tell him, or will I?" Charli spits at me, full of venom.

"There's an article in *The Sun*. Someone sent it to me, and I was just reading it when Charli came over. They're saying that we're together, that we've been having some kind of affair for months." I start trembling. I can feel Charli's glare burning into me. "They're saying that I'm the reason Sibella left."

Eddie snorts derisively. "That's ridiculous. Where would they even come up with a story like that?"

"Well, Your Highness," Charli says carefully, keeping her eyes on me, "there's enough truth in the coverage that I'm sure they have a source. They know quite a bit about Amelia, and they know that she's here with you. Are you sure you can trust her?"

"Uh, excuse me. I'm right here."

Eddie ignores me, speaking to Charli in a dark tone I haven't heard before. "Charlotte, are you seriously suggesting that Amelia has been leaking false stories about me to the tabloids?"

"We don't know what she's done."

Eddie puts his hand on my knee. "I am positive that this wasn't Amelia's doing. You need to trust my judgement. If you don't, there'll be no need for you to come back to work next week."

Charli opens her mouth to speak, then closes it again, obviously thinking better of whatever she was planning to say to Eddie. Instead, she simply nods and walks away, tapping furiously at her phone.

"Amelia, I can't apologise enough about all of this. This is exactly what I didn't want to happen."

"You don't need to apologise. I just don't understand how this got out so fast. Nothing was even happening until yesterday!"

"It's typical tabloid trash. I assume someone leaked to them that you came on this trip with us, and the papers have extrapolated from there. It's incredibly frustrating, but I don't want you to worry yourself about it. Their issue isn't with you, it's with me."

"Do you... does this change things?" I ask.

"No! Of course not. I don't care what this ridiculous article says. I care about you."

He *cares about me.*

I'VE ALMOST BEEN able to forget about the article by the time the plane touches down on the runway at London City.

"I know it's been a long day, but would you like to come back with me for dinner? Lucy and Emma are coming over for a post-trip debrief, and I'm sure they'd like to see you."

"I'd love to, but I promised Penny I'd have dinner with her. She'll disown me for sure if I stand her up."

"Are you sure? Am I going to have to get down on my knees and beg?"

Now that's an image. How am I meant to say no to that?

"Alright, I'll come for dinner. But I'm going to have to leave early—eight p.m. at the latest. Don't let me lose track of time."

"I wouldn't dream of it."

Walters is standing squinting out the window as the flight attendant disarms the door. He turns around and walks towards us.

"Excuse me, Your Highness. It seems we have an issue."

"What's the matter?"

"There are photographers on the runway. We've called airport security, but it may take a while to clear them."

"Are the cars ready to go outside?"

"Yes, sir."

"In that case, let's just get to the cars quickly and head out."

"Are you sure, sir?"

"Yes, quite sure. I don't want to spend an hour waiting for airport security to deal with it."

"As you wish, sir," Walters responds. He strides back down the aisle and nods to the flight attendant who disarms the door.

With the door open, Walters walks towards the stairs with Edmund and me following behind.

"What are we having for dinner then? Have you got your chef on standby?"

"I'll have you know that I don't have a chef."

"But you can order food from the kitchens at the other apartments, right?"

"Well, yes, Helena has extra kitchen staff, so they can cater for the rest of us. But that's not the same as having my own dedicated chef."

"Oh, of course not, Your Highness. You're the picture of the everyman. The public would never question the cost of the monarchy again if they knew you were here sharing chefs," I say, rolling my eyes.

No response. Eddie is frozen at the door with his back to me. Oops, maybe that one went too far.

"Hey, I'm sorry. It was just a joke..."

"It's not you," Eddie says stiffly. "It's them."

My gaze follows Eddie's hand as he gestures out the door to the runway. On the ground is a pack of at least forty people with cameras and microphones. There are flashbulbs going off everywhere and photographers and reporters jostling and yelling over each other, trying to get our attention. This is not what I pictured when Walters said there were photographers here.

Watching the scene down on the ground, I try to figure out how so many people got here so fast. Is this what it's always like when Eddie goes out? There were reporters following us around in Kenya, but it was nothing like this. They were a small group of pre-approved professionals. Something about this pack is far rougher and more volatile.

"What do we do?"

"They've already seen us, so I say we keep our heads down and get to the cars as fast as possible. You'd better head back to your flat. If they get photos of us going into KP together, things are going to escalate quickly."

"Right, of course. Okay, I guess I'll head home."

Eddie walks down the steep stairs and I follow, watching my feet and trying to pretend that this is a totally normal experience that I am completely fine with. The facade doesn't last long.

Halfway down the stairs, the wind dies down and I'm hit by a wall of sound. Everyone on the ground is yelling. Reporters are shouting questions, airport security officers are screaming at the reporters to move back and Walters and the PPOs are urging Eddie and I to move faster and get to the cars. Making my way across the tarmac to the car, I keep my head down and catch bits and pieces of the questions being hurled at Eddie through the chaos.

"Why did you cheat, Edmund?"

"What did Sibella say?"

"Give us a kiss!"

"How long have you been seeing her?"

After what seems like an hour, I make it to the car, and a PPO opens the door and starts pushing me in. As he does, I look up and see a lone reporter with floppy brown hair and tortoise-shell glasses staring at me. Not Eddie, me. "Oi, Amelia! How does it feel to finally catch a prince?" Before he can say anything else, I'm shoved into the backseat and the door slams shut next to me.

"Camden, is it, ma'am?" the driver asks, looking at me in the rear-view mirror.

"Pardon?"

"We're headed to an address in Camden?"

"Oh, yes. Thank you."

"Don't worry, ma'am," he says, his eyes softening. "You'll get used to it."

CHAPTER 19

As we drive along, I take my phone out to call Penny and find that my battery is dead. Damn. Why do I never remember to charge my phone? I used to carry one of those charge packs around with me, but then I'd forget to charge that, too, and just ended up with two paperweights in my bag.

How did the papers find out about us already? Was someone watching us last night? I haven't even had time to figure out if what happened last night makes Eddie and me an "us" yet. I definitely like Eddie, and I know he said that he cares about me, but it's not like we're dating. We kissed one time. One kiss, and people say we've been sleeping together for months. What in the world am I getting myself into?

"I'll get your bags for you, ma'am," the driver says as we pull out outside my flat.

He hops out of the car to open the boot.

I open the door and slide out on to the footpath, rummaging around in my bag trying to find my key.

"It's her!" someone hollers.

"Lads, it's the mistress!"

Lights flash, and people are running down the street towards me. Before I can get to the front door, I'm surrounded by photographers. I guess they've found out where I live now, too.

The flashes are blinding me, and people are calling out from all directions. How do I get past these guys? My chest tightens, and my heart is racing. Finally, I see a couple of police officers elbowing their way through the pack. They make their way to the centre, and one puts his hands on my shoulders and guides me through to the door. I fumble with my keys but eventually manage to unlock the door and stumble through into the lounge room.

"Oh my god, Mils, you're back!"

Penny runs over and slams the door shut behind me.

I fall to the ground, trembling with shock.

Even with the door closed, I can still hear people shouting outside.

"How did this happen? Are you okay? Can I get you anything?"

"Uh, I'm not sure. Some water?" I stammer. "I'm a bit rattled."

Penny disappears into the kitchen, and I pick myself up off the floor only to collapse onto the sofa. I'm staring at the ceiling, trying to breathe when Penny reappears with water and a tub of ice cream.

I take a swig of the water, shaking, and it slops everywhere. Looks like I'm more than a bit rattled.

Penny sits down next to me and puts her arm around me.

"Okay, babe," Penny says. "I'm feeling seriously out of the loop here. I let you out of my sight for five days, and suddenly you're a celebrity. Are you and Edmund *together*?"

"No! Well, maybe. I'm not sure."

"You're not sure? How are you not sure if you're dating a prince?"

"Well, we kissed, once."

"What! When did this happen? More importantly, why didn't you tell me immediately?"

"It only happened last night. I wanted to talk to you about it in person, so I was waiting until I got home. But then there was the article, and there were photographers at the airport, and here…"

I gasp for breath. I think I might be having a panic attack.

"Hey, shh, it's okay. This is a lot to deal with."

I nod, and Penny hugs me and strokes my hair until I calm down.

"How did the press find out about it if it only happened last night?"

"We haven't been able to figure it out. Eddie thinks they may not actually know anything. They might have just found out that I was on the trip and made up a story from there."

"Sounds about right. I swear the tabloids have a bunch of sixteen-year-olds sitting in a room somewhere making up ridiculous stories based on random paparazzi photos."

"They must. What a job! If I wasn't a lawyer, I'd love to do that. Although, now that I'm on the other end of it, I'm not enjoying it so much."

"Oh, I'd love to get paid to write celebrity gossip. Greatest job ever. I assume it pays terribly, though."

"Probably," I agree. "Guess I'll have to stick to lawyering for now."

"Poor thing." Penny laughs. "But, back to more important things, missy. Uh, you kissed Edmund?"

"Well, technically, he kissed me."

"Even better. And?"

"And what?"

"How was it? This might be the best gossip I ever get to hear first-hand, so I'm going to need a lot of adjectives here."

"It was good."

Penny looks at me expectantly. "Really, that's all you're telling me?"

"Yup."

"Ugh, you're the worst sometimes. But I'll give you a pass

because of the stress you've been under today. So what happens now? Are you going to see him again soon?"

"I think so. I hope so."

~

Monday 30 August

WHEN I WAKE UP, I check my phone and see a stream of Instagram notifications. Eddie has posted some pictures from the trip to his Frank Jones Insta. There's a photo of Eddie, Leo and me holding food out for the giraffes, and then an amazing shot of Eddie with a giraffe's tongue on his face.

Getting up close and personal with new friends #toomuchtongue #mouthwashtime #traumatised

I grin to myself. He's so funny.

"Have you seen the news?" Penny squeals when I emerge from my room.

"Not yet. I think I'm going to need a coffee before I can handle reading any more about my love life on the internet."

"I think you may need a few."

"That bad?"

"The articles aren't necessarily bad, but there are a lot of them."

Bracing myself for the worst, I open my *Daily Mail* app and there I am, front and centre. The main photo for the article is a shot of Eddie and me on the tarmac at London City last night. Eddie has his head down and I'm clinging to his arm, staring at a camera with a full deer-in-the-headlights expression. And bad plane hair. Great.

Edmund's new squeeze!

Yesterday it was revealed that Prince Edmund has moved on from long-time love Lady Sibella Cavendish with London-based lawyer

Amelia Glendale. The pair were pictured returning from a romantic getaway in Kenya last night on a private jet.

Sources close to the hot and heavy new couple have hinted that Amelia is the reason Lady Sibella sensationally turned runaway bride at her July wedding. Celebrity guests and royalty alike were left stunned when Lady Sibella ditched the wedding, which was reported to have cost taxpayers twenty-five million pounds. It now appears that Edmund's ongoing affair with another woman was the reason for the last-minute cancellation.

With the wedding behind him, Edmund has been flaunting his new relationship. The couple flew back into London last night on a twelve-seat Bombardier Challenger 605 valued at over fifteen million pounds. The Daily Mail *has not yet been unable to confirm who picked up the tab for the pricey jaunt.*

But who is Amelia Glendale, and how did she snag the country's most eligible bachelor?

...

I shake my head and put my phone down upside down on the table. I think I'm done with reading the news for today.

"I hate that they can print all these lies. They're making out like we spent a fortune going on some fancy holiday together. It was a work trip! And Leo chartered the plane!"

"I know it's frustrating, hon, but you're just going to have to try to ignore it," Penny says, putting her arm around my shoulder. "Have you spoken to him this morning?"

"Eddie? No, I haven't heard from him since we left the airport last night."

"Have you tried to call him?"

"No, I didn't want to seem too needy."

"Mils, the photographers outside last night were pretty intense. I don't think it's unreasonable to want to talk to him about it all."

"I guess so. It's the norm for him, though."

"What are you going to do then?"

I sit up tall and try to look confident. "I'm going to go to work and pretend everything is normal."

"Are you sure about that?"

"Yeah, I think it's the best thing to do."

Penny points towards the door. "Have you looked outside today?"

I walk over and peer around the curtain out the window next to the door. Outside there are a dozen paparazzi photographers camped out—sitting on the footpath, chatting, drinking thermoses of coffee, eating sandwiches. A couple of them have even brought folding chairs with them. All of them are holding cameras with ridiculously long lenses.

I breathe in and out rapidly. It feels unusually claustrophobic in here.

"I might work from home today."

"Good choice." Penny nods. "I really think you should try to call Eddie."

BETWEEN CHECKING NEWS sites and looking at my blank phone screen, willing it to ring, I get barely any work done during the day. By mid-afternoon, I decide work is a lost cause and give up. Lucky I've got episodes of *The Real Housewives of Beverly Hills* stockpiled. If a good housewives fight can't make me feel better about my life, I don't know what can. Other than possibly Lisa Rinna's face. Someone should really put her on a lip filler fast.

At least three hours after I start my *RHOBH* binge, Penny gets home from work and finds me on the sofa hidden under a pile of blankets.

"How long have you been watching this for?" Penny asks, stooping down and picking up piles of chocolate wrappers.

"Not sure. Netflix has asked me twice if I'm still watching, so probably a while."

Penny throws her hands up in the air. "What has the world come to when apps are judging us for watching too much TV?"

"Right! Stop shaming me for enjoying your product, Netflix! All I want to do is lie on the sofa without moving for many hours in a row eating chocolate. Is that so bad?"

"For your health? Yes. As a general concept? Not at all. You could be out joining a street gang if you didn't have an endless supply of TV to keep you entertained."

"I'm not sure they'd take me. I'm white, almost thirty, and a lawyer. Any self-respecting gang member would assume I was an undercover cop."

"True. But Netflix doesn't know that."

Just then, my phone rings. I lunge across the sofa for it and manage to fall onto the floor, multiple blankets tangled together around my legs. I'm still trying to extract myself from them when I answer.

"Hi, Eddie."

"Amelia, hi. I'm so sorry I didn't call earlier. Dad has had me locked in PR meetings all day."

"It's fine, honestly."

I'm almost out of the blankets when I pull one the wrong way and fall over again with a thump.

"What was that?" Eddie asks.

"I, er, dropped a book on the floor."

"Right. Anyway, as I was saying, I'm terribly sorry about all of this—dealing with these vultures is part of my job, but you didn't ask for any of it."

"It's not your fault. I can ignore the news for the most part, but it's a bit much having people camped out the front of my flat."

"They're outside your flat?"

"Yeah, about a dozen of them. They've been here since last night."

Before I can stop myself, I start sobbing.

"Oh, Amelia. I would have called sooner if I'd known. Do you want me to find you somewhere to stay? This is all my fault."

"No, that's okay. I'd rather be in my own bed, even if there are sleazy paparazzi outside."

"I completely understand. If you're going to stay, though, I'd be much more comfortable if you had some security there. Do you mind terribly if I send someone over?"

I hesitate. "I would feel better knowing there was someone here, but won't that make things even worse if you have taxpayer-funded security guarding your... whatever I am?"

"You're right, sending a PPO over wouldn't play well in the press. That's why I'm going to hire someone private and pay for it myself. Don't argue, Amelia. If you say no, I'm going to come over and guard your door myself. Do you want to find out what Piers Morgan thinks of that?"

I laugh, finally feeling the tension of the day start to lift. "I really don't."

"Excellent, it's settled then. I'll get Henry to send you the details. We should be able to have someone over by the morning."

"Thank you, Eddie, I really appreciate it."

"It's the least I can do to make this up to you. On the plus side, Charli and her team think this should blow over quickly. Reporters obviously don't have any proof of an affair and don't have much else to go on, so there's nothing for you to worry about."

"That's the best news I've heard all day."

"Before I forget, the actual reason I called was to ask if you'd like to come over for dinner tomorrow?"

"Sure, that would be great."

"I'll send a car to pick you up from work."

"Perfect," I say, grinning.

Turns out that being asked on a date by an attractive man who has a sense of humour and owns a ceremonial sword makes me feel even better about my life than judging celebrities for their bad plastic surgery does. Who knew?

CHAPTER 20

Tuesday 31 August

AFTER A GOOD SLEEP, I wake up much more relaxed about every-thing. Someone is going to deal with the creepy photographers outside, and I think Charli is right that the stories will disappear soon. What else can they possibly say about me? My life is so boring—I'm either at work or at home watching TV. Unless someone wants to run an expose on the sexism inherent in my preference for *The Bachelor* over *The Bachelorette*, the rumour mill is going to be out of luck with me.

My phone rings, and a number I don't recognise shows on the screen. I let it go to voicemail. Does anyone answer calls from numbers they don't know? I hate talking to people I don't know. In fact, I don't love talking to people in general. Surely everyone could just text each other? The less human interaction, the better.

The caller left a voicemail, so it obviously wasn't some kind of scam call or a reporter trying to catch me accidentally answering my phone.

"Good morning, Ms Glendale. Henry Buxton here from

Prince Edmund's office. A security officer named Michael Jones from Premier Security should arrive at your house within half an hour. Call me on my direct line if you encounter any issues."

See? Things are looking up today.

Ten minutes later, the doorbell rings, and I sneak a look through the window next to the door. There's a gigantic man in a black suit and dark glasses standing on the step.

"Ms Glendale," he says through the closed door. "I'm Michael Jones from Premier Security. Can I come in for a moment?"

I open the door a crack, and Michael shows me an ID badge and then steps inside. His shoulders are so broad he looks ridiculous squeezing through my average-sized door frame. That's the kind of muscle I want on my side.

"Thanks for coming. I'm not used to all of this attention." I say.

Michael is standing in my lounge room, back ramrod straight and arms crossed. "Yes, ma'am. Have you been briefed on logistics?"

"Uh, no. I was just told you'd be coming this morning."

"I will be your main protection officer, which means I will be travelling with you wherever you go and be stationed outside when you are at home. When we're not here, there will be another officer outside. We run three shifts a day—changeover is at six a.m., two p.m. and ten p.m. We've arranged a car, which will be your only form of transport. If you need to go anywhere, you tell me. You don't go anywhere without me, and we don't go anywhere by foot or in an unauthorised vehicle."

I blink a few times. This got serious all of a sudden.

"Any questions, ma'am?" Michael asks.

"How long are you going to be here for? Just for the next couple of weeks until the press attention blows over?"

"I'm not privy to that information, ma'am."

"Right. I'll have a chat with Henry about it then, I guess."

Michael gives a sharp nod. "I'll be outside. Our car will be here shortly. When you're ready to go to work, knock on the door, and I'll get you from the door to the car."

"Okay, thanks."

Michael turns and disappears back outside. This is surreal. A week ago, my life was pretty ordinary, and now I have four—four!—security officers and a driver. Thank god Charli thinks things will go back to normal soon.

With the help of Michael, I successfully manage to leave the flat and make it to work. A vast improvement on yesterday. I'm in the lift when I get a text from Eddie.

Eddie: *Morning, are you still okay to come over for dinner tonight?*

Me: *Yes, sounds great. What time?*

Eddie: *Just swing by whenever you finish work. You'll be on the list at the gate.*

Me: *Perfect, looking forward to it.*

Eddie: *Don't look forward to it too much—Lucy and Emma have invited themselves along.*

Oh. I was hoping this was going to be more of a one-on-one situation. Maybe Eddie's come to his senses and realised that he doesn't want to date me after all. This could be his way of trying to friend-zone me? But then, it would be a bit weird to hire security and a driver for someone you're trying to distance yourself from.

I don't have much time to think about it at work because people I've never met or have barely spoken to keep turning up at my office to talk to me. Some of them make flimsy work-related excuses, but others blatantly ask me questions about Eddie or stand outside my office staring at me through the window. It's exhausting.

I'M in the middle of reviewing a product disclosure document when I get a text from Edmund.

Hi, send me a message when you're on your way.

I check the time and realise that it's already past six. I was planning to go home and change and put on more make-up than I normally wear around the office, but looks like I'm out of time. Do men even notice the difference between work heels and trying-to-impress-someone heels anyway? Probably not. Boring black pumps, navy knit and black pencil skirt (featuring half the contents of a packet of soy sauce from my sushi at lunch) will have to do. This is why I shouldn't be involved with royalty—I can't even get through a meal without making a mess of everything. There's no chance I could survive a state dinner without causing some kind of international incident.

Michael accompanies me to the lift, and we make our way down to the increasingly familiar work basement. My car stops in front of the lifts, ready to take me to the palace. How did this become something that happens on my Tuesday nights?

Twenty minutes later, we pull up to the gates of KP—Michael and the nameless driver sitting up front in silence, me sitting in the back seat nervously playing on my phone—and a guard appears by the driver's door.

"Good evening," the driver says, showing the guard his ID. "I've got Ms. Glendale."

The guard checks a list on an iPad and peers into the back of the car.

"All clear. Up the drive, left at the roundabout, second house you come to," he says, waving us through the gates.

Past the roundabout, the driver stops in front of a three-storey red brick house with a slate roof and three dormer windows.

"Here we go, ma'am. Wren House."

"Thank you," I say, stepping out of the car.

A short cobblestone path leads to a black front door with an oversized brass knocker. As I walk up the path, I can see the lights glowing inside and hear laughter floating through the air. It's more like a warm country manor than a palace.

The door flies open almost as soon as I knock.

"Hello there, homewrecker!" Emma cries before leaning in to kiss me on the cheek. "Fantastic to see you."

"How's your week been? Steal anyone else's future husband?" Lucy asks, appearing around the corner.

I shake my head. "Ugh, I don't think I'm ready to joke about this yet."

"Don't worry, love, I'm sure no one believes the trash that they've printed about you. You didn't even meet poor Eddie here until after his heart was very publicly broken." Lucy says.

Emma sighs. "The papers run the most ridiculous stories, and nobody believes most of what they say. Did you know the *Daily Mirror* once ran an article claiming that I chartered a jet to courier a handbag from Paris to London?"

Edmund clears his throat. "Ah, Em. Wasn't that story true?"

"Hardly! It was *three* bags, and two of them were crocodile-skin Himalaya Birkins. Do you have any idea how expensive they are? There's no way I was putting those babies in a cargo hold."

"Good grief! The lack of truth in journalism these days is appalling," Eddie says sardonically.

"That's quite enough about my entirely reasonable and not at all newsworthy travel arrangements," Emma says. "What are you serving us for dinner, dear cousin?"

"Chicken," Eddie replies. "I thought we'd eat outside while the weather is still good."

When it comes to London weather, "good" is a very relative term. Having grown up in Australia, I'm used to summer days over forty degrees Celsius, but thirty degrees in London is basically unheard of. Tonight it's twenty and clear, which at home would mean sitting under a blanket if you were outside; in London, it's sunbathing weather.

Eddie leads us through the hallway and lounge room and out

into a walled garden behind the house. The garden is surrounded by six-foot-high red brick walls covered in ivy. A conifer hedge runs along one side wall, and raised wooden planter boxes full of herbs adorn the other. In the centre of the garden is a massive oak tree, strung with fairy lights. Under the tree, a long wooden dining table sits on the grass, flanked by benches and looking out over the lavender bushes and wildflowers that line the back of the garden.

"This garden is beautiful," I enthuse.

"Fab, isn't it?" Lucy replies, plonking herself down at the table which is set with a hessian table runner and raw linen napkins.

"It's my escape in the city," Eddie says. "I know that it's minuscule compared to Kensington Gardens and Hyde Park over the other side of the fence, but I like that it's just for me."

"I can see why. It feels like we're out in the country."

"That's what I'm aiming for—peace in the city. One day I'd love some fruit trees, but I don't have the space at the moment."

"There's a simple solution to that one, Edmund," Lucy says. "Move on up to 1A now that Bertie and Louisa have jumped ship to Buckingham."

"Dad's suggested it," Eddie replies. "I'm not interested in moving, though. I don't need all the space, and I only finished my renovations here earlier in the year. Let Dad's cousins fight over 1A."

"Oh, they will," Emma responds.

"Ooh, Eddie! Please tell old Margaret and Catherine that it's available and film the catfight," Lucy urges. "That'd be better than anything you can see on telly. Margaret's been dropping very unsubtle hints for years now that Apartment 10 isn't big enough for her."

Emma nods enthusiastically. "Are you aware that she only has five bedrooms, Edmund? Five! She can't be expected to live like this."

"Life is tough in a palace," I say, laughing.

"Darling, you haven't a clue," Lucy purrs. "The politics of living in a compound surrounded by your extended family are so draining. It's almost enough to make me want to move out. The location is just too good to leave though, so we endure."

"So brave. You might just be my new hero, Lucy," I say.

"Thank you. I deserve it."

Just then, an alarm on Eddie's phone starts beeping.

"That'll be the roast. I'll just pop into the kitchen and be back. Can you help with plates please, Emma?"

"Yes, sir!" Emma jumps up and follows Eddie back into the house.

"So!" Lucy exclaims, spinning around to face me as soon as Eddie and Emma are out of earshot. "Tell me everything. But not *everything* everything—he is my cousin after all."

I laugh awkwardly. "There's not much to tell, really. I assume you know that he didn't actually cheat on Sibella with me?"

"I do. Perhaps he should have."

"We didn't even meet each other until after the wedding!"

"What a shame. Better late than never, though."

"Nothing is really happening. We haven't even been on a date yet."

"Why are the two of you having dinner with us then?"

"Ah, you invited yourselves?"

Lucy throws back her head and lets out a peal of laughter. "We did. I'd do it again, too. I couldn't pass up a chance to see Eddie being all awkward on a date."

"I'm not sure this is even a date."

"We'll see, my dear."

Lucy falls quiet as Eddie and Emma re-emerge from the house. They walk over to the table and lay out a roast chicken, vegetables and salad.

"Smells delicious," I say, my stomach rumbling.

"He does a good job in the kitchen, our Eddie, doesn't he?" Emma says.

"You made all this yourself?"

"It's nothing special," Eddie replies, shrugging.

"It looks pretty special to me. I assumed you had all your food sent over from Princess Helena's kitchens."

"Oh no, Edmund's far too self-sufficient for that." Lucy says. "He's also an excellent cook so, unlike us, he has no need to order food from Mummy's place."

Eddie turns a deep shade of red. "I'm not that good. I just enjoy cooking. I find it relaxing. Anyway, less talk about me and more eating." He looks at me and rolls his eyes. "Please ignore everything these two say."

CHAPTER 21

WHEN THE SUN SETS, even the Londoners have to admit that it's now too cold to stay outside. We all pick up our plates and carry them back into the kitchen. When I walk into the room, I hear a mad barking, and next thing I know a big pile of golden fur has launched itself at me.

"Poppy! Down, please," Eddie says. He walks over and scoops the fur ball up into his arms. "Did you miss me, girl?"

He scratches the dog under her chin and rocks her back and forth like a baby. My heart melts.

"Naw, she's so cute," I say. "Can I pat her?"

"Of course! Come and have a cuddle."

My phone buzzes in my pocket. I pull it out and see a string of news alerts.

I look up at Eddie. "More articles. I can't believe that you've been living like this forever."

Eddie draws his lips into a line. "I'm afraid it comes with the territory."

"It's a lot."

"Mm, it is what it is."

"Do you wish sometimes that it were different, that you were someone else?"

"Never," Eddie says, shaking his head decisively. "There are certainly drawbacks and difficulties, but I would never wish my position in life away. I've been born into a life that allows me to help people on a scale that most people couldn't even imagine. It's what gives me purpose."

"I love that you're so passionate about using your position for good. Not everyone would be, especially given all the issues it creates for you."

"There are aspects of my life I don't enjoy, but ultimately my duty to the crown and to this country that has given me so much is bigger than any inconveniences I may suffer."

I look at Eddie, and his eyes smoulder. "I'm not sure that the country deserves you, but I'm glad they have you. I'm glad I have you."

Lucy appears in the doorway and coughs. "It's time for us to go home."

Edmund cocks his head. "You're not staying for dessert? I made a crumble."

Lucy shakes her head. "No, no. Time to make ourselves scarce while you two have your dessert."

Emma turns to me and winks. "Enjoy."

Eddie flushes again. "Do you both intentionally try to torture me, or does it just come naturally?"

"Oh, a bit of both," she says airily.

"We really are done with you for tonight though," Lucy adds. "Come on, Em, let's leave these two to it. Good to see you, Amelia. Don't be a stranger."

With that, the princesses sweep out of the room and show themselves out.

"Are they always like this?" I ask Eddie.

He nods emphatically. "Sometimes more."

"I kind of love it."

"They're both a bit ridiculous, but they're a laugh, and their hearts are always in the right place. I'm quite lucky to have them around."

"That's really sweet. On a more important topic, though, did you mention crumble?"

"That I did," Eddie says, turning to the oven. He opens one of the doors on the emerald-green four-door Falcon oven with brass knobs and retrieves a dish with a flourish. "Apple and rhubarb crumble with rhubarb from the garden."

"Look at you! So fancy."

"I do my best."

Eddie plates up two serves of crumble and leads me from the kitchen, through the dining room and into the main lounge room. There's a second lounge room hidden away at the back of the house overlooking the garden that I'm told is used almost exclusively for watching bad TV.

With the hurricane princesses having left the building, I'm able to have a proper look around the room we're sitting in. It's quite a traditional sitting room with high ceilings and intricate cornices, but it's been decorated in more of a mid-century style— all walnut, leather and velvet with brass accents. I take a seat next to Edmund on a cream leather Herman Miller sofa and gaze around the modern interior. As I do, the spectre of Sibella looms large. I know Eddie says that they were never really in love, but they were still "together" for over a decade, and this was her home too until not long ago. How many rainy days did she spend curled up in the navy velvet armchair by the fire? Did she side-line the palace designer to choose her own artfully mismatched throw pillows? Did she come back after the wedding to collect her books, or are they still sitting there on the shelves, waiting for me to unknowingly read them?

"Amelia? Have I lost you?" Eddie waves a hand in front of my face.

"Sorry, zoned out for a second there. What did you say?"

"I was just asking how your day at work was."

"It was fine."

"Are you okay, Amelia? You seem rather distant all of a sudden. With my cousins gone, have you realised that I'm deathly boring and you made a terrible mistake in coming here tonight?"

I laugh weakly. "No, it's not that. I just feel really strange sitting here chatting over crumble so soon after Sibella moved out. It's like I'm trying to just step into her life. You were together for so long—you can't be ready for another relationship."

"I can understand you feeling that way. But this is not a rebound or distraction for me—this is real. This is my house, my life. It never really belonged to Sibella, and she has no claim on it now."

"You say that, but as far as the world is concerned, she was your partner for over a decade. Also, didn't she live here for years?"

"Officially, she did. And I won't lie, she did stay here sometimes. She never thought of it as her home, though."

"So she didn't personally select this very elegant chair that I'm sitting on right now?"

"I'll let you in on a little secret: Sib had no input in the design of this place at all. This tasteful decor? All me."

I laugh. "You and your team of interior designers, I assume?"

"No, I'm serious. I went through a phase of bingeing HGTV home design shows and reading interior design blogs when I couldn't sleep. I once tried to apply to a casting call for a Netflix competitive reality show for interior decorators under a fake name. The palace caught the email on the way out. Charli had a field day with that one."

"Did you really?"

"Cross my heart."

"What were you going to do if they asked you to audition? I'm pretty sure the producers would have recognised you."

Eddie shifts his weight from side to side. "Oh, you know, the usual—fake name, wig, bad Scottish accent. Aye, wee lassie and all that."

I have to pretend to cough to mask my snort. "I'm not sure you'd be fooling anyone with that accent."

"No, neither was Charli. And thus my career as a star of the decor world was crushed before it even began."

"Tragic."

Eddie hangs his head. "I was devastated."

He reaches out and takes my hand. "The point of all of that is you're not stealing anyone's place in my house. Or in my life. I want you here."

Without waiting for a response, Eddie leans over and kisses me. It's a slow, deep kiss that I melt into.

"I want to be here," I say when we come up for air.

"I'm extremely glad to hear it," Edmund says, smiling and moving towards me again.

I move back and put my hand on his chest. Ugh, I'm going to regret this. "But, tonight, I should really go home."

"Do you have to?"

Eddie wants me to stay, and I'm going to say no? I'm *really* going to regret this. "I think—I—I just don't want to rush anything."

Eddie kisses me again. "I understand. I'm not saying I'm happy about it, but I understand. I'm going to let you go home now, but I expect you to come back for dinner again as soon as humanly possible. If not sooner."

I FLOAT HOME, replaying every moment of the last hour in my head. When we arrive at the flat, Michael opens the car door for me and walks me to the door. Tonight there are only a few photographers outside. It appears the security is working.

"Good night, ma'am. Lock the door once you're inside. If you need anything overnight, you have my number."

"Thanks, Michael. Have a good night."

"Yes, ma'am."

The lounge is dark when I walk in.

"Penny, are you here?" No answer.

It's not until I'm in my pyjamas and brushing my teeth that I hear the door open.

"Mils?"

"In the bathroom," I call out through a mouthful of toothpaste.

Penny appears in the doorway. "How was your dinner?"

"It was good," I say coyly.

"Ooh, how good?"

"Pretty, pretty good." I grin.

"Why are you home then?"

"Pen!"

"What? He's dreamy, and I wouldn't be passing up a chance to see what the crown's made of, if you know what I mean."

"All I've done is kiss him, and I'm already international tabloid fodder."

"Exactly, so what've you got to lose by getting some action?"

Penny shrieks as I throw a toothbrush at her.

"What? We're all grown-ups here."

"How was your night?" I ask, trying to change the topic.

"My night was also *good,* thank you, Amelia."

"Jack again?"

"Mm, yup. I am not constrained by tabloid attention, so I had a remarkably good night."

"How long have you been seeing him for now?"

"A couple weeks, ever since you started visiting Edmund at KP. It might be a record. I don't know how long it's going to last, though. Your bodyguard out there is pretty tempting..."

"Don't you dare! I need him to protect me from the journos. If you scare him off, I'm going to throw you out there to deal with them instead."

"Sticking with Jack it is, then."

~

Wednesday 1 September

REMEMBER how I said that my life is utterly boring and the rumour mill is out of luck with me? Turns out I was wrong.

Despite the shrinking paparazzi contingent, I wake up to another stream of articles. None of them are anything particularly new, other than *The Sun*'s headline story that is.

Has Edmund been had?

Since returning from Kenya on the weekend, sources report that Prince Edmund has been spending increasing amounts of time with new flame Amelia Glendale. Meanwhile, Lady Sibella was spotted yesterday in Greece looking downcast.

According to insiders, Sibella has good reason to feel threatened. The Sun can exclusively reveal that all may not be as it seems with lawyer Amelia. While some may see an earnest, hardworking professional who bonded with Edmund over their common passion for charity work, the truth is profoundly different. Amelia has in fact been an avid royal watcher since her childhood in Australia. She reportedly developed a particular interest in none other than Prince Leo. It was Amelia's obsession with Leo that motivated her to move from down under. Insiders claim that Amelia went so far as to decorate her desks at white-shoe law firm Linklaters and then the Queen's Charitable Foundation with photos of the playboy prince. Indeed, she could often be seen walking around the office sipping tea from a Leo mug.

Once in London, Amelia wormed her way into royal circles with the sole intention of nabbing Leo. The persistent expat took every opportunity she could to get closer to the prince, and obsessed over his TV appearances in the meantime. It was only after meeting Edmund that

Amelia decided that she'd found an easier mark and set her sights on the other prince. Edmund stood no chance when faced with the beautiful social climber who spent years planning her attack, determined to catch a prince.

...

This is so humiliating. Has Eddie seen this? Oh god, I hope he hasn't seen it. Or Lucy and Emma. Or Leo! I hadn't even considered that Leo would see it. He's the last person who needs an ego boost. It might be time to crawl up in a dark hole somewhere and die. That's really the only rational response to everyone you've ever met reading something like this about you.

I hear a scream from the other room. "Amelia!"

Clearly Penny has been doing her morning celebrity gossip check. A few seconds later, she barges into my room.

"Have you seen it?"

"I have. It's so embarrassing! What's Eddie going to think?"

"He will probably dump you immediately and never speak to you again."

I gulp. "He will, won't he?"

"I was joking. Of course he won't. Eddie knows better than to believe everything he reads, so I wouldn't worry about his reaction too much."

"True. It still makes me sound terrible, though. He's never going to want to be seen in public with me if this is what I'm known for. The palace might try to sweep me under the rug until I go away like Kayla."

"Probably."

"Who are these sources anyway?" I muse. "It's all ridiculous, obviously, but there's enough detail there that they must have gotten information from someone. Could someone at work have spoken to a reporter?"

"Maybe. That would be a bit weird though, wouldn't it? People at your office would have information about the royal family all the time. Why would they keep that under wraps for years and then decide to start selling stories about you?"

"It's really strange. Eddie did suspect there was a leak at KP after the wedding, but no one at the palace would have that kind of information about me. Unless it was one of his PPOs?"

"Seems unlikely. They'd have the most vetting of anyone."

I moan. "How did this get so complicated already?"

"That's what you get for making out with one of the most famous people in the country."

I groan and rub my temples. This isn't how I wanted to start my day.

CHAPTER 22

OPENING THE DOOR, I see that the small group of photographers from last night has multiplied. News that I'm a creepy prince stalker has reinvigorated their interest in me. Somehow Michael manages to get me through the throng and into the waiting car, but not before I'm hit with a barrage of questions and jeers.

"Hey Amelia, would you still prefer Leo?"

"Gold digger!"

"How does Edmund feel about being your second choice?"

"Any tips for other social climbers?"

"Amelia! Over here! Show us some leg, love."

Mercifully, the noise fades into the background when the door slams shut. I'm really not sure how much more of this I can deal with. Damn that stupid Leo mug.

As far as offices go, I'm normally an open door kind of girl unless I'm super stressed, but today I slam the door behind me. I'm not going to face one more person than absolutely necessary today. They can all judge me from a distance.

Once I'm safely ensconced in my office, I flop onto my chair and get out my phone to call Edmund.

He answers on the first ring. "Good morning."

"Are you having a good morning? Because mine has been anything but good."

"You've seen the papers then?"

"I'm so embarrassed. How is anyone going to take me seriously after this? Are you calling to say that you want nothing to do with me anymore?"

Eddie laughs. "Amelia, I've already seen your Leo memorabilia, and it didn't scare me off. I forgive you for having poor taste in your youth."

"You might be the only one who does."

"Try not to worry too much. Most people understand that everything these rags publish is rubbish."

I can hear the panic rising in my voice. "Some people do, but not many. I bet everyone is convinced I was stalking Leo for years and preyed on you when you were heartbroken."

"Not everyone thinks that."

"How can you be so sure about that?" I ask dramatically. "They might."

"Well, I for one don't think that. And I tend to think that my opinion on the topic is rather important. I believe I'd remember you preying on me."

"I'll give you that. But still, how do you deal with all of this? How do you fight the urge to put out statements refuting ridiculous stories? Or worse, the stories that are just believable enough that they might actually be true."

He sighs. "It's quite easy, in fact, because even if I wanted to respond to something in the press, I couldn't. I'm not the one in charge of my public image. That's for the palace PR team to handle. Charli and her team—heavily influenced by Dad's PR team—decide where I go and who I appear to be. I have very little say in the matter."

"That sounds awful."

"Oh, it's not all bad. In a way, there's a freedom in ceding control to someone else, and I don't spend much energy concerning myself with image problems these days. There's no point when both the problem and the response are out of my control."

"But surely the palace must give you some say in your public image—they work for you, not the other way round."

"I'm always involved—I have press clipping review meetings with the team three times a week, monthly profile strategy sessions, a messaging meeting before each official engagement and a debrief after. Charli and the others ask for my opinion, but over the years I've decided that it's simpler not to have one. If I have the 'wrong' opinion, it'll be ignored anyway."

"I never realised how much of your time is spent on publicity."

Eddie laughs. "I wish it wasn't, but that's how the machine works. We're a family, yes, but we're also a business. Dad will never let any of us forget it."

"I don't know if I could live like that."

"You get used to it. Anyway, would it cheer you up if we went out for dinner tonight on a real-life date in an actual restaurant?"

I chew my lip. "I'm not sure. Can I think about it? I don't want to attract more attention. You're not worried about how the PR team would react? I can't imagine they're thrilled about any of this."

"They'll live. Given that I have handed over complete control of my public life, I rather think I deserve to have some say in how I live my private life."

"It just sounds like something that could backfire."

"There's always that risk, but promise you will consider it. I'd really like to take you for a dinner that doesn't involve any of my family members. And we all know the chances of that happening at home are slim to none."

"I promise."

"Excellent. I'll call you later today to get your answer. In the meantime, do try not to let this get to you. I won't be giving it another thought."

"Thanks, Eddie. I'll speak to you later."

All morning I'm getting messages from friends teasing me about the Leo obsession. It's not making me feel better about the article, and it's definitely not helping me to focus on getting any work done. After lunch, I give up and decide I need a break, so I pick up my bag and walk to the lift. Michael follows me downstairs and then out through the lobby onto the street. I'm not sure where I'm going, but I need to walk some of this stress off.

After walking along the river at South Bank for a while with Michael trailing behind me, I decide to stop at a pop-up cafe for coffee. Coffee might help, right? And cake—today is definitely a day for cake. I order at the counter and then find a seat in front of the pop-up. It's an eco-friendly cafe in a shipping container covered in a giant vertical garden and surrounded by stools made from recycled shipping pallets. I'm busy trying to figure out how the plants are attached to the wall when I hear my name. I look up, assuming it's the waitress trying to find me to deliver my coffee and sugar hit, but instead I see a group of women in their early twenties standing at the door, pointing and staring at me.

"You're right, it is her."

"Who does she think she is? She's not nearly hot enough to date either of them."

"Totally. At least with Sibella, you could tell what Edmund saw in her. This just makes no sense."

"Terrible rebound choice."

None of the women seem to care at all that I'm sitting less than three meters away and can hear every awful word they're saying. I can't decide if I should go over there and confront them or try to make myself invisible through sheer force of will. Before I figure out what to do, my order arrives. I jump up and walk out of the cafe as quickly as I can without drawing any more attention to myself.

As I walk back to the office, I catch more people looking at me, nudging their friends and whispering to each other. I can't get back to my desk fast enough.

In the lift back upstairs, my phone buzzes with a text from Eddie

Eddie: *So, have you decided if I can take you out tonight?*

After my coffee experience? No chance.

Me: *Do you mind if I pass? I just picked up some coffee and had people pointing at me the whole time, so I've had enough public attention for one day.*

His reply comes through straight away.

Eddie: *Dinner at mine instead then?*

That I can handle.

Me: *Perfect. I'll come by when I finish up here. I expect something delicious, please.*

Eddie: *Yes, ma'am.*

Maybe this day won't be so bad after all.

～

A COUPLE OF HOURS LATER, my car pulls up outside Wren House. There's no answer when I knock on the door, so I try again. When there's still no answer, I call Eddie.

"Hey, are you at home? I'm at the front door."

"Sorry," Eddie says. "I didn't hear you. I'm out the back. I'll come and let you in."

Not long after I hang up, the door swings open and Edmund is standing there, dressed in jeans and a pale grey V-neck t-shirt.

"Hi there," he says, leaning against the door frame.

This day has definitely improved.

"Hi, thanks for agreeing to stay in. Today has been a bit intense."

"I'm never going to say no to you coming over here. I have to warn you, though," Eddie says as he moves aside for me to pass into the hall. "We have company."

"Oh?" I ask warily.

"Yes, Lucy invited herself over. I couldn't stop her," Eddie says, rolling his eyes. "And then she invited Emma, Leo and Kayla too."

"That is... more people than I expected to see tonight. Are you speaking to Leo again?"

"Yes, we're speaking. He cooled off pretty quickly once we got back to London. He loses his temper sometimes, but he doesn't hold a grudge."

"Well, I'm glad you two are okay."

"Leo and I are fine, but are you and I okay? I know you didn't want to be entertaining a crowd this evening. Although I did warn you it's hard to manage a dinner alone here."

"You did, you did."

"Last chance to run away. I can pretend you were a Mormon door-knocker trying to convert me."

"Do you often get door-knockers in a palace guarded by dozens of soldiers?" I ask, raising an eyebrow.

Eddie puts his hands up in defeat. "You got me. Confession, I've never seen someone door-knocking. I'd be basing my story entirely on *The Book of Mormon*."

I laugh. The knot in my stomach starts to unravel, and I feel more relaxed than I have all day. "That could be a problem. I'm sorry to be the one to tell you this, but door-knockers in real life are far less musical and not particularly funny."

"That is extremely disappointing news. Given that my cover story is a bust, you'll have to stay."

"I can't argue with that logic."

"Excellent, come through then."

Eddie peels off to check on dinner in the kitchen, and I walk out to the walled garden where Lucy, Leo and Kayla are sitting around under the oak tree with wine and cheese. Lucy jumps up from the table when she sees me.

"Hello, darling," she says, giving me a warm hug. "Read any interesting news lately?"

I cover my eyes with my hands. "Please don't," I say. "It's too raw!"

"Oh, Amelia, it could be far worse," Lucy cries. "No one could fault you for preferring Leo. He is the more attractive brother, after all."

"Too right I am," chimes in Leo from his seat at the table.

I uncover my eyes and clear my throat. "Er, Leo, while I'm here. You know that article wasn't true, don't you?"

"Whatever you say, Amelia. I know who the real catch in this family is."

Ick. How did I ever think he was the charming one?

Kayla is giggling and stroking Leo's arm, but she's also keeping her eyes trained on me.

"You are a catch, Leo," Emma says. "If we were still allowed to marry our cousins, you'd be my one of my top two picks. Maybe I should have a chat to Bertie about it."

Kayla's mouth drops open. "Gross!"

Clearly someone has no sense of humour.

"Calm down, Kayla, it was a joke."

"Oh," Kayla says, pursing her lips. "Why would you joke about something like that?"

Just then, Eddie emerges from the kitchen carrying a large roasting tray.

"What are we eating?" I ask, craning to look into the dish.

"An Ottolenghi couscous salad with lamb shanks," Eddie replies, placing the tray of lamb in the centre of the table. "It's lucky I made extra. One of these days I'm going to only cater for the people I've invited to dinner, and the rest of you interlopers will go hungry."

"Or, you could assume that you should always have enough

food to feed me. The rest of you can starve," Leo says, winking at Lucy and Kayla.

Kayla crosses her arms and huffs. Lucy ignores him.

"I appreciate your generosity, cousin. I would tell you that I'm sorry and will never invite myself to dinner at the last minute again, but we all know it would be a lie."

"How do you lot feed yourselves when I'm not here?" Eddie asks.

"Easy, we go out," Lucy replies, taking a sip of her champagne.

"Enough talk, more food," Leo says.

Eddie rolls his eyes and starts passing out plates. When everyone has one, Eddie takes a seat next to me on the bench, close enough that our legs are touching.

Eddie places his hand on my thigh, and I'm so distracted by the contact that I can't focus at all on the conversation over dinner. Lucy is telling a story that has something to do with a ferret and the king of Spain, but I couldn't for the life of me tell you what the ferret did to the king—or was it what the king did to the ferret?

We finish eating, and Eddie stands to clear the table.

"Leave it," I say, touching his arm. "You've made me dinner two nights in a row. The least I can do is take care of the dishes."

"If you insist."

I squeeze Eddie's arm and give him a lopsided smile. "I do."

He winks back at me. I'd better get into the house before I do something inappropriate to him in front of half his family.

When I pick up plates to take into the kitchen, I'm surprised to see Kayla stand too. She gathers up some glasses and follows me inside.

"How are you holding up, Amelia?"

"Sorry?"

"How are you coping with all the attention? You must not be used to it."

"I'm not used to it at all. It's been so sudden too, so it's pretty hard."

"I get it. I was only eighteen when I entered the public eye and had to learn how to deal with it all."

"You seem quite, uh, comfortable with the attention now."

Comfortable is an understatement. Kayla is one of those Instagram influencer reality stars who'll go to the opening of anything if she gets a goodie bag and her picture taken. You can't keep her away from a camera.

Kayla sighs, "It just takes practice. The public interest is the price I pay for my success."

The price she pays for her success? Give me a break. The girl is a D-grade celebrity at best.

"Well, you seem to deal with it well."

"We should have lunch sometime soon. I could help you with the press? I know what it's like trying to fit in with this family too."

"Thank you, Kayla, that's really nice of you."

"Are you free tomorrow? I'm on a break this week, but off to film a new project after that."

"I think so. I'll check my calendar."

"Great, meet me at Chiltern Firehouse tomorrow at midday."

I hadn't actually had a chance to check my calendar yet, but what could I have going on that's more important than Kayla's busy morning of selfies and Pilates? It's not like I have a real job or anything.

AFTER DINNER, Kayla and Leo retreat to Nottingham Cottage next door, but Lucy and Emma show no signs of leaving.

"What are we watching tonight?" Lucy asks.

"No reality TV, please!" I say. "After the last week, I don't think I can look at reality stars in the same way. It's all fun and games when you're sitting at home reading about their latest wardrobe malfunctions in the news, but it turns out it doesn't feel great at all to be on the other side. I'm developing some serious sympathy for celebrities."

Emma tuts. "Please, most reality shows are entirely scripted, and the stars are experts at attracting attention. Some shows are definitely more exploitative than others, though."

"Why don't we stick to something properly scripted? There's a new season of *The Crown* out this week. I've been saving it until we were all together," says Lucy.

Eddie groans. "Do we really have to put ourselves through more of that? I watch TV to escape from my life, not to waste my time on a fictionalised version of it."

"Yes, we have to watch it. I love it!" Emma says. "It's so much fun to see what parts of Mummy and Granny's lives were like before we were born."

"You're aware, I assume, that it's not a documentary, Emma?"

"I'm aware of that, cousin, but I think it's fun."

"I agree," Lucy says. "If I ever get married, I'm going to ask their costume designers to choose my wedding gown. Much like the rest of the show, it'll look better than real life."

Emma turns to Lucy. "Ooh, do you think that when they get to our bit, they'd let us play ourselves? It'd be such a laugh."

"That would be fabulous! I'll have to see if I have any connections at the production company."

"You could ask Kayla," I say. "I'd be amazed if she hasn't already tried to get them to cast her."

"You're so right!" Emma says. "One of her many attempts to force the king to let Leo go public with her."

Edmund shakes his head. "She should save her energy. Dad is never going to change his mind."

"Why is he so against her?" I ask. "I know that she's a bit ridiculous, but she seems harmless."

Eddie shakes his head again. "She's just not the right sort, see?

No one who chases the publicity will ever truly fit in with the family or be able to do the work without making it all about their own image."

"The way she calls photographers on herself is so gauche," Lucy says.

"Does she really?"

"She definitely does," Emma says. "I'm convinced she's taking free clothes in exchange for product placement on her social too."

Lucy grimaces. "Or worse," she says. "She could be taking money for posts."

"I wouldn't be shocked at all by that," Emma says, shrugging. "There's something inherently dubious about someone who chooses to get out at bed at five in the morning to exercise."

CHAPTER 23

"How was your date?" Penny asks when I walk into the flat after dinner and collapse on the sofa.

"It was great, other than Leo, Kayla, Emma and Lucy all inviting themselves along."

Penny's eyes widen. "Again? Is his family trying to make sure that you get no time alone with him?"

"It's starting to seem that way. I don't think they're doing it intentionally or anything—they just have this close family thing going."

"Intentional or not, it's some A-grade cock blocking."

"It really is. It's actually getting pretty frustrating to be honest, I like spending time with them, but there's so much going on. I could really do with some time to just talk to Eddie about everything."

"You need to sort that out."

"As soon as possible," I say, nodding. I stretch my arms and yawn. "Oh, guess what?"

"What?"

"Kayla asked me to lunch with her tomorrow."

"Did she?" Penny asks, leaning in. "Why would she do that?"

"No idea. I think she feels sorry for me because of all the media attention. She says she wants to help me."

"Well, taking her advice can't hurt."

I sigh. "Let's be honest, at this point I need all the help I can get. Even if it is from Kayla."

Thursday 2 September

MY MORNING MEETING the next day runs overtime, so at twelve fifteen, I'm in the car on my way to Chiltern Firehouse to meet Kayla. I'm still not quite sure why she wants to help me, but I'm not going to say no to any paparazzi-wrangling tips. I'm finding having people outside my flat waiting to see what I'm wearing or where I'm going incredibly stressful. I could barely sleep last night knowing they were still out there, wondering what ridiculous stories they're going to print next. I'll take help wherever I can get it.

I arrive at the restaurant in Marylebone half an hour late. I'm kicking myself because I'm guessing that Kayla isn't the kind of woman who likes to be kept waiting, and I don't want to put her offside. Enough people hate me already. The restaurant is in an imposing red brick building which was built as a fire station in the 1800s and is run by the same team as the Chateau Marmont. Exactly the sort of fancy celebrity magnet that I normally avoid at all costs.

A maître d' greets me when I walk through the door. "Good afternoon, madam. Do you have a reservation?"

"Yes, I'm meeting Kayla Monroe."

The maître d' nods and gestures towards the kitchen. "Right this way, madam."

I'm shown to an empty table in the centre of the room. There are plenty of discreet tables scattered around the dining room, but this is not one of them. This is an exhibitionist table. As I sit down, I try to avoid looking around at the patrons I can sense watching me. At least I got here before Kayla.

Ten minutes later, I'm studying the ceiling's exposed beams when I hear Kayla's voice. I turn and see her greeting the maître d' like an old friend. She stops at three tables to talk to people before finally appearing next to me.

"Hello, darling!" she says, leaning in and air kissing me on both cheeks.

That was unusually friendly.

"Hi Kayla, how are you?"

"Fine, thanks, babe. Just exhausted. I've been frantic all morning, you know how it is."

"What are you working on?"

"Oh, this and that. I had yoga this morning and then had my hair done. After that I had to choose a dress for an awards show next week, and I've got a call with my agent this afternoon."

"Wow," I say. "That sounds, uh... busy."

Kayla sighs and rolls her eyes. "You don't even know!"

She's right, I don't know what it must be like to think of that as being a busy day. On my busy days, I'm on two conference calls at once while sending emails on another project, or sitting at my desk for hours trying not to pee myself because I don't have time to go to the bathroom between meetings.

Before I can say anything I might regret, a waiter appears by the table.

"Good afternoon, ladies, what can I get for you today?"

"Can I please have a salami pizza and a side salad?"

I've been thinking about this pizza all morning. Is there anything better than hot carbs covered in cheese?

"Of course, madam. And for you, Ms. Monroe?"

Kayla gives me an amused look before turning to the waiter to order. "A gin and tonic and a side of steamed greens. No oil or dressing."

The waiter scrawls down our order and returns to the kitchen.

"Anything new in the papers today?" Kayla asks.

"No, nothing new. Just more of the same."

"It must be hard for you, not being someone who is used to being in the public eye. You don't have the poise or instincts of someone who has always attracted attention like I have."

"No, I suppose I don't."

"You'll never be a natural, but try to keep your head up and give the paps a little something for their effort. You want to keep up a good relationship with them."

"I don't think I want to do anything to encourage all this attention."

Kayla laughs and pats my arm. "Oh darling, you're so naïve. Of course you want attention—you just want the right kind."

"I'd rather just be anonymous, to be honest."

"We'll see about that," she says, smirking. "Anyway, tell me about how you met Edmund. Did you really want Leo?" she leans in with a conspiratorial grin. "You can tell me, I won't be jealous."

I almost choke on my water. "I was just hedging my bets. As long as I can wear a tiara to my wedding, I don't care who the groom is," I say sarcastically.

Kayla looks at me, eyes wide and her mouth hanging slightly open. I don't think sarcasm is for her.

"Don't worry, I was never trying to pursue Leo."

"Oh, I'm not worried," Kayla says, sitting taller and holding her hand out to admire her nails.

The awkward silence that follows is broken by our waiter returning with our meals and placing them on the table with a flourish. When I say "our meals", I mean my meal and Kayla's four stems of broccolini. No carbs and no sarcasm? What a depressing life. Note to self—never become an influencer.

"How long have you been seeing Leo for?" I ask, trying to

steer the conversation back to a topic that Kayla will be more comfortable with.

"Over six months now. We met at a mutual friend's private club, and we've been *obsessed* with each other ever since. It's just one of those deep, spiritual connections, you know? We're very in tune."

"That's great."

"We'll get married soon. We just need Albert to give us approval."

"Has Leo proposed?"

"Not yet, but he will."

I wish I had that kind of confidence about my relationship with Eddie. I'm not even sure if it *is* a relationship, and I don't have the guts to ask.

Kayla spends the next half an hour telling me stories about parties she's been to with various celebrities and complaining about how hard it is to decide which diet shake or fake tan company to work with for sponsored Instagram posts. The life of an influencer, am I right?

After lunch, there are a handful of photographers waiting outside. I don't know how they always seem to be able to find me. Did one of them inject me with a tracking chip in my sleep? I wouldn't put it past them. Or maybe Lucy was right about Kayla calling them herself?

Kayla, seeming unperturbed, makes a show of kissing me goodbye as the cameras snap away and then leaves me in a cloud of what smells like Ariana Grande-branded perfume. I'm not sure that was helpful at all.

∽

Friday 3 September

ON THE WAY TO work the next day, a Google alert pops up on my phone. I admit it, I set up Google alerts on my own name. Celebrities always claim that they don't read anything about themselves online, but that's definitely a lie, right?

Opening the article on the *Daily Mail* website, I groan.

Is Amelia using Edmund?

Amelia Glendale has wasted no time in taking advantage of her newfound notoriety. Since returning with Prince Edmund from Kenya, Amelia has been getting chummy with as many celebrities as possible. Yesterday she was spotted having lunch at notorious celeb-hotspot Chiltern Firehouse with influencer, model and reality star Kayla Monroe.

Kayla looked glamorous as always in an orange silk jumpsuit from her soon-to-be-released clothing line, while Amelia dressed down in a black skirt and cream cap-sleeved blouse. She also suffered a major wardrobe malfunction when she was seen exiting the restaurant with sauce splattered over her blouse.

Insiders have speculated that Amelia knows her time with the prince is limited and is trying to make as many connections as possible before being tossed to the curb.

...

The article is accompanied by the photos of Kayla and I leaving the restaurant. I can't believe I'm at the point where I can't go anywhere without being photographed and having my clothes judged. I'm not made for this. I selected my skirt yesterday because it was the cleanest thing I could find in the giant clothes pile on my floor.

I send the link to Penny

Me: *Not sure that I'm cut out for this royal girlfriend business.*

Penny: *You should at least make sure you wear clean clothes in public. I saw you wear that skirt three days in a row.*

Me: *It was clean enough until I spilt food on it at lunch!*

Penny: *I bet Kayla never recycles outfits two days in a row. She probably also doesn't store all her clothes in a floordrobe.*

Me: *I maintain that it's easier to throw things on the floor than put them away. I can always find them that way.*

Penny: *Whatever you want to tell yourself. We all know you're just lazy.*

Penny: *Are you home for dinner tonight?*

Me: *Yeah, I'll be home around 7.*

I think about sending the link to Edmund too, but I don't want to draw too much attention to the fact that there are more unflattering photos of me out there. Instead, I decide to pretend they don't exist instead, since that's clearly the mature response.

Me: *Morning, how was your night?*

Eddie: *Unbelievably tedious. Dad sent me to a dinner for the National Birdwatchers' Association. Four hours of listening to avian fanatics telling stories about the different birds they've seen in the city. I think he's trying to punish me for landing in the papers again.*

Me: *Sounds hideous. Are there any birds in London that aren't pigeons?*

Eddie: *I wish it was that simple. Want to come by after work so I can educate you about the many, many varieties of pigeons living in our midst?*

Hmm, how annoyed is Penny going to be if I stand her up? Probably very annoyed.

Me: *Sorry, promised Pen I'd be home for dinner tonight.*

Eddie: *That's OK. I'm meant to be going to a meeting of the National Horticultural Society so would need to leave by eight anyway.*

Me: *Free tomorrow instead? You'll be able to add some plant facts to your pigeon presentation. I expect a detailed slide deck.*

Eddie: *It's a date.*

WHEN I GET HOME after work, I'm confronted by a mountain of bags in the lounge room.

"Penny, are you here? I can't see you through all the stuff."

"In the kitchen. I'll be out in a sec," she calls from the other room.

"What is all of this? Are you making gift bags for a work event again?"

Penny emerges from the kitchen, her long skirt swishing around her legs. "No, these are for you."

"For me?"

"I'm going full Kanye on you and overhauling your wardrobe. I've already been through your room and thrown out everything I don't approve of, which was basically everything."

My mouth drops open. "Excuse me?"

"Amelia," Penny says, a determined glint in her eyes. "If you're going to keep seeing Edmund, the photographers aren't going to go anywhere. It's my duty as your best friend to make sure you don't look like a homeless person on the internet."

"Do I get a say in any of this?"

"No, none at all. My friend Jess, who is a buyer at Selfridges, and I went shopping this afternoon and bought you a new wardrobe. We've gone for a mix of tasteful high street and high-end basics so you can mix and match. We've got you covered for work, casual weekends, and a few fancier date outfits. If you're going to a proper event though, you'll need a dedicated outfit. We're working on lining up freebies from designers through some of Jess's contacts."

High-end basics? Designer freebies? I'm so far out of my depth here. I didn't think about any of this when I started spending time with Eddie.

I take a deep breath. "Okay, I take your point that I need to up my clothing game and at least wear something clean in public. But is all of this really necessary?"

"It absolutely is. Sibella wasn't walking around in the same pair of jeans every weekend. There are certain expectations when you're involved with the royal family. You don't want to give reporters any more ammunition."

She has a point there.

"Okay, you're right. One question though, how did you afford this?"

"Easy," Penny says, starting to pull garments out of bags. "I stole your credit card."

My stomach drops as I start mentally tallying the cost of everything around me. "Penny!"

"Shh, it's for your own good. Now strip. You need to start trying things on."

CHAPTER 24

Saturday 4 September

THE GROUNDS of the palace are uncharacteristically quiet when I arrive. I'm wearing one of Penny's new day-to-night approved outfit—a black pleated silk midi skirt from Theory teamed with a colourful printed blouse from Zara and kitten heels.

I ring the bell, and Eddie appears at the door, wearing a Union Jack apron, flour smudged on his forehead.

"Been busy in the kitchen, I see?" I say as Eddie leads me inside.

"Indeed. If I don't maintain my culinary standards, you might stop visiting."

"You're right, I *am* mainly here for the food."

"I don't blame you. I don't have much else going for me."

I shake my head and make a tutting noise. "Don't be too hard on yourself, Edmund. You've also got fantastic hair. Admirable lack of hair loss."

He runs his hand through his sandy hair. "I don't know, I'm only thirty-one—there's plenty of time for the bald genes to catch up with me."

"Fair warning, I'll have to re-evaluate our friendship if that happens. In the meantime, you can keep cooking for me."

"How magnanimous of you, Amelia."

"That's me, generous to a fault," I say, smoothing my skirt.

Eddie cackles with laughter. "I don't know what I've done to deserve the attentions of a saint such as yourself, but I hope I can keep it up."

He stoops down to open the oven door and I'm hit with the aroma of tomato, basil and cheese. Lots of cheese.

"Edmund," I say, hand on heart. "Did you make me lasagne?"

"I did."

"From scratch?" I ask incredulously.

Eddie bobs his head slightly.

"Okay, all jokes aside—I have no idea what I've done to deserve *your* attentions. You're a keeper."

"Just wait until you see dessert," he says, jerking his thumb towards the counter.

I look over and see a baking tray covered in a lumpy tea towel.

"What is this?" I ask, walking across the kitchen and drumming my fingers on the edge of the tray.

"See for yourself."

I lift the edge of the towel and then gape at Edmund, eyes wide. "Edmund... are these fresh croissants?"

"Yes, chocolate ones this time. They're almost finished proving."

"Were you baking all those pastries for me yourself this whole time?"

Eddie fidgets with his watch, eyes darting around.

"I thought you were bringing them from the palace kitchen."

"I never said that," says Eddie. "I said I was bringing them from home. You assumed that meant from the main kitchens. I just didn't correct you."

"Let me get this straight. You're a prince who is passionate about saving the world, and in your spare time you bake me incredible pastries? No wonder I love you."

Eddie's pupils flare, and my hand flies to my mouth. I can't believe I just said that. Quick, think of something else to say! The longer we stand here in silence, the more awkward this is going to be.

"I mean, I love that you have so many talents. Sorry, that was stupid, I didn't mean that."

Or did I? We've basically only just started dating, and I know I'm not in love with him, but there is something about the whole "dating a prince" thing that is easy to get swept up in. It's real life, but sometimes it doesn't feel like it.

"Why don't we eat?" Eddie says, picking up plates and walking off to the dining room, avoiding my gaze.

Good job, Amelia. You've well messed that up.

We sit down at the table and Edmund disappears to the kitchen before returning with a bottle of wine.

"It's strangely quiet around here tonight. We're not expecting anyone else to drop by?"

"No, not tonight. Lucy and Em are in Switzerland for a mountain break with Helena, and Leo's off on navy business."

"Does that mean I get you to myself for an entire night?"

"It does indeed," Eddie says, his eyes burning into mine.

"Can I talk to you about something?"

"Anything."

"About what I said before…"

His eyes twinkle. "That you love me, you mean?"

"Uh, yes, that's the one," I say, my cheeks flaming.

"What about it?"

He's not going to make this easy for me, is he?

"You know that I'm not in love with you, don't you?"

He chuckles. "I didn't take it literally. We've only been seeing each other for a couple of weeks. I'd be a tad concerned if you thought you were in love with me."

I wipe my brow. "Thank god! I mean, we haven't even talked about what this is, and I go and put my foot in it by accidentally saying 'I love you.' You'd be well within your rights to think I was insane and move on."

"You've got a point there, Amelia."

"It *would* be insane."

"No, not about that," Eddie says, shaking his head. "You're right that we haven't defined what's going on between us."

My chest squeezes. "Oh, don't worry about that. Like you said, it's really early days. We don't need to label anything."

Eddie's eyes bore into mine. "What if I want a label?"

"Did you have a particular label in mind?"

I feel like all the air has been sucked out of my lungs as I wait for him to respond.

"I was going to suggest girlfriend. For you that is, not for me."

My heart is beating a million miles an hour.

"So that would make you…"

"Your boyfriend, if you'll have me."

I cock my head and rub my chin. "Hm, I'll think about it."

"Not the overwhelmingly positive response I had anticipated, but I'll take it. You're a hard woman to please, Ms. Glendale."

My straight face breaks into a grin and I feel like I'm floating. "I'd love to be your girlfriend. Wait, not love! Why do I keep doing this? What I meant to say is, I would like that. Very much."

AFTER DINNER, we move into the lounge room.

"Can we light a fire?" I ask, gazing longingly at the oversized fireplace. I've always wanted a fireplace. Give me a fireplace, a bathtub and a patch of grass where I can read in the sun and I think I'd be happy forever. That's the dream. It's a shame that living in London is so eye-wateringly expensive that even on a decent (by not-for-profit standards) lawyer's salary, I can't afford any of those things.

Eddie kneels down by the fireplace and starts meticulously placing kindling in a little pyramid.

"You've done this before."

He sits back on his heels and puffs his cheeks out. "I have, you know. Army."

I slap my forehead. "Oh, of course, I forgot that you were in the army. I mean, I didn't forget as such. I just always assumed that you didn't have to do in-field work. I didn't expect you to have been out there doing survival training."

"Other than being given extra leave to attend important engagements, the army didn't give me any special treatment. I completed my basic training and deployments just like everyone else."

"How did you find that?"

Eddie strikes a match and leans in to light the little pile of sticks. "It was fantastic."

"I can't imagine many people can say that about military training."

He gives a lopsided grin. "Maybe not. There aren't a lot of times in my life when I've had that kind of consistency, though. It felt like I was just like everyone else. It was also strangely liberating to not have any responsibility. In my normal life, people are always looking to me for answers and asking me to make decisions I'm not remotely qualified to make. In the army, you just do what you're told. I take great comfort in a chain of command that I'm not at the head of."

"I can see the appeal of that," I say, nibbling my bottom lip. "But... you know that people ask you questions because you have something to say, and they value your opinion, right?"

"I'm not convinced." He leans back and stretches his legs out on the floor in front of him. "Sometimes I don't feel like I have a lot to contribute."

"This is going to sound super cheesy, but I think you have a lot to contribute. You're smart and kind and passionate. And if you think about it, you've been training your whole life for that role of leader."

"There are much more qualified people out there. The only formal qualification I have is a degree in British History, which is basically like having a degree in 'stories about great-uncle Edward.'"

"I'll concede, there are always going to be people out there who'll be more qualified on paper. Most of them don't look as good in an apron as you do, though."

Eddie laces his fingers together behind his head and looks up at me. "I have to have some skills in life."

The fire is crackling and popping, giving the room a cosy glow. I slide down onto the floor and lie next to Eddie, watching the flames dancing.

"This is so nice," I murmur.

Eddie props himself up on his elbow and strokes my cheek with his thumb. "It really is."

I gaze deeply into his eyes and feel a jolt of electricity shoot down my spine as his eyes bore into me. My skin tingles where his hand is resting.

I tilt my head up and linger momentarily before he closes the gap between us. He kisses me urgently, and the electricity spreads through my body.

He tugs my shirt over my head in one swift movement.

"You've done that before," I say.

"I never said that wearing an apron is my only skill."

"Is that so?" I say, as he kisses the nape of my neck.

"It is. I'd be happy to demonstrate some of my other specialties for you."

I run my hand through his hair and pull him closer, unbuttoning his shirt.

He shrugs his pants off, stopping to retrieve a small silver wrapper from his pocket.

"You were very prepared for dinner, weren't you?" I ask with an arched brow.

"What can I say?" Eddie says, sliding my skirt off. "I'm an optimist at heart."

∾

I TELL YOU WHAT, he was not kidding about those skills. He takes his time and gives me *quite* the demonstration.

When we're both completely exhausted, I lie back on the floor, arching my back and closing my eyes. I draw in a deep breath and then slowly exhale. "That. That was something else."

Eddie drapes his arm across my chest and nuzzles into my neck. "Something else good?"

"Mm. The best. Mind-blowing. Life-changing."

"I'll do anything to serve the public," he says, tugging at my earlobe with his teeth.

"Those skills of yours could do wonders for your public approval ratings."

"Oh, really?"

"Absolutely. I'd give you a solid nine out of ten."

Eddie jolts up next to me. "Only nine out of ten? Oh, we're going to have to do something about that."

"What do you propose, Your Highness?"

Eddie pulls me up so that I'm sitting on his lap, legs wrapped around his waist.

"I've got a few ideas."

∾

Sunday 5 September

I'M WOKEN by the smell of pastries wafting through the air. I open my eyes and see Eddie sitting in bed next to me, wearing boxers and reading a book. The sun is dappled on the bed, shining in through the branches of the oak tree outside the window.

"Morning," I say, rubbing my eyes.

"Morning, beautiful," Eddie says, his face lighting up.

I nestle down in a pile of soft white pillows and pull the heavy cotton sheets up to my chest. "Has anyone ever told you that your bed is amazing? The thread count on these sheets is so high I can hardly lift them."

Eddie laughs. "Really? After last night, my linen is what's made the biggest impression on you?"

"Hmm," I say, tilting my head and tapping my chin. "There have been a few highlights of this visit, but I think the bed tops the list. I've never been so comfortable."

"Wow," Eddie says, his mouth twitching. "You certainly know how to keep a man's ego in check."

I pat his arm. "Don't worry, you were also very good. Don't let it go to your head, though." I sniff the air. "More importantly, are there fresh pastries?"

"Yes," Eddie replies. "I kept some croissants out to pop in the oven this morning. Shall I bring them up?"

"Yes, please. You'd better go and grab them now before I start talking about how perfect you are. That could definitely go to your head."

Eddie grins. "Breakfast croissants, on their way."

He soon reappears, carrying a silver tray loaded with croissants, butter, jam and juice. My heart skips several beats, seeing him standing there, hair ruffled and breakfast in hand.

I'm in a lot of trouble here, aren't I?

The croissants smell amazing as always, especially warm out of the oven.

"Can I just stay here forever?"

Eddie juts out his bottom lip. "I'll consider it. In the meantime, though, I'm going to need to ask you to leave after breakfast."

"It's like that is it?" I ask, one eyebrow raised. "Is this just your typical 'invite a girl to your palace, take advantage of her, ply her with baked goods and then kick her out' deal? If I had a quid for every time that happened…"

He puts his hands up in mock surrender. "You've got me, I admit it—that was my plan all along."

"I knew it!"

"In all seriousness, Amelia, I am terribly sorry, but I am actually going to have to ask you to leave. Dad is coming by to talk to me in half an hour, and I want him to like you when you meet. Him finding you in my bedroom at eight a.m. is not the way to achieve that."

He said that he wants the king to like me when I meet him. Not if, *when*. I suddenly feel like I'm glowing on the inside. Maybe I'm not the only one getting a bit carried away with this.

"When you put it that way, it's not quite as insulting."

"I would never dream of insulting you."

"I'm glad we cleared that up. Do I have time to enjoy your fine breakfast offerings and have a shower?"

"Naturally. What kind of monster would bake croissants and then throw you out of the house before you have a chance to eat them?"

"Excellent," I say, taking a huge bite.

After breakfast I walk into the en suite to have a shower. The room is filled with a warm, familiar scent. I sniff the air trying to place it. It's not Eddie, and it's not the croissants but I know it from somewhere.

"Edmund!" I call out suddenly. "Your bathroom smells like the queen!"

He pops his head around the door.

"Pardon? Did you just say that my bathroom smells like my mother?"

I chuckle. "No, not your mother. Queen Alice!"

Eddie closes his eyes and takes a big breathe in through his nose. "Gardenias. It was her soap. I buy it because it reminds me of her."

"Do you miss her?"

"Every day. She was incredibly busy, obviously, but she always made time to see me."

"She must have been so proud of you."

"I hope so," he says, with a faraway look in his eyes. Suddenly his eyes focus back on me. "Wait a second, how do you know what she smelt like?"

"Uh... I guessed?"

"You guessed that the late queen used to smell like gardenias?" Eddie looks at me, eyebrows raised, corner of his mouth twitching.

"Okay. Promise you won't judge me too much if I tell you the truth?"

"I'll try not to judge, but I make no promises."

This is so humiliating. You're meant to pretend you don't know anything about his family, Amelia, not let him know that you're a complete royal family tragic.

I stare at my feet. "I smelt her once."

"Sorry, what was that?" Eddie asks.

"Queen Alice. I walked past her at a work gala once, and I sniffed her. I wanted to know what a queen smells like."

Eddie whoops with laughter. "You're so odd sometimes, Amelia. It's rather endearing."

Twenty minutes later, I'm dressed and ready to walk-of-shame it out of here.

"I know this sounds ridiculous, but could you send your driver a message and ask him to meet you over on the other end of the grounds? You can walk around behind the cottages here, just to make sure you don't run into anyone.

"Of course," I say, trying not to feel like a dirty secret. It's totally reasonable for him to try to hide me this one time so that I can make a better first impression on his family. It doesn't mean that he's ashamed of me. At least I don't think it does.

Eddie leans in and gives me a long, soft kiss goodbye and makes me promise to call him after lunch. I open the door and step outside, closing it quietly behind me. I search around and spot my car parked in the distance down the drive. Has the driver been waiting here all night in case I decided to leave? What a life.

I put my head down and scurry around the back of the building. Thank god so many people are away.

I'm wrapped up in thoughts about last night when I walk straight into someone with a smack. "Ow," I say, rubbing my forehead.

I look up to see who I've run into, willing it to be someone who has no idea who I am.

"Soph?" I say, scrunching up my face. "What are you doing here?"

"Amelia, good morning. I'm just on my way to visit Helena. How are you?"

"Ah, yes. Uh, well, thanks."

"Lovely. I'd best be getting on. Helena's expecting me for our morning yoga session. Let's meet for lunch soon."

"Yes, that sounds good."

With that, Soph glances around and keeps walking.

Wait, didn't Eddie say Helena is in Switzerland with Lucy and Emma? Weird.

CHAPTER 25

I DON'T SPOT anyone waiting with a camera outside the palace and miraculously the pack outside my flat seem to be on a coffee break or otherwise indisposed when I get home, giving me a chance to slink in the door unnoticed. Unnoticed by everyone other than Penny, that is.

When I walk in, she's is sitting on the sofa, cross-legged and sipping a cup of tea. "Oh hello there, Miss Amelia. I didn't hear you come home last night. Is there anything you'd care to share with the class?"

I purse my lips. "A lady never tells."

"Bugger that! You are my best friend, and you have been rampantly neglecting me since you came home from overseas. You owe me this."

"I owe you?" I ask, hands on hips.

"Yup, big time."

I bite my bottom lip. "Ugh, fine."

Penny pats the seat next to her on the sofa. "Good girl. Come, sit, tell Aunty Penny everything."

"I slept at Eddie's last night."

"And how much sleeping was involved?"

"Not very much," I say, smirking.

"You go, Mils! It's about time!"

"About time? I only kissed him for the first time a week ago."

"Exactly, you put this off for a full week. You've seen how hot he is, right? I might have lasted an hour. If that."

"Unlike you, I have some self-control. Or I did until last night. I'm now making up for lost time."

"So it was good?"

I run a hand through my hair and sigh. "It was very, very good. I'm in way too deep here, Pen. What am I going to do when he gets bored or meets the next pretty aristocrat?"

"Why do you assume that's going to happen?"

"Because he's him, and he has limitless options. He spent twelve years in a fake relationship so he could play the field in peace. Nothing about that says 'looking for a deep and meaningful relationship' to me."

"You can work on that," Penny says.

"Maybe. For now, I just want to work on not giving royal gossip blogs anything else bad to say about me." I yawn. "I need to go back to bed. Let's have lunch later."

"It's a date. If you change your mind later and run off to see him instead, you will be dead to me."

I collapse onto my bed and rub the threadbare sheets between my fingers. I could get used to the palace lifestyle.

~

Sunday 12 September

EDDIE and I are curled up in his TV room watching *Selling Sunset*. I'm still not feeling great about feeding the media beast by watching reality TV, but I'll make exceptions for things that are clearly scripted—no one property firm could have that many

Amazonian brokers, right? It's totally implausible, so my conscious is clear.

Eddie is sprawled out on the sofa with Poppy curled up at his feet. I'm lying on my side next to him, my head and arm on his chest. I can hear the thump of his heart beating and feel the rise and fall of each breath.

"Are you sure that's Christine?" he asks, wrinkling his nose.

"A hundred percent."

"They should consider including a before and after recap at the start of each season so that you can recognise people."

"Agreed," I say, leaning over him to grab a handful of popcorn.

Yet another blonde woman appears on screen, and Eddie leans forward, studying her face intently. "Do you think they take longer breaks between filming seasons than most shows to let everyone's surgeries heal?"

"They must. Fillers and Botox are one thing, but some of these women have definitely had structural work done between. Noses and chins take time to look normal again."

The camera cuts to Christine and her husband inspecting a tacky LA mansion, complete with basement dance floor and DJ booth.

I slap Eddie's chest. "Why don't you have one of those?"

"I've no idea. Enormous oversight on the part of my ancestors."

"It really was."

"Speaking of Christine, was that her real wedding?"

"Who knows," I say, throwing my hands up in the air. "But if it was, I respect her for going for it. Who doesn't want a wedding with swans, thrones and indoor snow?"

"You'd want a wedding like that, would you?" Eddie asks, starting to massage the back of my neck. "Did you know that my family owns all the unmarked swans in the country? We also happen to have some thrones. The snow, I can't help you with."

I jerk my head off his chest. Is he suggesting we get married?

No, surely not. Calm down, Amelia, he's just joking around. Other than about the swans, though—that bit is true. And the thrones, obviously. But still, whatever you do, do not read into this and start dreaming about your royal wedding.

Eddie is looking at me, confused.

"Sorry, there was, uh, a spider on me." I say, lying back down and trying to relax.

"Right. Well, don't get too comfortable here. I have to go up to the big house now for a meeting with Henry. But it should only take an hour, so you can stay here and make yourself at home."

"Sure, I'll keep watching TV and be here when you get back. It's not going to be easy, but I'll do it for you."

Eddie gives me a quick kiss and walks out of the room. "See you soon, beautiful."

He's trusting me to stay in his house by myself? That's brave. Not that I'm likely to pilfer the silverware, but I'm not sure that I'll be able to resist the urge to rifle through a few cupboards and drawers. It's not creepy to do that when you start dating someone, right? It's just good due diligence. What if he were a serial killer with a collection of trophies collected from his victims stashed in his bedside drawer? Wouldn't it be better for me to find out about it now and not in ten years' time? No one wants to be Ted Bundy's girlfriend.

The door clicks shut, and I wait a couple of minutes to make sure he's gone. When I'm sure he's not coming back, I grab my phone out of my bag and FaceTime Penny.

"Oh hi there! Guess where I am..." I flip the camera and pan around the room for her.

"Wait, is that... are you at Edmund's house?"

"I sure am."

"Where is he?"

"He's gone up to the palace for a meeting and left me here by myself until he's done."

Penny shrieks. "Show me everything!"

"Penny, I can't do that! That would be a total invasion of privacy."

"So you called me to gloat?"

I giggle. "I called because you're my best friend and I wanted to share a little of this with you. Don't worry, I'll try to score you an invite one day so that you can see it for yourself."

I'm busy talking to Penny when I hear a key rattling in the door.

"Eek, Pen, he's back early. I've gotta go."

I hang up, run over to the bookcase and grab a random book to pretend to read and then take a seat in one of the armchairs by the fire. The footsteps become louder as they approach the room. I smooth my skirt down and try to slow my breath. I glance down at the book—*British Army Field Manual, Countering Insurgency*. Well, that's not going to be very convincing is it? Too late now to find something else.

I'm busy trying to look absorbed in the field manual when Edmund clears his throat loudly. "Oh hey, I didn't hear you come in," I say, closing the book and looking up.

I drop the book and it falls to the floor with a thud. Those were not the footsteps and throaty sounds of Eddie. No, instead I'm sitting in front of Eddie's fireplace, gaping at none other than King Albert.

"I assume you are Amelia," he says, looking down his nose at me as if I'm something he stepped in on the street.

I fly up from the armchair and try to curtsy as gracefully as possible. "Your Majesty, it's a pleasure to meet you."

"I only wish I could say the same for you."

It doesn't appear that Eddie's plan to have me make a good first impression on his father is going very well.

I stand, jiggling my leg. "I'm sorry, Your Majesty. Ed... Prince Edmund isn't here right now."

"I'm aware, thank you. I had Henry schedule a meeting with Edmund this afternoon because I wanted to speak to you."

"Oh," I say, playing with a lock of my hair. "What did you want to speak to me about?"

The king draws himself up to full height and glares at me. "What do you think we have to discuss?"

I swallow hard and stare back at him in silence, desperately trying to form a coherent sentence in my head.

"I understand that you and my son are... involved," he says, his nostrils flaring.

Oh god. How do I respond to that? Also, where does the UK stand on beheadings these days? I don't think the king can order someone to be executed, but I can't be sure. This is when I regret not having taken any UK criminal or constitutional law classes when I moved here. No one has beheading rights back home in Australia, but we are a country built by criminals, so it's hardly surprising that the more cruel and unusual punishments fell out of favour.

I brace myself, taking a deep breath in and then exhaling— three seconds in, three seconds out. "We've been spending some time together recently, Your Majesty."

"Is that what you call it these days? I've been briefed by security, Ms. Glendale. I'm aware that you were here overnight on Friday."

Gulp.

He looks me in the eye, maintaining steely eye contact. "I've also been briefed by our public relations team. It seems you appearing in Edmund's life is no coincidence."

Fire rises in my chest. "I never targeted Edmund. I'm not a crazed fan or a gold digger. I've always admired your family, but I never meant to end up in this position."

The king snorts. "I'm not convinced that I believe you. But, in any case, what I believe doesn't matter. What matters is that the public believes it, and we can't have that. After the wedding disaster, Edmund's on thin ice with the public. His approval ratings have already taken a hit. If they fall any further, they're going to impact the rest of us."

"I promise you, I'm not thrilled about my relationship being tabloid fodder either. I'm not planning to give them any more ammunition against me."

"Silly girl," the king says, rolling his eyes. "The cat's out of the bag, and there's nothing you can do to stop the stories now. I had to tell my disappointment of a son the same thing when he came to me saying he was going to put out a statement telling the press to back off."

Eddie wants to do that for me? I'm touched by the gesture, but I don't want him to have to burn any of his goodwill with the media on my account. There must be more I can do to improve the coverage.

"Well, then what do you suggest I do? I'm happy to sit down with Charli and her team and come up with a PR strategy. We could work with a crisis firm, or I can do some media training? Whatever it takes. I don't want to cause any issues for Edmund."

"None of that will be necessary."

I screw up my face. "It won't?"

"No, it won't," King Albert says, his mouth set in a hard line. "You will stop seeing Edmund immediately. I won't risk any further damage to the family's reputation."

"Why should we have to break up when you let Leo date Kayla under the radar?"

He huffs.

"Because I say so! You know full well that Edmund and Leo are in very different situations. Edmund doesn't have the luxury of making poor choices."

"Eddie is his own man, you don't get to control every aspect of his life. I won't leave him just because you want me to. I'm sure he won't be thrilled to hear about you threatening me either."

"You're even more naïve than I thought. By all means, tell him about this conversation, it won't take long for you to see where his loyalties lie. He'll never openly defy my wishes."

My mouth falls open. I'm still trying to decide how to respond when King Albert turns to leave.

"I trust we won't need to speak again."

The door slams, and the house is quiet once more. I collapse back into the armchair like a deflated balloon and start to weep.

He wouldn't break up with me just to keep his father happy, would he?

CHAPTER 26

I'm still in tears when Eddie returns. "Amelia?" Eddie rushes over to me and brushes the hair out of my face. "Are you alright? What happened?"

I sniff and stutter, trying to stop crying long enough to speak. "Yes," I say, wiping my eyes on my sleeve. "I'm fine."

"Are you sure? I know us upper-crust types aren't well known for our emotional intelligence, so I may be wrong, but you don't look particularly fine."

I breathe out slowly and blink the tears away. There's no way that I'm going to tell Eddie about his father's visit and get myself involved in a palaver of family drama. Also, a not-so-small part of me is scared that if he knew the truth, he would side with his father. He's so loyal to his family and everything they represent, I can't imagine him wanting to go against the palace's wishes.

"Honestly, it's nothing."

Eddie furrows his brow. "Are you absolutely positive?"

"Positive."

He sighs and then shakes his head. "I'm fully aware of what's going on here, you know."

Oh god, maybe he saw Albert leaving and asking me about it was a test that I've just failed miserably.

I wince. "You are?"

"Yes, it's perfectly clear to me that when I went out you snooped around the house and discovered my deep, dark secret."

"Did I?"

"You must have, this is clearly the hysteria of someone who has realised that she's dating a man with multiple portraits of Elton John hanging in his guest room."

Despite my low mood, I let out a laugh.

"I never took you for an Elton fan."

"Oh yes, enormous fan."

I raise an eyebrow.

"Alright, maybe not so much a fan of Elton as a fan of the kitschy portraits in the guest room. They belonged to my great-aunt when she lived here, and I couldn't bear to have them taken away when I redecorated. Will you be able to keep seeing me, now that you know the truth?"

I lean my head against Eddie's shoulder and soak in his earthy scent. He smells like a mixture of sandalwood, fresh-cut grass and buttered popcorn. It's strangely reassuring. And makes me a little hungry.

"I'll find a way to get past it."

"I'm incredibly glad to hear it."

He strokes my cheek.

"To be serious for a minute, I know the media attention has been rough on you, but we'll get through it together."

Of course he thinks this is about the articles. Probably for the best.

I wipe my eyes. "Thank you, Eddie. Having you on my side means a lot to me."

He kisses me with a ferocity I haven't seen from him before. As he kisses me, he hoists me up and carries me to the bedroom.

Two hours and some rather, ah, *strenuous* activity later, we're sprawled on Eddie's bed, limbs entwined.

"I know how to cheer you up. We should go on a date tonight," Eddie declares, breaking the warm silence.

"I think you've already made some serious progress in the cheering-up department. Also, you've got things a bit backwards with the date idea, kiddo. You already got into my pants."

Eddie grins. "Twice."

"Even more reason it's a bit late to try to impress me with dinner."

"Think of it this way—if that's what I managed without a date, imagine what could happen after a fancy meal."

"You've got my attention. Keep talking."

"I want to take you out and show you off. We should go somewhere nice. Tonight."

"You're not worried about what your dad's going to say?" I wince just thinking about the king.

"He can say what he likes, but this is my life and my decision. I'm not going to run scared, and I'm not going to hide our relationship."

He wants to come to my place? That feels like a bad idea. I do a quick mental inventory of all the junk lying on the floor... and bed... and sofa... and table. Yup, this is definitely a bad idea.

"You should stay here and relax. I'll just meet you at the restaurant," I say, feigning disinterest.

"I'd rather spend the time with you," Eddie says, giving me a cheesy grin. "Let's go."

"No!"

"Why not?" he asks, eyebrows raised.

"Uh, Penny might be home."

"Great, I'd love to meet her."

Think, Amelia, think. Quick.

"She might be... uh, naked. Yes, she might be naked! She's basically a nudist. It's extremely uncomfortable for guests. Better just meet me at dinner."

Eddie's eyes sparkle. "You never thought to mention to me that you live with a nudist?"

"It never came up."

"I don't believe you," he says, narrowing his eyes. "What are you trying to hide?"

"I give up," I say, throwing my hands up. "My flat is a disaster, and I don't know if I want you to see how I live. Between work and hanging out with you, I haven't had time to tidy up for a while. A pretty long while."

Eddie laughs. "Is that all? Have you forgotten I go on overseas tours through actual slums? I'm sure I'll be fine. You should text ahead and make sure no one will be naked when we arrive though."

"Okay, but don't say I didn't warn you."

We take Eddie's car back to Camden and park outside my flat. Sitting in the car behind the tinted windows, I give it one more crack. "Are you sure you want to come in? Looks like there's a photographer outside."

"You're not getting out of showing me where you live that easily," Eddie says.

Ugh. I guess I'm going to have to let him come in. I tried texting Penny on the drive over to beg her to at least pick up the dirty underwear strewn all over my floor, but I didn't get a reply.

I lean over and open the door.

"Here we go!" I say, plastering a broad smile on my face.

Eddie steps out of the car after me, and the shutter speed goes crazy as the paparazzo on the street realises that he's won the "waiting outside Amelia's flat hoping she does something interesting and/or embarrassing" lottery and puts his camera into continuous shoot mode, not wanting to miss a second.

Eddie puts his hand on my lower back and leads me to the door with Walters trailing us. Our friend calls out to us,

"Edmund! Come to slum it with the common people for the night, have you? How do you feel about Leo being her first choice?"

Eddie ignores the photographer and keeps walking, eyes trained on my front door. When we reach it, I extract my keys from the bottom of my handbag and open the door. Side note—why do they always fall right to the bottom of my bag? One day I want to be grown-up enough to have an organised bag where my keys and phone are readily accessible and I never find random half-eaten muesli bars or used tissues floating around in it. I should really work on that.

Eddie gently nudges me through the door, and Walters slams it closed after us with a satisfying clunk.

"Does this paparazzi business ever get less stressful?" I ask.

"I've gotten more used to it over the years, but I must admit I do still find it quite difficult. Some of the others handle it much better than I do."

"Lucy and Emma don't seem too concerned about the attention," I say with a wry smile.

"I don't know. I don't think that they'd choose to live a public life if they had a choice, so they just try to make the most of the situation."

"They certainly do."

"Enough distractions though, Miss Amelia," Eddie says, poking me in the arm. "I demand a tour."

Right, time to face the judgement of a man who I'm going to guess even in the army never had to make his own bed. I know he says they didn't give him any special treatment, but there's no special treatment and then there's *no special treatment*. I like to imagine that if he'd been deployed, he would have taken a butler with him.

"Well," I say, waving my arm around the room, "this is the lounge room. That door over there is Penny's room." I walk towards the kitchen that opens off the lounge. "This is the kitchen, and through there is my room," I say pointing to the hallway that leads to the bathroom and my bedroom.

Eddie glances into the kitchen and does a double-take. He swoops into the room and laughs as he plucks a mug from the bench. A mug with his face on it.

"Amelia, you never told me that you had memorabilia with my picture on it too. I'm touched."

My cheeks burn. "It's Penny's, I swear."

"I don't buy that at all. Lucky I think it's adorable and not alarming."

Phew.

"You mentioned your bedroom? Is there a VIP tour available? I'm quite keen to explore it."

I try to block him from leaving the kitchen by standing in the doorway, but he pushes past and walks into my bedroom.

"Dear lord, have you been burgled?"

I cringe.

Eddie pokes his head back out into the hallway. "I can't even walk into this room without standing on something. Are all these clothes on the floor dirty?"

"Some of them are clean," I say defensively.

"How do you know which ones are clean and which ones are dirty?"

"Well, I normally remember."

"And what if you don't remember?"

"I see what smells clean."

"You choose what to wear based on what *smells clean?*" Eddie is back in the hall now, staring at me slack jawed.

"Only sometimes…"

"How is someone so successful and well-adjusted such a complete slob? Are you a genuine hoarder? This feels like an emergency. I may need to call in Marie Kondo. There's nothing a small, organised Japanese woman can't fix."

"I just don't have a lot of time to clean. I'll get around to it soon. I'll just live in my own filth until then."

"As you wish, Amelia. I don't think I'm going to need that VIP tour of your bedroom, though. Maybe we should just get to dinner."

Lucky, I need to get him out of here before he discovers the six-month deep pile of unopened mail and the shelf in the fridge where leftovers go to die.

～

AFTER A QUICK OUTFIT change and make-up refresh, Eddie and I are back in the car and on the way to the Mandarin Oriental to go to Dinner by Heston.

When we arrive, a valet opens the car door, and we make our way to the restaurant where the maître d' greets Prince Edmund like an old friend.

"Good evening, Your Highness. We haven't seen you in a while."

"No, I've had a bit going on."

"Of course, Your Highness. Come straight through." He steps out from behind the podium at the entry to the restaurant and leads the way to our table. We walk through the tasteful restaurant floor decorated in neutrals and leather. I try to stare straight ahead as I walk, but can't help noticing heads turning towards us and couples whispering to each other as we pass. Ignoring the attention, I focus on the rows of caramelised pineapples rotating on a spit behind a pane of glass. Who knew roast pineapple would be so delicious? That's why Heston is an insane genius.

When we pass the pineapples, we turn left towards the kitchen instead of right towards the tables. In the bowels of the kitchen, the maître d' motions to a chef's table sitting in the corner.

"Wow, very fancy."

"I love sitting here and watching the kitchen team work.

Sometimes I go in and watch, or ask them to teach me how to cook a dish."

I laugh. "And how do the very busy kitchen staff feel about that?"

"They've never complained."

"Do you think that has anything to do with you being *you*?"

Eddie's eyes twinkle. "Perhaps. I like to think it's just because I'm such a talented amateur chef and all-round nice guy though."

"A likely story."

Eddie's hand runs up my thigh and butterflies invade my stomach. "I'm so glad that we're here. I don't care what dad and his PR team say. I don't want us to run away from the attention."

"I don't want to cause problems for you, though. I don't want to drive a wedge between you and your family." I tense up and start chewing my lip.

"If my family has a problem with us dating, they'll be the ones driving a wedge between us, not the other way round. Let's talk about something else. I want to forget about family issues and just enjoy having dinner with you somewhere that isn't my house."

"What would you like to talk about instead?"

"Anything. Did you see the flat earth documentary on Netflix?"

My nose wrinkles. "No, what's it about?"

"Exactly what it sounds like: people who believe the earth is flat."

"Wait, there are people alive in 2021 in a world where the internet, planes and satellites exist who think the earth is flat?"

Edmund chuckles. "There certainly are. Convinced they'll just fall right off if they walk to the edge. After they climb the giant ice wall guarded by NASA, of course."

"I should watch this right away."

"You really should. It may be my favourite conspiracy."

"It sounds pretty good, but my personal favourite is that your family are actually reptilian aliens in skin suits."

"Shh!" Eddie hisses, putting his hand over my mouth, his eyes darting around the room madly. "You can't let them hear you talk about it!"

I dissolve into giggles and only stop laughing when Eddie starts kissing me. There's a lot to be said for this " real date" business.

CHAPTER 27

WHEN I GET HOME from dinner, I stumble into my room and flip the light switch. Wait, did I accidentally walk into Penny's room? I'll admit, I'm a bit tipsy, but I didn't have that much to drink at dinner. I see my photos on the wall. Nope, definitely not Penny's room. Now it really does look like I've been robbed. There's nothing on the floor, my faded floral bedding has been replaced with crisp white linens, and I think someone has cleaned my window?

I stride out into the lounge room looking for Penny. "Pen? Are you here?"

Her bedroom door is closed, so I knock. I hear shuffling sounds, and Penny appears at the door. She pulls an ear pod out. "Hey, what's up? Sorry I missed your text earlier. I was out with Jack, and my phone died. How was dinner?"

"Dinner was great. It was intense being out in public. We sat off the kitchen so not too many people could see us, but even the staff were kind of staring."

"I'm afraid that's the price you pay for dating a prince, my dear."

"Ugh, I wish it wasn't. Hey, did you clean my room while I was out in case Eddie came back here or something?"

Penny's eyes narrow, and she tugs at her earlobe. "Didn't he tell you?"

"Didn't who tell me what?" I ask.

"Edmund," Penny replies, rolling her eyes at me. "He sent a maid over here while you were at dinner to clean up. The security guy out the front said it had all been cleared, so I assumed you knew about it."

"Are you serious?"

"Deadly serious. I definitely didn't pick up your dirty clothes myself."

He sent a maid to my house, to clean up my bedroom without asking me. I do not feel great about that. At all.

I grit my teeth. "Is that a normal thing for people like him to do? I could have had private things in my room. The maid could have found my enormous dildo collection."

"Mils, I know how boring you are. You don't have a dildo collection. Or anything else worth hiding."

"He doesn't know that though!" I fume. "I just don't get how he didn't see this as a huge invasion of privacy."

"I don't know, he probably thought you'd appreciate it. I'm not the person to ask."

"You're right, I'm going to call him right now and get to the bottom of this."

Penny puts her arm around me and leans her head on my shoulder. "Mils, you should wait. So you don't say something you'll regret later. Why don't we go binge-watch some *Great British Bake Off* and eat our feelings? You can call him in the morning when you've calmed down a bit."

"Thanks, Pen. What would I do without you?"

"For one thing, you'd have to buy your own stress ice cream."

~

Monday 13 September

BASED on my morning tabloid check, it seems there's going to be a lot of stress ice cream in my future. I'd almost managed to forget about the photographer who caught Eddie visiting yesterday. The photographer on the other hand clearly hadn't forgotten. He was probably going to be eating expensive steak tonight on the back of the photos.

Duke of Camden!

Prince Edmund was spotted yesterday heading into the Camden home of new love Amelia Glendale. The Prince tried to keep a low profile in dark glasses, but eagle-eyed onlookers saw it all.

Sources say the couple are wasting no time in getting hot and heavy. As well as the Prince's visit to Amelia's modest flat, insiders have revealed that Amelia has been spending increasing amounts of time at Edmund's somewhat more comfortable Kensington Palace digs.

The Prince lives in Wren House, a grace-and-favour home at the palace that was previously occupied by the late queen's cousin, the Duke of Kent. Until recently, it was also home to Lady Sibella Cavendish, who completed a pricey renovation of the dated interiors not long before ditching Edmund at the altar. She is said to be devastated about Amelia taking her place with the bed barely cold.

Amelia, on the other hand, seems to have no qualms about stepping into Sibella's shoes. After their rendezvous in Camden, she and the prince were spotted on a very public dinner date at Dinner by Heston where they engaged in what other diners described as "excessive" and "off-putting" public displays of affection.

...

The article includes a whole gallery of photos of Eddie and me entering and exiting my flat, as well as grainy photos of us walking through the dining room at Heston's. Thankfully there are no photos of our supposedly excessive PDA.

I toss my phone down on my bed and creep out to the front door. I groan when I peer through the window and see that it's another big paparazzi pack day. This is too much. I'm going back to bed.

I really hope he issues that statement soon and tells the vultures to back off.

Two hours later, I'm woken by my phone buzzing next to my head.

"Hello?" I say, yawning.

"Hi Amelia, it's Daisy. Just checking if you're coming in today? We're meant to be in a meeting with Lloyds Bank in five minutes…"

"Sorry, I totally forgot. I'm not feeling well, so I'm going to stay home today. Can you please put them off for a few days?"

"Of course, I'll see if I can reschedule them for next week. I hope you feel better soon. Do you think you'll be in tomorrow?"

I squeeze my eyes shut and puff out my cheeks. "I'm not sure, probably not."

"OK, just let me know."

"I will, I promise."

I check my phone and see that I've had a missed call from Eddie and three from Charli. Argh, I should call them back. I hate that my life now feels like a constant cycle of crisis management when I haven't even done anything wrong! Here I was all my life, thinking that I was a respectable, inoffensive—hey, maybe even likeable—member of society. Clearly I was wrong. It kills me that everyone I know has been inundated with these stories about me —colleagues, friends, family. Does it change how they see me? Do any of them believe the lies?

I'm mid anxiety-spiral when my phone rings again, and I see Eddie's name appear on the screen.

My finger hovers over the reject call button before I think better of it and answer. "Hey."

"Hi there, beautiful," he says, his voice warm. "How are you this morning?"

"Honestly? I've been better."

"Was our date that bad? Is it because I didn't walk you to the door? I should never have let a security guard do a gentleman's job."

"No, nothing like that."

"Have you been reading the papers again?"

I murmur in agreement.

"Oh, Mils," Eddie says. His voice is soft when he speaks again. "You can't keep doing this to yourself."

"I'm having a hard time ignoring it. The articles just keep coming." I sniff and try not to cry.

"I understand. Listen, I'm in the car on my way to a hospital wing opening, but I'll be home by lunchtime. Do you want to come over? We can talk about it."

"Sure, that sounds good."

"Anytime. It was a selfish offer anyway. I was looking for an excuse to lure you back to my house."

I laugh. "Consider me lured."

I ARRIVE at Wren House just before midday and am let in by a maid. Eddie's engagement has run overtime, and he's just about to head back now. I'd never seen domestic staff in here before, but today there seem to be two women here, buzzing around cleaning and organising various things around the house. Did one of them deal with my dirty underwear last night? I am not feeling great about that. I know it's normal for Eddie to have people handle all his things and know about every aspect of his life, but it's not how I'm used to living. It's not how I want to live.

I'm still spiralling a little wondering what else Eddie's maids saw when they were going through my room when there's a commotion by the front door.

Rounding the corner into the foyer, I see Eddie, Lucy, Leo and Emma pile into the room.

"Amelia!" Emma shrieks, swooping in to kiss me on the cheek. "What a fabulous surprise. How are you darling?"

I suck in a deep breath. I love Lucy and Emma, but I was not prepared for this—they can be a lot.

Eddie steps in and slips his arm around my waist. "She's had a bit of a rough day."

He kisses me on the head and leans in to whisper into my ear, "I'm sorry. I ran into them on my way home, and they invited themselves to lunch."

I squeeze his hand and nod.

"Oh no!" Lucy says. "What's wrong, poppet? Life of a working girl got you down?"

Leo guffaws in the corner.

"Uh... I don't think you know what working girl means."

Lucy frowns. "Is that not the term you women with jobs prefer these days? I can't keep up."

"Only if you're talking to Julia Roberts's character in *Pretty Woman*."

"Well," Lucy says. "Definitely not the right term then—you are as far from a nineties call girl as Edmund here is from nineties Richard Gere."

Emma nods vehemently. "Eddie wishes he had Gere-esque hair."

Eddie's hand flies to the back of his head. Leo meanwhile is now cackling with laughter.

I rub Eddie's arm. "Call me biased, but I love your hair."

He drops his hand and threads his fingers through mine.

"Well, aren't you two just the cutest?" Lucy says, cocking her head and making puppy dog eyes.

My cheeks burn.

"Aren't they just?" Emma says. "I can't wait to see you being all lovey-dovey together at the show on Saturday."

Show? I've learnt to ignore some of the more nonsensical things that the princesses say, but I genuinely have no idea what she's talking about this time.

"What show?"

Leo smirks while Lucy's jaw drops.

"Edmund! You haven't neglected to invite dear Amelia, have you?"

I narrow my eyes. "Invite me to what?"

"Windsor, obviously," Emma says.

"The castle?"

"No. Well, yes. The Royal Windsor Horse Show, hosted at the castle. It's one of the premier events of the equestrian calendar, don't you know? It's an annual tradition for us to go together."

"We assumed you'd be coming," Lucy adds.

I turn to Eddie and look at him, searchingly. His expression is blank.

"Let's talk about this later," he says. "Now, you lot, are you here for lunch or to interrogate poor Amelia? There's chicken and some salads in the fridge. Let's go and dish up."

"I thought you'd never offer," Emma says, fanning herself. "I'm famished."

And with that, the group disappears into the kitchen on the hunt for food. I hang back in the foyer and grab Eddie's arm.

"Hey, what's this Windsor business all about? I thought you said you had engagements on Saturday."

"It's nothing," he says, shaking his head. "The family and I are going along, but I didn't think you'd be interested so I didn't mention it to you."

"You didn't think I'd be interested in spending the day with you and your family?"

"Let me rephrase. I didn't think you'd be interested in the attention that would come with attending a public event together. Dinner last night was one thing, but an official engagement is a whole other kettle of fish. I've seen how much strain the attention has put on you since we started seeing each other. The last thing I want is for you to become more involved in my public life and realise that it's all too much."

My eyes soften. "Oh, Eddie. I know I've been upset about all the press, but I'll find a way to deal with it. I want to be part of your life so that I can support you."

If I'm going to stand up to King Albert and show him that he hasn't scared me off, I may as well do it in a fancy hat.

"I don't have to come though, I'll do whatever you want."

"I'd love you to be there, but are you ready for us to go public?"

"Our relationship isn't exactly private at the moment, in case you hadn't noticed the pack of reporters living on my doorstep. People know about us."

"Be that as it may, the attention is only going to get worse if we start appearing at official events together. Are you absolutely sure?"

"I'm a big girl, and I can handle it. I'm going to stop reading the articles."

"You've said that before, Mils."

"I mean it this time, I swear."

Besides, I'm hoping things will calm down once he tells reporters to back off and makes it look like the palace doesn't want more lies about me printed.

A smile spreads across Eddie's face. I feel good about this. It's going to be great.

CHAPTER 28

Saturday 18 September

"Last chance to change your mind—do you really want me to come to a horse show with you and Eddie and all his intimidatingly famous family?" Penny asks, twirling around in a floral silk dress.

"I do."

"Have you thought this through? Are you sure you trust me to meet these people?"

"Of course I do! You're my family here, lady, and I want you to meet my boyfriend. Also, Eddie and the others are arriving together in a procession, and I don't want to be hanging around awkwardly by myself until they get there."

"I'm going to go right ahead and ignore the second part of that explanation."

"Whatever you need to do."

A car horn honks outside the door.

"Time to go!"

In the car Penny pulls out a mirror. "Does my make-up look

okay? I need to be photo ready if I'm going out with my famous friend."

"I'm not famous," I say, scrunching up my face.

"Uh, you kind of are."

"Please. There have been a couple of trashy tabloid articles about me, but I'm hardly a celebrity."

"Are you serious, Mils? Firstly, it's been way more than a couple of articles. Secondly, you're dating the next king of England. This attention isn't going anywhere. As long as you're with Eddie, you're going to be famous."

A shiver runs down my spine. She might be right. I've been so focused on getting through the initial rush of attention triggered by Eddie moving on from Sibella that I haven't really stopped to consider that it might always be like this.

An hour later, our car pulls to a stop to the side of Windsor Castle where a series of marquees have been erected overlooking a lawn dotted with obstacles and jumps. The marquees are festooned with oversized floral garlands, and there are striped umbrellas and picnic blankets set in front of them for spectators wanting to be closer to the equine action.

Penny whistles. "This is definitely not your average backyard party."

We do a lap of the general admission area while we wait for Eddie to arrive. I'll tell you what, the Royal Windsor Horse Show has attracted an eclectic crowd. It's a particularly British mix of women in eye-wateringly expensive dresses and women in rubber boots and sensible trousers. Royal enthusiasts meet horse enthusiasts.

We're drinking Pimms and watching groomers preparing horses across the field when a sudden hush descends over the crowd. I look around and see a pair of horse-drawn carriages winding their way down the drive.

The carriages circle around the lawn. Eddie and Leo are front and centre, followed by Lucy, Emma and Princess Helena bringing up the rear. They're all waving and smiling, some more enthusiastically than others. Eddie, as always, looks particularly stiff and uncomfortable.

The carriages stop next to a large marquee with a stage set up in front of it. The family alight and climb the stairs onto the stage. Everyone in the crowd stands to attention and watches as Eddie takes the microphone and gives a stitled welcome.

The crowd applauds politely, and the family disappear into the marquee behind them.

Penny turns to me, eyes shining. "Let's go find them."

"You're not wasting any time, are you?"

"That tent he just walked into is filled with some of the most eligible men in the country. You'd better bloody believe I'm going to spend as much time in there as possible."

I raise an eyebrow. "What happened to your boyfriend?"

"Oh, he's still around," Penny says, waving her hand dismissively. "You can never have too many options, though."

After weaving through the crowd, we arrive at the entrance to the royal marquee. The door is flanked by security.

As I approach, a security guard gives me a once over and nods, gesturing for me to enter. Penny and I are almost inside when a security guard thrusts his arm out in front of Penny.

"Name?"

Penny scoffs. "I'm with Amelia."

"That's nice, but I can't let you in unless your name is on the list."

"I believe it is. Penny March."

The officer scans a list on an iPad and glances back up. "Go right through, ma'am."

Penny grabs my arm. "See, you got through without even giving your name. Famous."

I huff. Penny's insistence on calling me famous is rubbing me the wrong way. She knows full well I have no interest in people knowing who I am.

"There he is!"

I jerk my head up and see Eddie gazing at me across the room, a soft smile on his face. When I wave, he breaks into a wide grin, and my heart melts.

Eddie bounds across the room and pulls me into a hug.

"Amelia, I'm so glad you're here. And you," he says, spinning around, "must be Penny. It's a pleasure to meet you."

Penny curtsies. "It's great to meet you too, Your Highness." When she stands again, Eddie leans in to hug her as well.

"I feel like I know you already, I've heard an awful lot about you."

Penny fans herself. "Why, thank you, Your Highness. All fantastic things, I assume."

Eddie chuckles. "Naturally. And please, call me Eddie. Now, shall we locate some drinks?"

Walking through the marquee, I can feel hundreds of eyeballs following me around the room. Quite a few of the well-heeled attendees quickly look away when I catch their eye, but more still stare openly and whisper to each other when I pass by.

Looks like even in the relative privacy of a royal enclosure, I need to keep my guard up. I can't imagine the aristocratic set covertly taking photos of me to sell to the press, but you never know—they've got to get the money to maintain those leaky old houses from somewhere.

Maybe I shouldn't have that drink after all.

With champagne procured for Eddie and Penny, we join Lucy, Emma and Leo.

"Amelia! So glad you made it," Lucy says when she spots us.

"Hi," I say before hugging her.

Leo clears his throat sharply.

"Amelia, as we're in public, it's expected that you greet us appropriately."

"I'm sorry," I stammer. "I didn't think."

He glares at me, lips pursed, and I feel my cheeks burn.

I draw back and drop into a curtsy facing Lucy.

"Not her," Leo says.

"Sorry?"

"You're meant to agree us in order of rank. Me first, then Lucy, then Emma."

He's raised his voice loud enough what feels like half the room as stopped talking and are instead staring at us, waiting to see what I do next. This is so humiliating. I'd really appreciate a giant sinkhole opening up and swallowing me right about now.

I curtsy to Leo silently, followed by Lucy again and then Emma.

"This is my friend Penny by the way. "

Penny follows my lead and curtsies to everyone in the correct order.

Leo nods and promptly leaves to go to the bar. What was even the point of that? Does he just enjoy embarrassing me, or was he trying to remind me that I don't belong here? Either way, he succeeded in making me feel awful.

Eddie smiles sympathetically. "Don't worry about him. He's put out because Dad banned Kayla from attending today."

"But he was fine with me coming?"

After my conversation with the king, I can't imagine he would have been particularly thrilled about me finding my way onto the guest list.

"Eddie, am I not meant to be here?"

He coughs and plays with his cufflinks.

"You didn't tell him that you were bringing me, did you?"

"I didn't tell him, because I don't care what he thinks. Also, he's not here—what he doesn't see won't hurt him."

"Good job," Emma says with a nod.

"Hear, hear!" Lucy adds. "It's about time you stopped playing into his power delusions. You've got just as much right as he does to invite guests of your choosing to watch people parade around in tight pants and make horses do odd things."

Penny snorts. "Dressage is so weird, right? What's up with the bits where they try to make their horses look like they're dancing on the spot?"

Emma clicks her tongue. "Penny is it? I'll have you know that I was *quite* prominent on the London dressage scene for a number of years."

Penny snaps her jaw shut and makes a strange strangled sound.

Emma giggles and pats her arm. "Don't worry, darling, I only ever trained because I'm rather fond of horsey types. My old dressage instructor in particular."

"He was dreamy," Lucy says. "Shame he was ten years too old and conveniently given a very prestigious military posting as far from London as possible. I'm sure Mummy had a hand in that."

Penny laughs. "My dad wishes he had that kind of power! He's always had to settle for giving my bad boyfriends the evil eye and hoping they take the hint."

"Ah, the perks of being a princess. I can't wait to infuriate my own children with those kind of shenanigans. Of course I need Mummy to back off long enough for me to find a husband first," Emma says, sighing.

"Speaking of which," Lucy adds with a glint in her eye. "Are you on the hunt for your own thoroughbred today, Penny? We're distantly related to most of the men here, but I'm sure we could find you someone eligible."

Penny shakes her head. "No, I'm seeing someone. If it doesn't work out, though, I'll definitely let you know. I'd make a great baroness."

"We'll keep it in mind," Lucy says, winking.

～

THREE HOURS of fun (and surprisingly little horse-watching) later, Eddie pulls me aside.

"Amelia, I want to ask you something, and I don't want you to feel like you need to say yes."

What is he going to ask? He's probably gotten cold feet and wants me to quietly slip out before there are too many photos taken. Especially after the drama with Leo earlier. I bet he's wishing I was a lot more like Sibella now. He may not have been in love with her, but at least she wouldn't totally embarrass him in public.

Okay, breathe. If he asks you to leave, just go without a fuss. At least I can maintain my dignity and make a graceful exit

"Amelia?"

"Oh yes, sorry, got distracted for a sec. What did you want to ask?"

"I'm due back on stage shortly to present the awards from the morning's events."

"Good luck. I know these things always make you anxious."

"They do. That's why I'd like you to come on stage with me."

"Are you serious?"

"As you said, public appearances always make me nervous, and I'd be rather less nervous if you were there with me."

"Really? The press will have a field day—everyone would take it as a public declaration that we're together."

King Albert would also be livid.

He chuckles. "As you pointed out to me recently, people already know that we're together."

"Yes, but a member of your family appearing at an official event with a new partner means something. It means that it's a serious relationship, and they're going to be around long term."

"Amelia," he says, taking my hand. "I am serious about you, and I want people to know that. An official appearance is the natural next step in our relationship. Why not take it now? I'm ready. I want to make you part of my public life."

The man has a point—if we are going to be together, then

we're going to have to cross this bridge eventually. It feels like too much too soon though.

"Look, I want to help, but I think we should take this slow. Why don't I walk you to the stage and watch from the front of the crowd?"

He looks into my eyes. "I'd rather you were standing next to me the whole time, but I'll take what I can get."

～

WE'RE STANDING by the entrance to the marquee when an announcement comes over the speakers.

Ladies and gentlemen, please be standing for His Royal Highness, Prince Edmund.

Eddie squeezes my hand. "This is it."

My heart is beating out of my chest, and the noise of the crowd has morphed into a strange buzzing noise in my ears. Somehow, Eddie and I make it to the side of the stage. Eddie kisses me on the cheek and I feel hundreds (thousands?) of people gaping at me. This is starting to feel way too real.

The crowd cheers and claps as Eddie climbs the stairs to the microphone. He fumbles pulling a piece of paper from his pocket.

"Good morn... pardon, good afternoon, ladies and gentlemen."

Cue an awkward pause.

He looks down at me and I give him an encouraging smile. He takes a deep breath and flashes a grin.

"I'd like to invite up the winners of this morning's elementary, medium and advanced dressage events to receive your trophies."

Two women and a man in jodhpurs and tailored blazers stand to the side of the stage. Eddie makes his way down the line handing out trophies, shaking hands and making easy conversation with the competitors.

He then resumes his place at the microphone. "Thank you to

everyone here today for making the effort to join my family and me for such a fantastic day. We hope you have a cracking afternoon."

Eddie waves enthusiastically to the crowd who cheer and whoop. It may be my imagination, but the applause sounds far louder than before.

CHAPTER 29

Monday 20 September

RIGHT, so here's the deal. I thought, having dated Eddie for the last month or so, that I knew what the media was like. But I was wrong. Really, really wrong.

Ever since our official debut at the horse show, the spotlight has been taken to the next level. On Saturday I woke up and was on the cover of every daily newspaper in the UK. Literally every one. I checked.

At this point, I want to curl up in bed under a blanket and hide forever so no one can photograph or scrutinise me ever again. It stresses me out. Sadly, it's Monday, and I'm a grown-up so I need to get out of bed and go to work.

An hour later, I'm sitting in the car waiting to arrive at work. The trip is taking much longer than normal. We must have been less than a kilometre from my office for ten minutes now.

"Apologies, ma'am," my driver calls back to me. "Traffic in South Bank is awful this morning."

"No worries, it's not your fault. Any idea what's going on?"

"Not sure, ma'am. There may be an accident."

Another ten minutes later, we make it to the foundation's offices and see what was causing the traffic. There are people and flashing lights everywhere. Sirens are blaring, and traffic barriers have been set up on the footpaths and across the road. The police wave us over to the side of the road, and my driver lowers his window.

"You're going to have to turn around, sir."

"I'm just dropping off at this building here and then I'll head back around, if that's alright?"

"Right-o, make it quick. We're trying to get things moving again."

Michael strains his neck to look out the window and starts muttering into his earpiece.

"I'll hop out now. I won't be leaving the building during the day so no need to come back until around six. Whatever this is should all be cleared up by then."

I open the door and realise with a rush that only some of the flashing lights belong to the police cars. Some of them—most of them—belong to cameras. Hundreds of them. There are more reporters here than I've ever seen before. It makes my airport ambush look like amateur hour.

I start walking from the car to the building, but freeze in the middle of the footpath. There are reporters trying to jump over the barriers and at least a dozen police officers trying to hold back the surge. I'm still in shock when Michael firmly grabs both my shoulders and guides me into the building.

"What was that?"

"Saturday's engagement appears to have attracted some additional attention, ma'am," Michael replies.

"I'll say."

When I'm sitting at my desk, I look down and realise that my hands are shaking. None of the articles over the weekend had any awful new stories in them. Most of them just rehashed the same information about me that has already been splashed around, and some of them were even positive—it looks like people noticed how relaxed Eddie was with me by his side. And yet, the pressure feels immense. I never thought it would be like this.

I need a cup of tea to calm my nerves.

I'm rummaging around in the kitchen for a teabag, back to the door when I hear high heels clip into the room behind me.

"What a nightmare getting in today!"

"Oh I know, such a pain. I wanted to go out for coffee, but it's still a disaster down there. I don't want to fight my way through throngs of people just to get to the cafe."

"Ugh. I hope the police have cleared them away by lunch. I don't want to be stuck eating the stale muesli bar from the bottom on my handbag."

"She should quit. Her being here is a huge distraction from the foundation's work."

Well, this has just gotten significantly more awkward.

"It's making everything so much harder for the rest of us. It felt like harmless excitement at first, but how are we meant to work like this? It's not fair."

I suck in a deep breath. So this is what people think of me. People who used to respect me now think of me as nothing more than a problem to get rid of.

"She's doing more harm than good. Surely she must know that."

I feel tears welling up in my eyes. I can't listen to any more of this, I'm going to have to turn around and walk out. Keep it together, Amelia, chin up and eyes straight ahead. Don't let them see you cry.

I spin around and try to ignore the sudden, crushing silence as the women standing by the fridge stare openly at me.

Back at my desk, I wipe my eyes and try to put it all behind me by getting stuck into reviewing the longest contract I can find in my to-do pile.

A FEW HOURS later I finish reviewing the document and feel a rush of satisfaction. There's very little that makes me as happy as knowing that I've done a good job. I know that work isn't everything and that I'm more than what I do, but it's such a big part of what makes me feel like a successful human being. Even when I think I'm not good enough.

I'm scanning my list, trying to decide what to tackle next when there's a knock on my door. Hopefully it's not another staff member I barely know coming to gawk at me.

Before I can answer the knock, the door flies open, and William, the foundation's CEO, strides in. He closes the door behind him and takes a seat.

"William, hi. I'm so sorry about the traffic issues downstairs. I've asked my security officer to talk to the palace and police to see if there's anything they can do."

"No issue at all, Amelia."

"I just feel bad. It's causing everyone else so much inconvenience."

"Don't even mention it. You didn't invite them all here."

"I didn't, but I'm still going to try and sort it out."

"Well, that would be excellent, thank you. But that's not what I came here to talk to you about."

"Oh, of course. What did you want to talk about?"

"We need to have a conversation about your role here at the foundation."

Wait, what? Is he going to fire me because of the press downstairs? He literally *just* said that it wasn't an issue.

"What about my role?" I ask carefully.

"There are a number of high-profile new projects I'd like to get you involved in."

"Great," I say enthusiastically. "I know I've had some things going on in my personal life lately, but I'm very committed to my work here and would love to take on new projects. Do you want to give me a briefing now so that I can get started on thinking about the legal arrangements we need to put in place?"

"No, no," William says with a chuckle. "There's no need for you to think about the legal details. I've already asked Daisy to brief an external firm to help with that side of things."

"Oh. What can I do to help then? Are you sure you want to spend budget on briefing external lawyers? My team and I have some capacity, and we're more than capable of dealing with the initial analysis."

"I'm quite sure this is the best allocation of resources. I need you to do something far more important than contract negotiations."

"Right…"

"I'd like you to be involved as an ambassador for these projects."

"I'm sorry?"

"You know, an ambassador. We'll put some quotes from you and photos in promotional materials, you can attend press conferences, take some meetings with high-value donors. Whatever needs to be done to draw attention to the causes."

"You want to use me as a figurehead?"

"Yes, exactly. It's going to be great for the foundation, an enormous contribution."

"Are you seriously suggesting that instead of using me to do the legal work that I am paid for—and, might I add, highly qualified to do—you want to use me as bait for the press?"

William coughs, looking taken aback.

"Calm down, dear. I simply think that in your current *situation*, the best thing we can do is harness the public's fascination with you to draw attention to our projects. I'd like you to step away from legal work and focus your efforts on this."

"First off, don't tell me to calm down. Second, you want to use me and my connection to Prince Edmund for your own benefit?"

"Not for my benefit, Amelia, for the benefit of the foundation and all the causes we support. Surely you see the value in that?"

I give a joyless bark of laughter. "William, I'm not comfortable with what you're asking of me. My job here is head of legal, and that's exactly the job I'd like to keep doing."

William drums his fingers on my desk. "I don't think you quite understand. An ambassador position is the role that is available to you. Between all the attention and the time commitments you're sure to have with royal engagements, I don't think it's appropriate that you continue as head of legal. You'll stay on until we find a replacement, of course, but it hopefully won't take too long. The role will be advertised tomorrow."

"I… William…"

"No need to say anything, Amelia. HR will sort out all the details."

William stands and starts towards the door.

"William, this isn't what I want. I'm a lawyer! I do important work here. I'm not just someone's girlfriend."

He just shakes his head and closes the door behind him. By some miracle I manage to hold in the tears until he does, but once the door closes, the floodgates open.

I cry for what feels like hours. I can't believe that five years of university, six years as a lawyer and thousands upon thousands of hours of concentration and bloody hard work mean nothing. I've sacrificed so much life for work, and for what? After all of that, my only value is as someone's plus-one.

I can't do this anymore.

~

WHEN I COLLECT MYSELF, I ask Michael to call the car back and slip down to the basement. I'm going to see Eddie.

When I arrive at Wren House, I knock on the door and Eddie opens, phone held between his shoulder and chin.

"Hi, I wasn't expecting you. Come in—I'll just be a minute."

I let myself into the den and settle into a corner of the sofa, curling my legs up to my chest. I wrap myself in a cashmere blanket I find draped over the arm of the sofa and scan around the room, soaking in the atmosphere. The oak leaves are rustling out in the garden, and the scent of Eddie's morning baking is hanging in the air. A wave of melancholy sweeps over me. There's something incredibly comfortable about this place and about Eddie, but I'm sure of what I need to do.

If ever there was a moment for me to gracefully cry a single tear, this would be it.

When Eddie arrives, he looks at me, brow creased with worry. He comes to sit next to me and pulls my head to his chest. For a while, we sit together in silence, Eddie stroking my hair. When I feel strong enough, I raise my head and move ever so slightly away from him.

"Edmund, we need to talk."

"Is it about these stories? Can I make this better by suing someone? I could get injunctions against the papers. Surely we can lawyer our way out of this."

"Calm down there. I don't want to sue anyone."

"Are you sure? I was joking, but it's actually not a bad idea."

"I promise, I don't want to sue anyone. And I couldn't afford it anyway."

Eddie waves his hand as if swatting away a fly. "Don't worry about the money. I'd take care of it."

"I don't want to rely on your money to fix my problems."

"Pfft, it's just money. It wouldn't be an issue at all."

I draw further back from Eddie. "It would be an issue to me. I'm not someone who has grown up leaching off of other people.

I'm a hard-working, independent woman—I'm used to taking care of myself."

"But I can help, so why wouldn't I?"

"Because that's just not the way I operate," I say, raising my voice. "Speaking of, I don't appreciate you sending someone to my house to clean my bedroom without asking me first."

"Why not? You were busy, your room was a mess, so I dealt with it."

"Like I said, I don't need you fixing my problems for me."

Eddie's whole body tenses up. "I thought you'd appreciate the gesture. It was no effort."

"It was no effort for you, but it was an effort for whoever you sent over there."

"She was just doing her job!"

"Her job is to manage things here. It's not her job to clean your girlfriend's house. If you consider that was a normal thing to do, we come from two very different worlds."

Eddie grabs my hand. "Yes, our situations are somewhat different. But it's not an issue. I want you to be part of my world. Why don't you move in with me? It would simplify the security issue, and you'd have staff here to help with errands so you'd barely have to leave the grounds other than for work."

"Eddie, I like my world. I don't want to hide out here forever. I love spending time with you, but it's not that easy. Despite what you and my boss seem to think, there's more going on in my life than being your girlfriend!"

"What does William have to do with this?"

"He's demoting me. He came to see me today and told me that given my *personal situation* he's hiring a replacement head of legal and wants me to focus on photo opportunities. It was so degrading."

"Well that's just absurd, I'll call him in the morning and tell him that he's to do no such thing."

I shake my head and squeeze my eyes shut tight. "Eddie, it's not just about that. If I'm honest, I can't take the pressure of being with you. I can't spend every day with people watching my every move and judging me. I want to go back to my old life."

Eddie stares at me. "Amelia, you don't mean that. You're just overwhelmed. I understand, it's a lot to get used to. But I have so much faith in you, you can do it."

I say nothing.

"And look, I've heard you—you don't want to sue anyone. But we can still improve the situation. I'll talk to Dad again and get his approval to issue a palace statement asking the media to leave you alone. You'll feel so much better when you get a break from the people waiting outside your house and the fresh stories popping up all the time."

"Eddie, you've had weeks to issue a statement. I kept thinking you were going to, but you didn't. If you don't want to make your life more complicated and strain your relationship with the press for me that's fine, but you can't expect me to hang around for the media feeding frenzy. This isn't something I asked for, and it's not okay."

"You don't make my life more complicated, you make my life better. You make me laugh, and you make me want to be a better man, a better leader."

He grabs my hand and continues. "You don't have to move in here right now, even though I'd love you to. I'm not going to make you take any steps you're not ready for, we can take things slow."

"Eddie..." I say, my voice trailing off. "Trust me, this is for the best. It's going to make things easier."

"How on earth would us breaking up make anything easier?"

"It will make things easier with your family."

Eddie dips his head and rubs his temples. "My family? My family loves you."

I give a hollow laugh. "Emma and Lucy love me. Your father, on the other hand…"

"What about my father?"

"I didn't tell you this earlier, but your father came to see me a while ago."

"Why did he come to see you?"

"Because he wants us to stop seeing each other. Apparently, I'm bad for your reputation and approval ratings and could bring down the monarchy and ruin everyone's lives."

"Well, that's just ridiculous! Why didn't you tell me?"

My eyes are swimming in tears. "Because on some level, I knew he was right. We don't belong together."

Eddie stands and draws me into a hug, stroking my hair. "Shh, shh, it's okay. I promise it's all going to be alright. I don't care what my father or any stupid approval ratings say. I want you in my life, and I won't let you go without a fight."

"It's not going to be okay," I say, sobbing. "Your parents are never going to approve of me, and I'm never going to be ready to make this my life. I'm drowning in your world and turning into someone I don't even recognise. I think we should stop seeing each other."

Eddie clenches his jaw and his eyes glaze over. "You don't mean that. It's been a hard few weeks. Take a couple of days off, get some sleep, and then we can figure it all out."

"Edmund, it's not going to change my mind. You're amazing, but this life just isn't for me."

"Amelia," Eddie pleads. "I've never had a relationship like this before. When I'm with you, I'm so comfortable and content. You make me feel like I'm enough, just being me."

He paces back and forth in front of me.

"Amelia, I'm falling in love with you. I can't let you go."

Oof. Right in the feels.

"Eddie," I say softly. "I'd be lying if I said I wasn't falling for you too, but that's exactly why I need to end this now. I'm never going to be able to fit into this world, but if I let myself stay any longer, I don't know that I'll ever have the strength to leave."

"I hear what you're saying, Amelia, but I'm not going to give up on you. I'm not going to give up on us."

"I should go."

Eddie pulls my limp body into a bear hug and kisses my forehead. "Go home and get some rest, Mils. I'll call you tomorrow."

CHAPTER 30

Tuesday 21 September

TRUE TO HIS WORD, Eddie calls me the next morning. Seven times. I let all of them go to voicemail.

I've called in sick again and have convinced Penny to do the same. It was my snotty, hyperventilating tears last night that did the trick. After weeping until I passed out in the early hours of the morning, I'm now much calmer. Hideously depressed, but calm. Penny and I are curled up in my bed, binge-watching terrible reality TV on my iPad and surrounded by empty ice cream tubs and chocolate wrappers.

My phone rings again. This time, I don't even bother to pick it up to check who it is.

"You're really not going to answer any of his calls?" Penny asks.

"No, it's too hard. If I talk to him, I might change my mind and go running back over there to see him."

Penny shifts uncomfortably. "Would that be such a bad thing?"

"Yes, it would be a bad thing! Dumping a prince who is also a great person who I have a lot in common with may sound like a stupid thing to do on paper, but in reality, it's for the best."

"Remind me why that is again?"

"Because this is real life, not a fairy tale. In real life, being a prince's girlfriend means constant pressure from the media and public, crushing expectations from the royal family and no chance of leading a normal life. If I let myself get in any deeper, I won't be able to get out."

"Mm," Penny mumbles, sounding unconvinced.

"I'm telling you, it's a slippery slope. One minute you're having amazing sex in front of a fireplace in a palace, and the next minute you're being forced to quit your job and spend your days having tea with octogenarians while wearing sensible heels and pantyhose."

"Mils, I know that there are drawbacks, but are you sure that leaving him is what you want?"

"Honestly, Sibella had the right idea. She realised—albeit a teensy bit too late—that she didn't want that life, and I've realised I don't want it either. At least I'm not leading him on all the way down the aisle."

"You can't compare yourself to Sibella. Her situation was completely different."

"You're right, her situation was different—she'd grown up in this world, and she still couldn't handle it!" I snap. "How am I meant to deal with it?"

"That's not the difference I was talking about," Penny says, looking at me pointedly.

"I don't know what you're talking about."

"Oh, I think you do. Sibella was never in love with Eddie."

I scoff. "And you're saying I am?"

"Yup," says Penny, nodding.

"That's ridiculous. We've barely been dating for a month."

"I don't think it's ridiculous at all. I've seen how happy you are when you talk to him, or talk about him, or even just think about him. And those tears last night weren't tears of casual indifference. Admit it, Mils—you've got it bad."

"I admit, we get along really well and had a strong connection. But as I said, it's only been a month. I'm a big girl. I'll get over it."

"Okay, well, I don't accept that at all, but I'm glad to hear you sounding so positive because I'm about to abandon you—Jack called and asked if I was free for lunch."

My jaw drops. "You're abandoning me, your best friend and extremely low-maintenance housemate, in my hour of need for a *man?*"

"I am, but I'll be back in a couple of hours. Can you manage here by yourself until then without doing anything stupid?"

"Hmm," I say, tapping my chin. "I think I'll be okay. But only if you bring me some more chocolate before you go."

"Deal," says Penny, extracting herself from my blanket cocoon.

A WHILE LATER—AN hour? three days?—I'm woken by Penny's "slightly drunk but not drunk enough for karaoke" laugh, and the sound of her wrestling with the lock on the front door. I haul myself out of bed and peel a chocolate wrapper off my forehead as I pad out into the lounge room to open the door for her.

When I open the door, Penny spills into the room, followed by a man with dark, floppy hair and tortoise-shell glasses.

I freeze, still holding the door. I was not expecting company, and I'm not at all prepared to see other humans. I can't even say for sure that I don't have more food wrappers stuck to my body. There's definitely mascara all over my face, and I probably look like a crazy version of Helena Bonham-Carter.

I'm still clutching the door when the man sticks out his hand. "Hi, I'm Jack. You must be Amelia. I've heard so much about you."

"Uh, hi," I stammer. "Sorry, you've caught me on a bit of a bad day. Good to meet you."

"Don't worry," he says, giving me a sad smile. "Penny told me all about it."

I shoot mental daggers at Penny, who cheerfully ignores my rage.

"Make yourself at home, Jack. Do you want a cuppa?" she asks.

"Sounds good, thanks, love," he says, taking a seat on the sofa.

"I'll help you in the kitchen," I say to Penny through a tight smile.

"Penny," I hiss when we're out of Jack's earshot. "Are you kidding me with this? I'm a complete wreck, and you bring a random guy home?"

Penny winces. "Sorry, I didn't mean to, but he had the afternoon off and was keen to come over for a bit. Also, he's not a random guy—he and I have been seeing each other since just before you started dating Edmund, remember? It may not seem like long, but it is for me. Can you please pull it together and have one brief conversation with him, for my sake?"

"Ugh. Fine, but only because I love you more than almost anything in the world. I'm going to go and quickly try to make myself presentable, or at least slightly less horrifying."

I fume as I walk back to my bedroom and close the door. Penny is my best friend, but how did she think that throwing her happiness in my face after a devastating break-up was a good idea? Looking in the mirror, I see that the mascara has fallen on the Helena Bonham-Carter playing Bellatrix Lestrange but also homeless end of the spectrum. What a look. I make a perfunctory attempt at fixing my hair and making my face less scary, then pull on some clean jeans and slip a bra on under my pyjama T-shirt. Nothing says "I've got my life together, thank you very much" like wearing a bra at home.

I don't want to deal with Jack right now, but it's for Penny. If I go out there now and play nice for half an hour, I'll be able to retreat to my pillow fort for the rest of the day to wallow in peace.

Back in the lounge room, Penny and Jack are sitting on the sofa with cups of tea. I put on a cheerful face and carry out a dining chair to sit on.

"It's great to meet you finally," I say to Jack as I sit down.

"You too, Amelia, Penny never stops talking about you."

I give Jack a once-over. He's tall and bookishly good-looking. He looks vaguely familiar. Pen said he does something finance-y. Maybe I've come across him through work?

"What is it that you do again, Jack? I'm sure Penny's told me, but I've forgotten sorry."

"I'm in finance, very boring. It's all just moving paper and money around. Even I get bored talking about it." He rolls his eyes.

"No, I'm really interested," I say. "I'm a finance lawyer, so I'm one of the rare people who genuinely wants to talk about it. Where do you work?"

Jack shifts around in his seat. "I'm at a private equity firm."

"Which one? I might have dealt with you guys through work."

"Probably not," Jack says, shaking his head. "Anyway, enough about me. How do you find working at the princes' foundation?"

"It's great," I say, smiling broadly. "I love the work."

I'm going to have to quit now though, aren't I? I can't exactly keep working for Eddie—I'm sure he'd prefer not to see me pop up in meetings, and I don't know if I could manage to see him in person without crying.

Penny leans over and pats my arm.

"Everything okay?" Jack asks. "Pen told me about your break-up. Will you stop working at the foundation now? Could be awkward seeing the ex around the office."

I shake my head. "I'm not sure. I haven't really figured that out yet."

"How long have you worked there? When exactly did you first meet Edmund?"

"I started there about four years ago now, but didn't meet Edmund until recently. After his wedding," I say, my smile faltering. "I'd rather not talk about it, to be honest."

"Of course, of course." Jack puts his mug down on the floor and stands up. "I'm just going to pop to the loo, ladies."

"So, what do you think?" Penny asks me, after Jack disappears into the hall.

"He seems nice," I say.

"He's great," Penny replies, beaming.

"Which fund does he work for? He looks really familiar, and I'm trying to figure out if I've met him through work—maybe back when I was at the firm?"

Penny scratches her nose. "You know, I've never actually asked. I'm just not that interested in finance stuff, I guess."

"No worries. I'm sure I'll figure out where I recognise him from."

"By the way," Penny says, "you've still got a bit of mascara on your cheek."

"Ugh, this is what I get for crying all night without removing my make-up first. I'll be back."

I jump up and head towards my bedroom to fix my face. When I open the door, I stop in my tracks. Jack is standing in the middle of my bedroom, phone out and taking photos.

"What are you doing?" I shriek.

"Uh, nothing."

"That's not nothing! You were taking photos of my bedroom! What, were you going to sell them to the papers?"

Jack's eyes dart around the room.

"Oh my god. I've just realised where I know you from—you were at the airport when I got back from Kenya. You're one of them! Who do you write for? *The Mirror*? *The Sun*? *The Daily*

Mail?" I'm vaguely aware that I'm becoming increasingly hysterical as I shout questions at him.

Then Penny appears in the doorway. "What's going on?" she asks, her brow creased.

I spin around. "Penny," I say. "Your *boyfriend* is a fake. He's a reporter. He's just been using you to get to me."

Penny scoffs. "Mils, that's ridiculous."

"She's got it all wrong. It's just a misunderstanding," Jack says, shrugging.

"Oh, it's a misunderstanding, is it, Jack? I found you in here, taking photos. How many ways are there to understand that? And Penny," I say, turning back to face her. "I figured out where I recognise him from. It's not from work. It's from the paparazzi pack! Don't you think the timing of him running into you at a bar right before articles started appearing about me is suspicious?"

"No, I don't. I meet people all the time. Has your ego really gotten so big that you think everything is about you?"

I feel like I've been slapped in the face. My ego? None of this is about my ego. My best friend has been conned by a sleazy reporter—and she's taking his side over mine?

"Right, well, I should be going," Jack says as he tries to squeeze past Penny and me.

Penny rounds on him. "You're leaving?"

"No way I'm getting stuck in the middle of this one."

He pushes past me and saunters out into the hallway. Halfway down the hall, he turns back and calls over his shoulder, "Oh, Amelia? It's *The Sun*. Care to give me a quote for my readers before I go?"

All I can do in response is let out a guttural scream.

"I'll take that as a no," Jack—if that is even his real name—says, before disappearing down the hall. A moment later the front door slams shuts, and Penny and I are left standing in my room in shocked silence.

"Mils," Penny finally says, shaking. "I'm so sorry, I had no idea."

"How much did you tell him today about the break-up?" I ask.

"Er," Penny says, avoiding eye contact. "Quite a bit."

"Great, so I've got another exclusive exposé to look forward to tomorrow."

Penny hangs her head. "Probably."

"Do you have any idea how bad he could make me look? I can't believe that you'd do this to me. You swore you wouldn't tell anyone anything about Eddie!"

"What?" she asks, scrunching up her face.

"You've been the leak this whole time. Even if you didn't realise he was a reporter, you told him all these personal things that could be used against me. I can't even look at you."

"What do you mean 'even if I didn't realise'? Do you seriously think I might have done this on purpose?"

"I don't know," I say, shaking my head. "And to be perfectly honest, I don't care. I have bigger problems right now."

Penny snorts. "You have bigger problems? Mils, you chose to end a relationship. Meanwhile, I just found out that my boyfriend is an undercover reporter who was using me to get to you. I slept with this guy, and the whole time he was busy mining me for information. For all I know, he could have been recording our conversations to take notes from later. That's a problem!"

"Penny, I have very limited sympathy for you here. You should have known not to tell some random guy all about my private life."

"He wasn't a random guy! He was my boyfriend, or I thought he was anyway. My best friend dating a prince is easily the most exciting thing that has ever happened to me. You can't blame me for wanting to talk about it."

I squeeze my eyes shut, trying to hold back the tears. "I trusted you."

Penny throws her hands up in the air. "And I thought you cared about me more than your public image. I guess I was wrong."

Penny storms off to her room and slams the door.

I can't believe that I've somehow managed to lose my boyfriend and my best friend all within the span of twenty-four hours.

On the plus side, at least this is as bad as it gets. Things can't possibly get any worse from here.

CHAPTER 31

Thursday 23 September

DEAR DIARY, things have gotten worse. Much worse.

It's been two days since Penny and I stopped talking to each other, and everything is awful. Barely an hour after Jack left, the news of me dumping Eddie hit the internet—along with the photos that Jack took of my breakup bunker. In the end, it was lucky that someone had picked up all those dirty clothes for me.

The papers and blogs have been having a field day. Some articles have claimed it was actually Edmund who broke up with me when he came to his senses and realised that I was a heartless gold digger. Most of them though have been speculating about what could be so terrible about Eddie that two women have left him in less than six months—does he have bad breath? Erectile dysfunction? Is he secretly gay? Was he planning to abdicate and leave becoming king to the much more popular Leo?

Obviously none of it is true, but I feel terrible. Eddie has a thick skin when it comes to gossip, but it must be tough for even him to handle. I don't know for sure how he's coping because I'm still ignoring his calls and have been completely avoiding Penny. I'm not ready to speak to either of them. I'm not ready to go to work either, but Eddie followed through on asking William to give me my job back, so unfortunately I have to keep turning up. So that's why I'm here this morning, putting on real clothes and preparing to brave the outside world. Or at least the bit of the outside world between my front door and the car waiting for me across the road. Not long after Penny and I had our fight, Michael came to the door to tell me that Edmund had arranged for the security team and driver to stay on "until things calm down." Thank god for that—even just the idea of being on the Tube right now with everyone staring and whispering is giving me hives.

I'm now dressed and looking about as presentable as I'm going to. People will be able to spot my puffy eyes from miles away, but there's not much else I can do about it. I stand in the lounge room, frozen with my hand on the doorknob. Come on, Amelia, you can do this. Time to be a grown-up and get on with life. With a deep breath, I open the door and am assaulted by an onslaught of flash bulbs and shouts from reporters. It's like that scene in *Notting Hill* when Hugh Grant opens the door to one million paparazzi, except in real life, it's much less entertaining and I'm far less attractive than Julia Roberts—even nineties-hair Julia Roberts.

Michael is waiting by the door and immediately puts his arm around me and helps propel me through the crowd. I don't breathe again until I'm safely deposited in the car with the doors closed and Michael riding up front. This is short-term pain for long-term gain. Now that Eddie and I have broken up, the paps will get tired of me very quickly and I'll be able to go back to a normal life. If we stayed together, it wouldn't be this crazy all the time, but I'd never truly be able to escape the attention again. It's all for the best. Right?

I make it to my office and thank the office design gods once more for giving me a door—which today I take full advantage of, and close behind me as soon as I walk in.

It will have to get easier from here. The first step is the hardest and all that.

~

I'M SITTING at my desk eating a sandwich for lunch—I was going to go out to buy it myself, but I wimped out and asked Michael to pick it up for me instead—when there's a knock on the door.

"Come in," I call out.

The door swings open, and I see Daisy standing there, chewing her bottom lip.

"Hey Amelia, do you have a minute?"

"Sure, come and have a seat."

"Thanks," she says, sitting in the chair facing my desk. "How are you holding up?"

"Oh, you know..." I say, avoiding eye contact. "It's been a stressful few days."

"Yes, I imagine it has been."

"It's okay, it'll get a bit easier each day from here. The news will realise I'm immensely boring and move on pretty quickly."

Daisy taps her foot on the ground and looks at me with a sad smile. "The news is what I wanted to talk to you about actually."

"What about it?"

"I can't remember if I've ever told you that my sister is an arts editor at *The Times*?"

I shrug. "No, you hadn't. That sounds like fun. Way better than working for a piece-of-scum tabloid."

"Yes, she's lucky she got an opportunity there a few years ago. Anyway, she just called me about you."

"I'm not really interested in doing any interviews right now, sorry," I say.

Daisy's eyes go wide. "Oh no! That's not why she called. She, er, thought you might appreciate some warning about a story that's going to run in the next half hour."

"What's it going to say? Have things really gotten so bad that even *The Times* is publishing gossip about Edmund and me?"

"No, not exactly. They are going to run an article about Edmund, though. Apparently they've just had a press release from Buckingham Palace. I hate to be the one to tell you this, but Edmund's engaged."

I blink. "Engaged?"

"Yes, to Sibella. Again. They're going to be giving a re-engagement interview on the BBC news tonight."

Engaged to Sibella? I feel like I've been hit by a train. There's a pressure crushing my chest.

I gulp for air. "But I... I don't..." I shake my head. "I don't understand."

There must be some mistake. I thought he said that he never loved her. Why would he put himself through the public humiliation of taking back the woman who left him at the altar if he didn't love her? Was our whole relationship some kind of act for him? Or a way to act out against his father?

"I don't have any other details, sorry. My sister just thought you might want a heads-up before they publish the story."

Stay calm, stay calm.

"Of course. Thanks, Daisy. I really appreciate it."

Daisy looks down and picks at some invisible lint on her skirt. "Well, I might get back to work then."

Keep it together, Amelia.

"Yes, you should do that."

She stands up and bounds towards the door. "Would you like me to leave the door open or closed?"

"Closed," I say. Definitely closed.

As soon as the door closes behind Daisy, I fall apart. I feel like I've been hit by a freight train.

What is going on? How can he be marrying Sibella after

everything that happened last time? And what happened to her boyfriend? This can't be true. We've been broken up for less than three days. *Three days!* I refuse to believe that he would get engaged to someone else three days after we broke up, even if it is a relationship of convenience. Shouldn't he still be devastated? Maybe he just never cared that much about me and, after a quick attempt at a relationship with a commoner, decided that life with Sibella was the better option.

Oh god, is that why he's been trying to call me? Not to beg for me to come back, but to tell me he's moved on?

So this is what rock bottom feels like. It's a pain like nothing I've ever experienced before. Tears well up in my eyes, and I start breathing much faster than normal. I really wish Penny were here to talk me off the ledge.

I empty the remnants of my sandwich into the bin under my desk, place my head on my knees and start breathing into the paper bag. I have no idea how this is meant to help to calm people down, but they seem to do it a lot in movies. Unlike in the movies though, my paper bag still had sandwich crumbs in it which I'm now somewhat choking on. I throw the bag away and gulp down some water instead. Breathe, Amelia, just breathe. Surely it's some kind of misunderstanding.

Just then, my phone beeps. It's one of my wretched Google alerts. I open the link and feel my heart sink.

Prince Edmund to wed

The Times *is pleased to exclusively report that Prince Edmund is once again engaged to Lady Sibella Cavendish.*

Buckingham Palace announced the happy news in a statement released just minutes ago. "His Majesty the King is delighted to announce the engagement of his son, Prince Edmund to Lady Sibella Cavendish," the statement read. It went on to confirm that after some time apart, the Prince and his fiancée, both 32, have reconciled and hope to marry as soon as possible.

...

I bet Albert is "delighted" to announce that Eddie has gone crawling back to Sibella. He's gotten exactly what he wanted. Give them a few years to pop out some genetically blessed, appropriately pedigreed heirs, and the king will be able to die happy. Not that I think he's planning on dying anytime soon. He's only just managed to get his hot little hands on the power position, he's not going anywhere for a long time.

I drop my head onto my desk. Ouch. I hit the surface much harder than I was planning to. I dig around the bottom of my handbag and find a mirror. Great, now I'm forever alone and have a big bruise coming up in the middle of my forehead. At least this day can't get any worse, right? I know, I really shouldn't say that after last time.

And right on cue, here comes the flood of news notifications on my phone. Looks like *The Times* article has taken about sixteen seconds to be picked up worldwide.

I flip through the list of headlines until one catches my eye.

Amelia loses her tiara

Prince Edmund's former fling Amelia Glendale has been left in the cold by Edmund's recent re-engagement.

Amelia is likely to be kicking herself now for pursuing Edmund— who she saw as the easy target—instead of his brother. Amelia, who has been quoted as saying that she didn't care which prince she married as long as she got to wear a tiara at her wedding, had been focused on Leo until Edmund became available earlier this year.

...

I don't understand how they even make these insane stories up. Don't care who I marry as long as I get to wear a tiara? It sounds like something I'd say as a joke. Actually... that is something I said as a joke—to Kayla. What a snake! It dawns on me that she must be the palace leak Eddie was trying to avoid. If it wasn't for her driving Eddie out of his KP office, I would never have ended up in this situation.

~

ON MY WAY home from work, with tears streaming down my face, I torture myself scouring Eddie's private Instagram, trying to find clues about how he got back together with Sibella. How dare he have not posted anything since last week? How am I meant to stalk him effectively?

When I make it home, I open the door and see Penny sitting on the sofa. Instantly I burst into tears.

"Mils," Penny says, jumping up and running over to give me a hug. "I heard the news. I'm so sorry. Are you alright?"

I sob into Penny's hair.

"It's going to be okay. I'm sorry about Jack and my part in everything too. I never wanted to see you hurt like this."

I sniffle and pull myself away from her. "Don't be sorry. I'm the one who should be apologising. I know that the Jack disaster wasn't your fault. I was just upset and took it out on you."

"Are you admitting that I didn't deserve to be yelled at?"

"I am."

"Well, look at that! Amelia Perfectionist Glendale, acknowledging that she made a mistake. I never thought I'd see the day."

I smile weakly. "I've missed you like crazy the last few days."

Penny laughs. "I've been right here."

"I know, I know. I was just being stubborn, I didn't want to admit that I was wrong to be mad at you."

"You were a bit of a git."

"I was," I say, letting out a big sigh. "I'm sorry. Do you forgive me?"

Penny leans in and hugs me again. "Of course I do. You were under so much pressure, and I messed up and made it worse. I can't hold your reaction against you. Do you forgive me though? I'm so sorry, I should never have told Jack anything about you and Eddie. I knew you didn't want me talking about it but I couldn't help myself."

"Consider yourself forgiven. I need my best friend back."

"You've always got me, Mils."

HALF AN HOUR LATER, Penny and I are sitting on the sofa eating a takeaway curry that I'm pretty sure I'm going to regret later.

"So, are we going to watch the interview?"

I shake my head. "No, definitely not. I'm not going to torture myself by watching it. I'm better than that."

At least I hope I am.

"Are you sure? It might be better to see it first-hand."

"I'm sure. Find something else for us to watch. I need some mindless fluff to take my mind off he who shall not be named."

Penny opens Netflix, and I see that the new season of *Emily in Paris* has just landed. Things are looking up.

An hour later though, the ridiculous outfits and French clichés aren't bringing any joy to my cold, dead heart. I wonder where Eddie and Sibella will go on their honeymoon. Maybe Paris? I can picture them now, strolling along the banks of the Seine, dining by candlelight in a chic bistro, riding bikes with baguettes in the baskets…

"Mils? Amelia?"

"Sorry, what?"

Penny looks at me, eyebrow raised. "Have you been paying attention to anything I've been saying?"

Oops, I didn't even realise she was talking.

"Uh, no, not really. How I meant to be able to pay attention to anything when I know that right now, the BBC is playing an interview where Eddie and Sibella?"

An interview where they profess their undying love for each other and start raucously making out on national television to really drive home to me that I'm out of the picture. At least that's what I assume they're doing.

Penny wrings her hands. "Don't get mad at me, but I think we should watch it."

I sit there, tapping my foot on the ground and take a big gulp of my wine. My hand twitching over the remote. Maybe Penny's right—maybe we should just watch the interview and get it over with? I'm going to see it eventually. Or at least read about it. Granted, I wouldn't have to read about it if I did the sensible thing and stopped reading endless news about my ex, but we all know there's no chance of that happening.

I clutch at the remote like I've been bitten by a snake and it's a lifesaving dose of anti-venom. I give up, I'm going to watch it. It'll be like ripping a Band-Aid off—get the pain over and done with.

I turn to Penny. "Hold my hand while we watch?"

"Anything you need, love. We'll get through this together," Penny says, taking my hand and squeezing.

I flip on the BBC and am confronted by an image of Eddie and Sibella sitting in front of the fireplace at Wren House. The fireplace where Eddie showed off his fire-making skills for me a few weeks ago. That stings. More than stings. It feels like my heart has been ripped from my chest and torn into a million pieces.

Eddie is looking dapper in a charcoal suit, while Sibella is wearing what I recognise from Penny's fashion training as a red, raw silk Valentino gown with a tasteful scoop neck and short sleeves. They're sitting side by side on Eddie's Goetz sofa that has been rotated to allow the bookcases and fireplace in the background to better frame the couple.

"We couldn't be happier to announce our engagement," Eddie says without any trace of happiness in his voice.

"We may have had a bit of a false start," Sibella adds. "But we have an incredible amount of history together and are stronger than ever. I'm very much looking forward to becoming Eddie's wife."

An interviewer off-screen speaks. "When did you pop the question, Your Highness?"

"Last night," Eddie says, staring blankly at the camera.

Sibella places her hand lightly on Eddie's knee. "Edmund proposed over dinner. He'd made a roast for me here at home. Not many people know this, but Edmund is a fabulous cook."

Ugh. I knew that about him! How dare he cook dinner for her when he was cooking for me only days ago? It's just not right.

"Making dinner together over a bottle of wine is one of our favourite things to do," Sibella says.

Eddie gives a slight nod.

"That sounds very romantic," the interviewer says. "When are you planning to get married?"

"As soon as we can organise the wedding," Sibella says.

"Yes, I expect it will be quite soon," says Eddie. His lips drawn into a line.

"Why wait when we've been here before?" Sibella asks, gazing up at Eddie.

I study his face, desperately trying to figure out what he's thinking. Despite the warm words, Eddie and Sibella look stiff, and there's a small but noticeable space between the two of them on the sofa.

"Turn it off. I don't think I can handle watching the rest."

"Are you sure?"

"Positive, I've tortured myself enough for one night."

"Alright," she says before turning the TV off. She swivels around to face me. "So, what did you think?"

"I'm so confused. He looked totally uncomfortable sitting there with her."

"Well, you always said that he doesn't like the attention. Maybe he was just feeling awkward about doing an interview."

"Hm, maybe. I was expecting him to be relaxed and confident now that he's put the drama of dating me behind him and has his safe, uncomplicated life back."

"I don't know, he's never been great at interviews. He's probably just being awkward."

I shake my head. "No, it's more than that. He's put his walls up again. I don't think he's happy."

"Why would he be marrying her if he didn't want to?"

"I don't know. He might have proposed again because it was what his father and the palace wanted. I wonder…" I trail off, starting at the blank TV screen.

"Wonder what?"

I shrug. "Nothing. I'm sure it's nothing."

But what if it is something? What if he looks unhappy because he's not over me?

CHAPTER 32

Wednesday 29 September

A WEEK LATER, my life has not improved. After the announcement, I told work that I needed a break and took all my leave.
After everything that's happened, William was more than happy
to see the back of me for a while. So far I've spent my "holiday" in
bed with the lights off, surrounded by empty bottles and food
containers. If I can convince the food delivery drivers to pass
food through my bedroom window so I don't have to answer the
door, I will have reached peak wallow.

The only upside of the last two weeks is that the unexpected
news of Eddie and Sibella's re-engagement has taken all attention
off me. Stories about my social climbing have been replaced with
glowing tributes to Sibella's grace and unnaturally shiny hair.
After four straight days of not so much as a tourist with an
iPhone hanging around outside the flat, Michael and his team
deemed me safe to carry on without them and finished up yesterday. And so here I am, alone. Just me and my stress calories and
depression spiral. It's all for the best, though. I broke things off

because I don't want a life of public scrutiny. Let Sibella have it. It'll all be far less painful with time. I hope.

My phone starts ringing somewhere in the pile of wrappers on my bed. When it stops buzzing, I dig it out of the detritus and look to see who called—wondering if it was Eddie and I can tell myself that I've missed my last-ever chance to talk to him, because I'm a sadist like that—and am surprised to see that it was Soph.

She's left me a voicemail instead of just sending a text. Why do people do that? I don't want to have to listen to voicemail—it's far too close to actual human interaction for my liking. Still, I should check why she was calling.

"Amelia, it's Soph. Can we talk? Call me back when you can, darling."

I don't really want to talk to anyone, but I decide to send her a text to acknowledge that I heard the message—even if just so that she doesn't keep calling.

Hi Soph, got your message. I'm taking a bit of a social detox at the moment, but happy to catch up in a few weeks.

Three little dots appear on my screen, followed quickly by her response.

We should really talk. I'll be at your place in half an hour.

I go to call her and insist that she not come over, but I know that once she decides to do something, there's no changing her mind. Argh, this means I have to get out of bed, doesn't it? I give myself a quick sniff. Yup, I'm going to have to shower too.

I drag myself out of bed and close the door on my bedroom of shame. The advantage of hibernating in bed is that the rest of the flat still looks vaguely clean. Must keep this in mind for next time my life collapses.

I shower for the first time in an embarrassing number of days and put on non-athleisure clothes just in time for the doorbell to ring.

I open the door, and Soph air-kisses me on each cheek and then steps back.

"Let me get a good look at you, darling," she says.

I stand in front of her and give a weary smile.

"Well, it's official—you look dreadful."

"Thanks, Soph, great to see you too," I say, rolling my eyes.

"Are you going to invite me in?"

"Sorry, yes—I'm a bit out of it at the moment. Please come in."

I stand aside to let Soph pass through the door and gesture towards the sofa where she takes a seat.

"Can I get you anything?" I ask. "Tea? Coffee?"

"No, no, that's not necessary. Come and sit with me."

I sit next to Soph, and she pats my knee. She looks at me, her eyes full of sorrow. "Oh, darling, I understand how it feels."

"I'm sure you do. You grew up with the attention, though. And to be fair, I don't know that you've ever had paparazzi camped outside your house day and night."

Soph gently places her hand on mine. "That's not what I meant."

"Oh, what did you mean?" I ask, squinting at her.

"I know what it's like to love one of them."

I cock my head and try to process what she's saying. "Did you leave your husband for Princess Helena?"

Soph's eyes wrinkle, and she shakes her head. "I almost wish I did. At least she's single." She gives a long sigh. "Bertie and I... we've been involved for some time."

I blink furiously. Soph is having an affair with the king? I would never have picked her as the type to cause a potential scandal. She's always so aware of her reputation.

"I had no idea," I say.

"No," Soph says, giving a small smile and gazing into the distance. "Very few people do. Helena does obviously, but not the boys or Caro. I trust that you won't tell Eddie about this, by the way. It would be needlessly upsetting for him."

"We're not speaking, so there's no risk of me telling him anything at the moment."

"Still, promise me?"

"Of course, I promise."

I look at Soph and try to decide how to ask for more details without saying anything too offensive. I'm not entirely sure how I feel about the double standards of King Albert disapproving of me dating Eddie because of the optics when he's been having an affair all along.

"So when I ran into you at KP that morning..."

"Yes, I was heading home after staying overnight with Bertie. He keeps an apartment there where we stay when Louisa is away."

"When did you start, uh, seeing him? When you moved to his trust?"

Soph laughs. "Oh no, a long time before that. We've been together in one way or another since I was nineteen."

Wait, what? They've been dating since before he met Queen Louisa? I wonder if she knows? She must, surely. And what about Barry? Is that why they separated?

Sensing my confusion, Soph explains. "We dated when we were young and were very much in love. He wanted to marry me. He proposed when I was twenty-one, and I thought about marrying him, I really did. In the end, I just couldn't do it. Because I'd grown up in his world, I knew the pressure and responsibilities of the role and didn't think that I could make the sacrifices required of me, even if I wanted to."

"Wow. But when did things start again?"

"Oh, almost straight away. We both went off and found appropriate partners, and we tried to stay away from each other, we truly did. It never lasted long. There's always been something holding us together."

Soph dabs at her misty eyes. "Barry always turned a blind eye, bless him. But he knew. With Queen Alice passing away and

Bertie feeling like he had a bit more freedom to do as he pleased, Barry decided he was shot of there being three people in the marriage."

"What about Queen Louisa?"

"Louisa never wanted to bring the family into disrepute by leaving. She also loves Bertie in her own way."

"I... I don't know what to say."

"You don't need to say anything, dear. The reason I tell you this story and trust you with my secret is so that you can learn from it. Not a day goes by when I don't regret my decision to turn down his proposal. All my life, I've wondered what could have been. Don't make the same mistake I did. If you truly love him, it's worth the sacrifices."

I sit, staring at Soph and seeing versions of my future flashing before my eyes—a life without Eddie, sad and empty; one with Eddie, sometimes hard, but full of love and laughter; and, worst of all, the awful kind of half-life that Soph and King Albert have. The thought of a life without Eddie... it breaks my heart.

The last week has taught me that my life isn't the same without Eddie in it. I love him, and I want him back. The problems I faced when we were together didn't make me feel nearly as depressed as I've felt without him.

Tears well up in my eyes. "Oh, Soph, I do love him, but I can't give up my work and everything I want to do in life to just support Eddie and be his girlfriend."

"Has Eddie asked you to do that? Because I've known him since he was a baby, and I can't imagine that's what he wants."

"He hasn't said it in so many words, but even if he doesn't expect me to take on that role, everyone else does. I've already had William try to relegate me to ceremonial duties. What else could life as his girlfriend be?"

"Amelia, a good partnership isn't about one person supporting the other. It's about lifting each other up. Together, you can both achieve more than you could alone."

"Even if that were true, it's too late. He's marrying Sibella for real this time. I lost my chance."

"Darling, if Edmund's first wedding showed us anything, it's that it's not over until it's over. Go and get your man."

MY MIND IS RACING as I close the door behind Soph. How am I going to fix this? I could do the big romantic gesture and just turn up on his doorstep and beg him not to marry Sibella, but that's a bit hard to pull off when you have to find a way past a dozen guards to get to the doorstep. I'm *pretty* sure I'm not on the permitted visitor list anymore.

Then it hits me.

I pull out my phone and send a message.

I've made a terrible mistake. Can you help?

A couple of minutes later, my phone rings and Lucy's name flashes on the screen. I hit the answer button and hear her voice before I have a chance to speak.

"About bloody time, darling! I take it you've finally come to your senses?"

"I have. But I have no idea how to get him back. And he's engaged. Again."

"Are you at home right now?" she asks.

"Yup."

"Alright then, don't move. We're on our way."

I'm pacing around the lounge room when there's a knock on the door. I peek through the window and see two women in trench coats, enormous floppy hats and sunglasses. I guess that's the princesses' idea of keeping a low profile.

CHAPTER 33

"WHAT ON EARTH have you been doing, woman?" Lucy says in greeting when I open the door.

I glance around to make sure that there are no camera phones in sight and usher the sisters inside.

"Mainly binge-eating," I say sheepishly.

"What I meant is," Lucy says slowly, as if speaking to someone half deaf, "why did you break up with Edmund?"

"He didn't tell you?"

"No," Lucy replies. "We were up in Scotland when it happened. The night we got home, we realised that we didn't have any food, so we invited ourselves to dinner. I asked if you'd be joining us, and Eddie just said that you'd ended things."

"I was so overwhelmed by the attention. I took some time to think about what a life with Eddie would look like on a day-to-day level, and I didn't think I could do it. I'm not built to deal with that kind of pressure."

"I can appreciate that," Lucy says. "Royal life certainly isn't for everyone. I'm not sure Eddie would have chosen it for himself, if given the chance."

"But that's part of why he needs you. He was so much more

centred when you were around. He's been a total wreck since the break-up," Emma says. "You really did a number on him."

"What about what I need though? If I'm going to be with him, I need him to stand up for me."

"Give him a chance. He's had a lifetime of being a good little prince and going along with whatever the palace tells him to do, it may take a while for him to find the courage to take control, but I believe that he'll do it for you."

I clench my jaw. "I'm not convinced that he'll do anything for me. After all, he proposed to someone else immediately after we broke up."

Emma sighs. "We weren't particularly impressed by that, either. Eddie's been avoiding us ever since the news broke, so we haven't had a chance to grill him yet."

"I think he was probably just trying to protect himself," Lucy says. "In some ways, it's much safer being with someone you have no feelings for. Much harder to get your heart broken that way."

"Do you think I've blown my chance?" I ask, biting my lip.

Lucy's eyes sparkle. "There's only one way to find out, my dear. We need to get you in to see him."

"How? I'm pretty sure I'm the last person he wants to see. And Sibella isn't about to invite me over for tea."

"Leave that to us," Emma says, grinning. "But first, we need to find you a better outfit. Lead me to your closet, please!"

Lucy and Emma proceed to rifle through every item of clothing I own before they decide on an acceptable outfit for me —a red wrap dress with a V-neck deep enough to show that I mean business. I can't even imagine how they would have reacted to my wardrobe before Penny threw out everything I'd ever bought.

～

LUCY AND EMMA sign me in at the front gate at KP and take me in through the side door to Ivy Cottage.

We're in the sitting room trying to figure out if Edmund is at home when I hear a loud rap on the door. Emma gets up to answer the door, and my stomach leaps into my throat when I hear his voice.

"Thank god you're here," he says.

"Edmund! What are you doing here?" Emma asks.

Lucy looks around the room wildly, then points to the corner of the room behind the sofa.

"You want me to hide behind the sofa?" I whisper.

Lucy nods and starts pushing me towards the corner. This is ridiculous, but what's a girl to do when her ex is about to walk into the room and there's no way out? That's right, crouch down on the floor behind the sofa and try to make herself invisible.

"Is Lucy here? I need your help," Eddie says.

Goosebumps spring up on my arms, and I can feel my heart beating through my chest as I hear him walk into the room.

"Oh, hi there, cousin," Lucy says, walking over to hug Edmund. "I didn't realise you were here."

"I just arrived. I need your help."

Lucy wags her finger at Edmund. "Do you now? Last time I checked, you weren't answering my calls, so I'm not sure if you deserve my help at the moment."

"Please..." he says, his voice breaking. "Everything is ruined, and I don't know how to fix it. I'm begging you."

Lucy stands up and wraps Eddie in a tight hug. "Well, when you put it that way. How can we assist?"

"I need to figure out how to see Amelia without Sibella or Dad finding out."

Lucy and Emma exchange glances before Emma gives a small nod.

"It's your lucky day," Lucy says. She strides over to the corner where I'm hidden and yanks me up by the arm.

I wave to Eddie, who is standing across the room, mouth open and eyes wide.

"Hi," I say.

"Er, hi," says Eddie. "What are you doing here?"

Emma puts her arm around Lucy's waist. "I think we need to check on that thing in the kitchen now."

Lucy starts walking towards the door and then turns to me and mouths, "Good luck."

"Were you hiding from me behind the furniture?" Eddie asks.

I pull at my earlobe. "No, I... uh, was looking for something I dropped."

Eddie squints and rubs his jaw.

"Okay," I say, flushing. "I was hiding from you."

"Why?"

"I'm not really sure. I asked Lucy and Emma to bring me here to help me try to see you, but then we heard you come in and panicked."

"You came to see me?" Eddie asks, giving me a quizzical smile.

"I did."

"Does this mean you've changed your mind about us?"

I nod slowly. Eddie breaks into a broad grin, and my heart melts. I rush across the room and throw my arms around him.

"I've missed you so much," I say into his chest.

"I've missed you, too."

Eddie leans down and kisses me, running his hands over my back. As soon as he kisses me, all the pain and stress of the last few weeks disappears. My lungs are filled with his earthy scent, and I can feel the strength and safety of his arms. Kissing him feels like being home.

"Wait," I say, breaking away from him. "You're engaged."

He takes a big breath in. "It looks that way."

"It doesn't just look that way—it *is* that way. I watched you give an interview about it last night."

"I'm so sorry you had to see that. Let me explain."

"Please, enlighten me. Because from where I'm standing, it looks like we broke up and then three days later you proposed to someone else."

"I can see how it would look that way, but that's not what happened. I didn't propose to Sibella."

"What do you mean you didn't propose?" I say, narrowing my eyes. "I saw the statement. I saw the interview."

"I should start at the start. Not long after we broke up, I met with Dad and told him to stay out of our relationship. I said that I didn't care what other people say—you're a smart, kind, funny woman, and I wasn't going to let him ruin my happiness. I told him that I was going to fight to win you back."

"How did he take that?"

"Not well. He was rather apoplectic, actually."

I give a joyless bark of laughter. "I'll bet. He really isn't a big fan of mine."

"No, he isn't. Anyway, he got very angry and threatened to strip me of every privilege he can legally remove unless I broke things off with you and settled down with a 'more appropriate' match. He said he'd cut off my income from the sovereign grant, toss me out of my house, the lot."

My face screws up. "Can he even do that?"

"He can't strip me of my title, but everything else is fair game."

"What did you say?"

"I told him that he could threaten me all he liked, but I wasn't going to stop seeing you."

I put my hand on my heart. "You were willing to give up all of that for me?"

"In a heartbeat. All that matters to me is you and being able to serve as king one day. Luckily for me, he can't take either of those things away from me."

"I can't believe I broke up with you. Here you were going out on a limb for me, and I just left. You must have been crushed."

Eddie laughs. "Yes, it was unfortunate. I kept calling, trying to explain, but you wouldn't answer."

"I've really messed things up, haven't I?"

"Just a bit." Eddie smiles.

This is a lot to process. Eddie was willing to give up his money and home and who knows what else to be with me. And I completely ignored him. I have not covered myself in glory here.

"I'm confused—if you wanted to be with me and told your father that you would give up your home and everything else, how did you wind up engaged to Sibella again?"

"On the day the engagement was announced, Dad called me to his office for a meeting. I wasn't going to go, but then I decided I'd take the chance to yell at him some more. When I got there, he just gave me a piece of paper. It was a copy of the engagement announcement. It'd been released to *The Times* under an embargo before I even saw it."

"He announced an engagement that you didn't know about?"

"He did. It was his ultimate power move. He knew that once the statement had been released, I wouldn't be able to retract it without causing enormous embarrassment for the family."

"So you just went along with it?"

Eddie looks at the ground and wrings his hands. "I didn't feel like I had a choice. And you weren't answering my calls, so it all seemed a bit hopeless."

"I understand," I say, lacing my fingers through his. "But why did Sibella agree to it? I thought she was happy with her new boyfriend."

"She was. Turns out that Sib's father has a nasty gambling habit that he can't afford. Dad offered to pay off the debts, and Sib agreed to save her family's estate and reputation."

"So," I say. "What were you going to ask Lucy and Emma for help with tonight?"

"I wanted to see you in person so that I could explain. And if things went well and you agreed to take me back, I was going to ask them to help me figure out how to call off the engagement. Again."

"You'd really do that for me?"

"Amelia, I love you. I'd do anything for you."

I'm sorry, did I imagine that, or did he really just say that he loves me?

"Will you give life with me another chance?" he asks.

I definitely didn't mishear. Okay, girl, it's now or never. Is he worth dealing with all the inconveniences and pressures of royal life for?

Duh, of course he is. I'm not going to make that mistake twice.

"I love you so much, Eddie. You're one of the kindest and most driven people I know. I love that you want to use your position to do something good, and I love that when you're not saving the world, you watch bad TV and make lame puns. You're also the best pastry chef I know. I'd be stupid to give you up."

Eddie grins, dimple flashing. "Yes, you really would be."

"Can we come back in and stop eavesdropping through the door?" Lucy calls out from the foyer.

Eddie and I both laugh.

"Yes," he says. "You've pretended to give us privacy for long enough."

Lucy and Emma rush back into the room and hug us both.

"We're so happy for you," Lucy says.

"Thank you," I say, beaming. "I'm glad I called you today."

"Darling, calling us is always a good idea."

"That it is," Eddie says.

"So," Emma says, clapping her hands together. "What's the plan here? We've got an engagement to cancel."

"I'm so proud of you, Amelia. Who knew that you'd turn out to be a homewrecker after all?" Lucy says.

"What *are* we going to do?" I ask Eddie. I'd been so swept up in the moment that I hadn't thought about the logistics of the situation at all. Very un-lawyerly of me.

"First things first, I need to tell Sib. I'm sure she'll be more than happy to escape again if we can cover her father's debts."

Emma raises her hand. "If she needs someone to pay the debts, I believe we can take care of that. Uncle Bertie hasn't threatened to take *our* trust funds away."

"Thank you, I'll pay you back unless Dad follows through with taking all my money away. If that happens, I'll have to pay you in meals and haikus."

"We'll pass on the poetry, but your culinary skills will do nicely as payment," Emma says.

Eddie puffs out his chest. "That takes care of Sib. Our next issue will be Dad. I'll call him tonight and tell him that I won't be going through with it. I can handle the fallout. Whatever happens, it'll all be worth it."

I squeeze his hand. "We're going to get through this together."

CHAPTER 34

Eddie called Sibella and told her the news. To say that she was relieved is an understatement. She actually cried tears of joy at not having to marry him. To his credit, he was far less offended by her reaction than some men would have been.

After the call, he suggested that we head back to Wren House for some privacy, and I jumped at the chance. As much as I like Emma and Lucy, I haven't seen Eddie in ages, and there are a few things I'd like to catch up on without an audience.

When he opens the door, we basically run to the bedroom. I'm glad to report that what they say about absence making the heart grow fonder is definitely true.

Eddie kisses my neck as we're lying in bed, exhausted and bound together in a tangle of limbs and expensive linens. "Come away with me."

"Where do you want to go?" I ask, lazily tracing circles on his chest.

"Kenya. I want to go back, just you and me this time."

I give a low whistle. "Sounds amazing. We should start planning."

"No planning," he says. "We should go first thing in the morning. I would say tonight, but I'm not planning to let you leave this room for the next twelve hours."

"Tomorrow? You haven't even told your father about calling things off with Sibella yet!"

"I'll call him from the airport. He can yell at me in person when we get home."

I bite my lip. "Can we actually just go? Won't we need to book flights and hotels?"

"I know last time I said that I never fly private, but this is a special occasion. I've got a friend from uni with a jet who's always offering to lend it to me. I think it's time to take him up on the offer."

"Where will we stay?"

"There's an amazing eco lodge near the Tanzanian border, overlooking Mount Kilimanjaro that I've stayed at quite a few times now. It's off-season at the moment, so I'm sure they'll be able to find us a room." He looks at me with puppy dog eyes. "Please? I'm so happy right now, and I want to live in this bubble for a little while."

"Okay." I sigh. "Why not? I'm already on leave from work. I may as well spend some of it on an actual holiday."

Eddie grins. "Fantastic! You stay here, and I'll go and make the magic happen."

~

Thursday 30 September

BY EIGHT AM the next morning, we've swung by my flat to pick up some clothes and are back in the private airport lounge at London City. If any of the lounge staff are surprised to see Eddie there, drinking breakfast mimosas with a woman who isn't his fiancée, they don't show it. That's the kind of discretion you pay the big bucks for.

We're sitting in the lounge, catching up on everything that's happened in the last few days when Eddie's phone rings.

"It's Dad. I'm going to ignore it." He holds his phone, starting at his father's name on the screen until it rings out.

"Maybe you should call back." I say. "You're going to have to talk to him eventually."

"I know, I was just hoping to avoid it for as long as humanly possible. Preferably for another fifty years or so." Eddie rubs his temples. "You're right. I should speak to him and be done with it."

"You don't have to talk to him right now, but if you call soon, we can have a break without it hanging over our heads," I say.

"That's true," he says, thinking. "It would also give him some space to cool off while we're abroad. From a safety perspective, it may be advisable if we're in different countries when he hears the news." He takes a deep breath and breathes out through his nose. "Alright, I'll call him. I'm going to make him wait until tomorrow though. I've only just gotten you back, and I'll be damned if I'm going to let him try to ruin it again."

"Deal. Let's forget all about your dad for today and face reality tomorrow."

It's a nine-hour flight to Kenya, so we settle in for a movie marathon, and the cabin crew keep us fed with a steady supply of fresh snacks. I know that flying private is hideously expensive, terrible for the environment and all-round unnecessary... but I could really get used to it. It's not even the privacy or the cushy seats I like. The best things about flying private are the airport lounges where someone takes care of the check-in process for you while you have a snack, and the cashmere blankets. Give me kerbside check-in and cashmere accessories on British Airways, and I'd be happy to never fly private again. Is that really so much to ask?

~

WHEN WE LAND at the airport in Kilaguni—if you can call it an airport; it's really just a landing strip in the middle of the desert—there's nothing in sight but red dirt and scrub. Oh, and a jeep waiting for us, driven by what appears to be a *very* heavily armed guide from the lodge in traditional Maasai robes. We jump in the back of the jeep and set off towards the border with Tanzania.

Half an hour later, we arrive at Campi ya Kanzi, a small collection of round stone pavilions with thatched roofs and cream canvas tents. The guide drops us at our tent, set in a surprisingly green field and looking out over Mount Kilimanjaro. The scenery is breath-taking, even before I spot a tower of giraffes on the horizon. Let's hope they don't get close enough to lick anyone this time.

"If you'd told me that you were bringing me to stay in a tent, I'm not sure I would have agreed to come," I say. "I don't really do camping. Or the outdoors in general."

Eddie laughs. "I had a suspicion that may be the case, but I knew that you'd love this when we got here. Besides, it's hardly camping."

I walk through the entrance to the tent and see that he's right. The walls and ceiling may be made of canvas, but I'm not sure the structure really qualifies as a tent. The interior of the "tent" features hardwood floors, a large canopy bed, a stone bathroom and quite a few power points. A tent where I can sleep in a proper bed and use a hairdryer is my kind of camping. If the Wi-Fi's good, I might never leave.

We spend the morning on a tour around the wildlife reserve surrounding the resort. We get to see the giraffes up close and spot two elephants, a rhino and a cheetah. I'm glad to report that the Wi-Fi is good enough that I manage to send Penny update pictures without issue.

"So what now?" I ask Edmund after the safari and lunch. "What else do you do at an African eco lodge?"

"Whatever you like, really."

"Are there other activities here?"

"There are," he says. "You can do local village tours, conservation tours, cooking and craft activities with the Maasai. There are plenty of options."

"What do you normally do when you're here?"

Eddie narrows his eyes. "Honest answer?"

"Of course. I won't judge."

"Listen to true crime podcasts and take naps in the middle of the day."

I laugh. "You come halfway around the world to one of the most stunning places I've ever seen to listen to podcasts and nap?"

"I thought you said that you wouldn't judge me..."

"I did, and I don't. It just seems like such a waste."

"Is it a waste, or is it the best possible use of time? Those are the things I never get to do at home—with all the staff and engagements and people insisting that I read seven newspapers a day to make sure I don't miss any important issues."

"I get it," I say. "Luckily, I love a good nap too."

AFTER A LONG AFTERNOON NAP, Edmund leads me to the central pavilion with its tall, thatched roof. Inside, the rough stone walls are bathed in the warm glow of a roaring fire and lanterns. Eddie takes a seat on a sofa in front of the fireplace and beckons for me to sit next to him.

"Amelia, I wanted to say thank you."

"There's nothing to thank me for."

Eddie brushes a stray lock of hair off my face. "I have so much to thank you for. I honestly don't think you understand how happy you've made me. Spending time with you, it makes me feel like I have a whole life that belongs just to me—not to my family, or the rest of the country. I love you."

"I love you so much. I just wish we could stay in this bubble forever. When we're together, everything is great. It's when we go out into the world that things get difficult."

"Maybe we can," Eddie says, clutching my hands. "Well, not *forever* forever," he continues. "But for a good long while. I'll be king one day and lose a lot of my freedoms, but Dad's only just turned sixty. Based on my family history, we've got at least thirty years before we have to worry about any of that. He's already threatened to cut off my duties and income, so what do we have to lose?"

My nose wrinkles. "What are you suggesting we do?"

"Create a new life for ourselves, away from the complications. We could move to Africa, or a cottage in Scotland, or a riverboat in Bath. Whatever makes us happy."

"Would you really leave London? I don't want to take you away from your work—you're so passionate about it and are helping so many people. I couldn't live with myself if I made you choose between me and your duties. And, to be frank, I don't want to give up my work, either. I've always enjoyed it, but this year I've really come into my own. I feel like I'm achieving a lot, and I don't want to throw that away."

"Neither of us have to give up what we're doing. I'm not sure if you've heard of it, but there's this thing now called the internet. Thanks to that, we don't have to be in London to work. Name the place, and I'll be there."

"I thought you said your parents would never let you move away from the city."

"That was before they threatened to cut me off. Since he took the throne, my father thinks he can control everything, but I've had enough. If he won't accept our relationship, he doesn't get to decide how I live."

My heart swells. "It all sounds almost too good to be true."

"I'm not promising that everything will be perfect, but I am promising that we can build a real life together."

"Could we move to Australia?" I ask. "I was so excited to live in London, but after the last couple of months, the shine has well and truly worn off. It would be so nice to be back with my family and away from all the London chaos."

Eddie grabs my face and kisses me hard. "Australia! It's perfect, I don't know why I didn't think of it first. The palace can spin it as a way for me to focus on broader Commonwealth duties, and it's about as far away from Dad as you can get. The weather and beaches are a bonus."

"Australia then?" I say, grinning. "We can live in Melbourne, or Sydney, wherever you prefer. Either way, we can get a little place down the coast and spend weekends at the beach, away from everything."

"It's a deal," Eddie says before smiling and reaching into his pocket. When he draws his hand back out of his pocket, he's holding a small black velvet box.

"Amelia, I want to spend the rest of my life with you…"

Suddenly a sharp knock raps on the pillar by the entry to the pavilion, and Henry enters the room ashen-faced, without waiting for a response. I didn't even know he was here.

"Henry. What are you doing here?" Eddie asks.

Looks like Eddie didn't know that he'd followed us either.

"Excuse me, sir, but I need to speak to you privately."

"I'll find you when I'm free," says Eddie.

Henry clears his throat. "I'm afraid we need to speak now."

"Henry, this isn't a good time," says Eddie. "I'll come and see you as soon as I can."

"With all due respect, sir, this can't wait."

Edmund rolls his eyes and flashes me an apologetic smile. "Henry, I'm giving you ninety seconds. Talk."

"This is a private matter," Henry says, giving me a pointed look.

I stand to leave, but Eddie grabs my hand and tugs me back down to the sofa. Looking increasingly frustrated, Eddie snaps,

"Henry, whatever you need to say to me during my incredibly private holiday, you can say in front of Amelia. Out with it."

Henry clears his throat again and looks around nervously. After a long pause, he gulps and then speaks. "There's been an accident. Your father's helicopter went down. I'm afraid he didn't make it."

An earth-shattering silence falls over the pavilion, and the world seems to move in slow motion as Edmund drops my hand. His expression moves from confusion to shock, before he hangs his head and his face crumples.

After what feels like hours, Henry speaks quietly. "Your Majesty, I know this must be a shock, so I'll give you a few moments before we talk about what happens next."

With that, Henry turns and walks to the door where he bows before standing tall and addressing Eddie.

"God save the King."

THE END

THANK you so much for reading The Other Prince. I hope that you enjoyed reading this story as much as I enjoyed writing it. If you did, I'd love for you to let me know by either leaving a review or getting in touch at Facebook or Instagram.

To continue Amelia and Eddie's story, pre-order the next instalment, God Save the King, now on Amazon.

To keep up to date with new releases and other news, join my mailing list at www.alicedolman.com

ACKNOWLEDGMENTS

When I set out to write this book I was coming to the end a lock-down where I had spent over a hundred days looking after (and occasionally hiding from) my three children under five without any of the help I normally have. I started writing for an escape, but I never believed that I would finish. I probably wouldn't have without the support of a lot of people.

Firstly I'd like to thank Lucy and Emma who told me to stop saying I should write a book and just do it already. I love you both always.

To Josh, thank you for reading your first romcom for me. I appreciated your comments and help so much.

To my family - Mum, Dad, Clare, Caitlyn, Joe, Julia, Dette, Scott, Peter and Concetta - and friends, thank you for always being there.

To my lovely CRR colleagues who barely laughed at all at the idea of me writing a novel instead of a contract, I'm not planning to quit and go work for a charity. Promise.

These acknowledgements wouldn't be complete if I didn't thank my high school english and literature teachers - Mrs Bennett and Ms Thompson. I'm not entirely convinced that you'd enjoy this book, but I couldn't have written it (or anything else) without you.

While I couldn't have written this book without the support of the people I've already mentioned, I couldn't have taken it from an ugly first draft to something readable without my amazing editor Sarah. Her understanding of my story and characters had nothing to do with my writing skills and everything to do with her editing skills.

Last, but far from least, huge thanks to my husband and biggest cheerleader, Gerard. You're an Eddie, just FYI.

ABOUT THE AUTHOR

Hi! I'm Alice. I'm so glad you're here.

I write funny stories about people falling in love. Mainly princes and princesses because I'm a bit of a royal family tragic. Also because writing about royalty is the closest I'll ever come to wearing a tiara that isn't made of plastic.

I live in Australia with my husband and three small humans. In my seventeen seconds of free time each day I love reading romantic comedies, watching cheesy Netflix movies and baking cakes which I absolutely do not eat most of myself.

Made in the USA
Coppell, TX
13 March 2022